Representations of Aggression and Their Dynamics in D. H. Lawrence's Fiction

Representations of Aggression and Their Dynamics in D. H. Lawrence's Fiction

by

MIYO OYAMA

Miyo Oyama was born in 1990. She received her BA (2014) and MA (2016), and Ph.D. (2019) in English literature from Hiroshima University. She has published a number of articles on D. H. Lawrence, from the perspectives of post-colonialism, psychoanalysis, and the relation of body and mind, which are collected in this book. She is planning to enter the University of Nottingham in 2019 in order to gain a Master's degree.

ALL RIGHTS RESERVED. No part of this work may be reproduced, redistributed, or used in any form or by any means without prior written permission of the publisher and copy-right owner.

Published by KEISUISHA co., ltd.
1-4 Komachi Naka-ku Hiroshima 730-0041 Japan

ISBN978-4-86327-488-4 C3098

Acknowledgements

I would like first of all to express my gratitude to Dr. David Vallins who has supervised me for six years since the time when I was an undergraduate student. He always listened closely to the plans for my study and owing to his responsible and generous manner, I could complete my work.

And I feel an obligation to Dr. Kenichi Kurata, who was my discussion partner during my doctoral course and who has stimulated my intellectual curiosity. It cannot be forgotten that he gave me extensive advice when I was working on the first draft of this study and I depended upon him a lot in those days.

I have been greatly supported by the professors of Hiroshima University in which I spent seven years. There is nowhere like this homely atmosphere which let me be myself and freely devote myself to study and thus it makes me feel that I was right to choose to study here. However, it was Dr. Osamu Takeuchi, whom I met in my Kansai University days before, who led me to enter the way of living as a scholar of English literature. If it had not been for his suggestion that I had an aptitude for becoming a scholar, during our idle chat about our favourite books, perhaps I might have been unaware of this interesting and exciting way of life.

In addition, I am grateful to Dr. Masashi Asai and the members of the D. H. Lawrence Society of Japan for assisting me by introducing books and giving critical opinions about my presentation at the conference and my essays in journals. I am eager to contribute more as a member of the society from now on.

It is my supreme happiness that I have come through all my

studies with the love of my parents and grandparents. I appreciate them above everything for cheering me and supporting my life all the time. I would like to express much love to my mother, who has always been my best counsellor and my best friend for twenty-eight years. And I am also grateful that I met my understanding friends, who keep heartening me by saying that they support whatever I have in my mind.

Dedicated to Yone Okuura

My grandmother is an unusual person. I had a doubt about her way of living from my childhood: why is she not a mere gentle old woman? Why does she get involved with other people quite irrationally and love to attack and challenge them, even though they are her blood relatives? The problem of how to get along with her was a challenge for me as her granddaughter, for as long as I can remember.

However, I found the answer to the impasse since I discovered the novelist, D. H. Lawrence. It is because I saw my grandmother many times in the concept of 'aggression' which is strikingly prominent in Lawrence's works. And I understood that my grandmother was actually giving affirmation to her life by not communicating sympathetically or intellectually with others but starting a fight with them in an intuitive way. She looks oddly delighted whenever she offends people and sees how they react. One day she assuredly said, 'I'm done with somebody who does not retaliate: it's simply not fun'. By a curious coincidence, it resembled what Juana says in Lawrence's novel, *The Plumed Serpent*.

Isn't it because I was observing her through my fixed rationality that it seemed that there was nothing for it but to label her as an extraordinary woman? I discarded that idea. Since I discovered Lawrence and came in touch with his thoughts, I feel that now I can understand my grandmother, or the 'other', approve her existence, and even respect and laugh at her intuitive way of living as when Lawrence smiled at the curious natives and animals in the land of Mexico.

Thanks Grandma, for making me take up this abstruse and stimulating theme.

Contents

Acknowledgements i
Dedicated to Yone Okuura................................... iii
List of Abbreviations vii

INTRODUCTION 1

CHAPTER ONE: Unrepresentable Experiences in the Early Works
1. Bridging Social Differential by Dynamic Consciousness 13
2. The Psychodynamics of Affect 29
3. Transmitting Epiphany by Affect: The Effect of Ecstasy 45
4. The Symbolical Gap between Death and Resurrection 57

CHAPTER TWO: The Ambiguity of 'Stillness' and Finding a Remedy in 'Aggression'
1. Conflicting Texts — Desirable or Undesirable Inertia? 71
2. Stillness in Islands: The Abandonment of External Desire......... 81
3. Islands and Regression 92
4. The Introversion of Aggression and Necessity of the Other 101

CHAPTER THREE: Facing the 'External' Other in the Late Works
1. The Heroines' Quests and the Mystic Figure of the External Other 111
2. Conflicting Desires and Identities between Racial Others 121
3. *Ressentiment* or the Natural Life Competition 130

4. Friction and Reconciliation in *The Plumed Serpent* 144

CHAPTER FOUR: Discovering the 'Internal' Other and a New Vista on Human Relationships
1. The Return to the Interior 159
2. Encountering the Pan, or the Internal Other 171
3. The Pure Animal Man 183
4. 'Be tender to it, and that will be its future' 193

CONCLUSION 209

Endnotes 219
Works Cited 225
Index 237

List of Abbreviations

EME	*England, My England and Other Stories*
1L	*Letters of D. H. Lawrence* Vol.1
2L	*Letters of D. H. Lawrence* Vol.2
5L	*Letters of D. H. Lawrence* Vol.5
LCL	*Lady Chatterley's Lover: A Propos of 'Lady Chatterley's Lover'*
MM	*Mornings in Mexico and Etruscan Places*
P	*Phoenix: The Posthumous Papers of D. H. Lawrence*
PO	*The Prussian Officer and Other Stories*
PS	*The Plumed Serpent*
PUFU	*Psychoanalysis and the Unconscious and Fantasia of the Unconscious*
R	*The Rainbow*
RDP	*Reflections on the Death of a Porcupine and Other Essays*
SE	*The Complete Psychological Works of Sigmund Freud*
SL	*Sons and Lovers*
STH	*Study of Thomas Hardy and Other Essays*
StM	*St. Mawr and Other Stories*
T	*The Trespasser*
VG	*The Virgin and the Gipsy*
WL	*Women in Love*
WP	*The White Peacock*
WWRA	*The Woman Who Rode Away and Other Stories*

INTRODUCTION

It is unusual to appreciate the English novelist, D. H. Lawrence (1885-1930), as a writer concerned with human love. For a long period, there have been numerous readers who know the writer only for his dissident and extremist face, including his distinctive anti-Christian tenets and criticism of democracy, his prophecies of Fascist power politics, and his recommendation of sexual freedom, which in his own period was mostly seen as obscenity. However, the true quality which I find at the root of these images is Lawrence's sincere attitude and enthusiasm for removing the mental obstacles which hinder people from communicating with each other on a deeper level. What he devoted himself to was overcoming the confusion caused by the incompatibilities between individuals which differences of social class result in. The disparities exist in such areas as wealth, education, values and customs, which invest intelligence with superiority and physicality with inferiority. Therefore, social modernization has caused a significant change in our mental consciousness: people have become especially bound to the fixed ego — a multilayered form with historical, cultural, social, and sexual elements — and tend to appreciate the others' existence merely through superficial mental relationships. Through this study I aim to demonstrate that Lawrence's fiction gives literal expression to his ideas about the release of modernized people from their hardened egos and emotions and the acceptance of others. The most important thing I would like to propose is Lawrence's humanistic focus on harmony, which has been underestimated in spite of its fundamental role in most of his works.

However, it is not 'humanism' in the sense of the attitude with which modern Western society since the Enlightenment in the eighteenth century has determined the dominance of humanity through reason. Lawrence includes in his works many representations of the 'inhuman' or the 'impersonal' in order to resist the firmly implanted tendency of 'humanism'. Lawrence is thus sometimes regarded as among the post-humanist writers, though what we should notice is that he does not have a bloodless orientation towards power with a lack of human love, as he is often misconceived as doing. On the other hand, as Del Ivan Janik suggests, he does not criticize human beings as mere destroyers of the natural world but celebrates all the life forces in the universe as constituents of it (359). He tries to revitalize the organic, dynamic relationship between mankind and material nature in the way it existed before rationality became ingrained, and he also develops the same kind of fundamental communion between human beings. The 'inhuman' or the 'impersonal' bond, as a counterpart to 'humanism', is obtained by a dynamic consciousness which is deeper than mental consciousness.

Lawrence sought to revitalize the stagnant, old human relationships, so that rather than mentally fettering each other, individuals could have a lively exchange. He writes, 'The business of art is to reveal the relation between man and his circumambient universe, at the living moment' (*STH* 171), emphasizing the necessity of grasping the active instability of 'in-between everything' (*STH* 171). Lawrence calls this lively and changing flux the 'fourth dimension', and describes it as being recognized by one's blood and physical sense, and not by visual sensation, which works in conspiracy with intelligence.[1]

> [The man and the object] both pass away from the moment, in the process of forming a new relationship. The relation between all things changes from day to day, in a subtle stealth of change. . . . and morality is that delicate, forever trembling and changing *balance* between me and my circumambient universe, which precedes and accompanies a true relatedness. (*STH* 171-72)

Hence, while he intended to break away from modern humanism, Lawrence is a writer who demonstrates his insight into human beings by continuing to present better lives and a realization of better specimens of parent-child relationships, friendships, and love and sexual relationships to his readers. I would argue that this could not be done at all without his own profound human love.

As a preliminary remark, I would like to note the distinctiveness of my usage of the term, 'dynamic consciousness'. Many scholars have discussed the notion at length, and 'blood-consciousness' is the most popular term among them for its symbolical implications (the reason for which I will explain in the next chapter). Although I will occasionally follow this convention, I prefer to call it dynamic consciousness — a phrase which Lawrence himself often makes use of. The reason is that this phrase highlights the adjectives 'dynamic' and 'static', which Lawrence originally associated with physical consciousness, in contrast to mental consciousness: because this is significantly related to the contention of my entire study, I will use this specific term for the most part. Since, as I have mentioned, our socially-structured emotions and mental consciousness have fixed human relationships into static forms, it can be argued that Lawrence attempted to show that it is dynamic consciousness that has the power to dynamically change and reconstruct these relationships with its active and aggressive power.

The main perspective of my study is a duality of the dynamic and the static which I have already indicated. A large number of critics have already discussed Lawrence's condemnation of the reason-centered, anthropocentric world that brings about the collapse of a living relatedness with nature. However, what I particularly focus on is Lawrence's reference to the notion of fixedness as having a harmful effect on mental consciousness, and his contrasting emphasis on the necessity of motion, which is related to dynamic consciousness.

> There is nothing to do, but to maintain a true relationship to the things [contiguous universe] we move with and amongst and against. . . .
> Each thing, living or unliving, streams in its own odd, intertwining flux, and nothing, not even man nor the God of man, nor anything that man has thought or felt or known, is fixed or abiding. All moves. And nothing is true, or good, or right, except in its own living relatedness to its own circumambient universe; to the things that are in the stream with it. (*STH* 167)

Lawrence observes that the self and the circumambient universe, wherein the other lives exist, should be active and in a continual transition. What is described as 'never static' is 'the powerful blood-feeling' (*STH* 167) perceived by dynamic consciousness. Besides, it is the educational intelligence implanted in one's mind which makes one lose the motive for dynamic motion and recoil through the fear of change. John Clayton's words seem accurately to represent Lawrence's thoughts: 'the "voice of my education" — that is afraid to open the door when the angels knock. It is the voice that refuses new life, that fears the breaking open of the self' (203). Lawrence warns that the 'voice of my education' makes one flinch from freeing one's self and also having a rich relationship, uninterfered with by egoism, with other human beings, or with animals sometimes. Through this study, I will examine to what extent his thoughts are expressed in the concrete relationships depicted in his works. I am especially interested in the fact that his inclination towards motion is significant in his ideas and writings, and I argue that it has an important connection with the theories of physicality and affect which have attracted growing interest worldwide in recent Lawrence studies.

I would suggest that Lawrence's idea of human beings as conscious subjects and their relation to the motion of others resembles the analysis of Henri Bergson — a French philosopher and a flag-bearer of psychophysics. On the perception and expectation of the motion of external things, Bergson states that the subject tends to feel pleasure by 'mastering the flow of time and of holding the future in the present' (*Time and Free Will*, 12). The regularity of the rhythm establishes a kind of communication which allows the subject to foresee the objects' movement and it 'make[s] us believe that we now control them' (*Time and Free Will*, 12). Therefore, we feel pleasure when the object or the other 'seems to obey us when he really takes [makes] it [the movement]' (*Time and Free Will*, 12), and indulge in the thought of the reversal of the mastery and becoming the servant of the motion. Bergson continues that through this physical sympathy, when it has 'taken complete possession of our thought and will', one finds that 'it pleases you through its affinity with moral sympathy' (*Time and Free Will*, 12-13). In other words, the subject avoids displeasing stimuli and makes the other easily manageable by setting him up as a being who is inside the realm of one's recognition and expectation. There is an epistemological mechanism which tries to grasp the object's movement in the progression of time and one feels pleasure or displeasure with the relationship with others by the sympathetic nerves of thought and will. However, when the perception of ease toward the existence or movement of the other is hindered — that is, when the expectation is betrayed by the disorder of the movement — Bergson writes that we get impatient to replace the object in the stream of movement by forcing our mind and will. This analysis in Bergson, I would argue, is analogous to Lawrence's dynamism of fixed mind versus intuition. Bergson argues that the 'reflective consciousness . . . delights in clean cut distinctions, which are easily expressed in words, and in things with well-defined outlines, like those which are perceived in space' (*Time and Free Will*, 9) so that one is reluctant to accept the image of an object which has a dynamic representation because the dynamic way occasionally changes the nuances of the subject's myriads of perceptions and memories and thus causes an aggressive attack on one's cognition. It can go beyond the successive sense of time and space and what is realized by the total reliance on mental consciousness, which is the key to a fresh change for the life of human beings in Lawrence's vision.

It is obvious that cleansing the individual's consciousness is required prior to the process of regenerating the human relationships. In order to achieve this, I argue, Lawrence's works express the importance of awakening the active energy which has a potential for breaking many shackles which the modernized world imposes on our egoism. By resisting and destroying the fetters of rationality and making one's experience of life existential, 'another ego' is drawn out from the social

INTRODUCTION

ego. It is a pursuit of the direct experience of physicality and intuition against mind and it is presented as a means of overturning the power of hierarchy regulated by the modern epistemic scheme. However, Lawrence also squarely faces the issue of people's difficulty with and torment at dissipating the social consciousness which constructs one's being, and therefore most of the human relationships in his works do not see a fulfilment. Still, the important thing is the dynamism that is needed to unsettle the stagnant condition. It is a vital aggression that includes the energy for destruction, which accompanies the release from the social self, and also the energy for active communication with others: this is why I used the term 'aggression' in the title of the book. Through this study, I will examine how the paths to rebuilding the human relationships are presented in their vicissitudes in Lawrence's various works. The reason why I analyze his short stories for the most part is because they are a vast and active expression of the writer's thoughts and experiments. It is interesting that Lawrence usually develops a theme into several stories; we can trace the path of his thoughts since he displays different degrees of progress in the respective tales, representing examples of the characters' relationships, ending up in failure.

This book consists of four chapters. The first half of the study will mostly treat Lawrence's works from the earliest part of his career between 1907 and the 1910s. It is the time when he repeated his experimental explorations of the reformation of the relationships of English people until he obtained an exit permit at last in 1919 and started to wander through countries outside England with his wife Frieda Lawrence.

In the first chapter, I will discuss the characters' mental transformation through physical revival, by their experience of affect, epiphany, and intuitive communication with the other by introducing the arguments of Georges Bataille, alongside an analysis of Lawrence's texts, *The White Peacock* (1911), *Sons and Lovers* (1913), 'The White Stocking' (1907), 'Goose Fair' (1909), 'Hadrian' (1919), 'Second-Best' (1914), and 'The Horse-Dealer's Daughter' (1917). The tales depict the confrontations between man and woman caused by class consciousness or social egoism and the separation of mind and body which brings about another breaking of the interpersonal bond, which Lawrence depicts as a pathological state of modern society. Through activating their physical senses, the characters experience the cleansing of mind through the revitalization of their bodies. Thus the body and mind are organically integrated, which makes the understanding of the other possible in the new relationship. Those critics who read Lawrence from the perspective of 'affect theory' emphasize that aiming to break away from traditional novelistic style, Lawrence's writing deviates from expressing the subject's realistic viewpoint by presenting an 'unrepresentable experience'. However, their criticisms tend to remain in the realm of theoretical study and it can be said that studies which read Lawrence's texts in detail according to affect theory can still hardly be found. Therefore, in this study, I will work on the textual analysis and then clarify the purpose for which the remarkable 'unrepresentable experience' is expressed. I assume that it is not only in order to fulfil the author's stylistic intention; but viewing it from Lawrence's humanistic perspective, it offers the prospect of a social reorganization from the level of the individuals' bodies and sensations.

In the second chapter, I will focus on the notion of stillness and inertia, which counteracts the notion of aggression and active energy that is the pivot of this study. Although I have insisted on the radical significance of the movement against stasis, it has a close connection

INTRODUCTION

with Lawrence's own life and psychological inclination in the First World War period, and this notion is unavoidable when discussing his works in the middle period of his career. This strategy of exploring a counterbalancing perspective by presenting a notion which offers resistance to the pivotal idea is actually a kind of dialectical argument which Lawrence himself frequently engages in, and which is familiar to Lawrence critics. He often makes his characters express ideas which oppose the central idea and displays the struggle between the two contradictory thoughts. Therefore, in this chapter, I will follow Lawrence by examining to what extent the notion of stillness has a meaning in his works as a counterpart to motion, particularly focusing on the enclosure of space and time which is a common feature in *The Rainbow* (1915), *The Trespasser* (1912), 'The Man Who Loved Islands' (1927), and 'The Prussian Officer' (1914). Reconsidering the mutual desire of the characters and the discrepancy in their trajectories, this chapter will examine the texts from several psychoanalytic viewpoints such as Sigmund Freud's arguments and Jacques Lacan's model of the relation between human beings' mental development and powers of representation. As Kimberly Coates suggests, Lawrence disliked the diagnostic interpretation of his works by psychoanalysts who 'negate the art and leave merely a litany of symptoms that subscribe to a preordained complex' (145). Here, we see again the distaste for the expectation and adjustment which I have suggested earlier. Lawrence was also anxious about 'shoving the vital, kinetic, alive body into the deadening limitations of intellectual constructions' (Coates 145). However, the reason why I introduce the theoretical analysis is that whenever he tries to describe the incapacity for bodily experience which occurs in the failure of the interpersonal relationships and the mental discordance, the psychoanalytical theories seems to fit in a strange coincidence. Therefore, in the first half of my study, I will deal with the human relationships which are damaged in terms of the disharmony of mind and body which is produced by the system of social differences, and will discuss the challenges to and failure of the active relationships within Western modernization, and the role of the aggressive energy as a dynamo to transform the self.

In the latter part of the study, I will mainly treat the post-colonial works which Lawrence wrote in the 1920s by visiting foreign countries. In these works, in which the Western protagonists encounter people of alien races, the perspective from the outside of modernized Western society is introduced. What is distinctly different from the earlier part of the study is that because of the introduction of bigger differences such as those of race and culture, entering into the viewpoint of the other becomes harder to achieve.

The third chapter will focus more closely on the struggle with the external others who direct their critical gaze at the protagonist's Western egoism, which did not happen in the domestic tales examined so far, mainly by analyzing 'The Woman Who Rode Away' (1925), *St. Mawr* (1925), 'The Princess' (1925), and *The Plumed Serpent* (1926). In the history of Lawrence studies, the understanding of the critics has cemented around the interpretation of these texts in terms of the white heroine being deprived of her identity through the primeval events and rituals of the inhuman others, or being negated by their dark power and passively accepting the violent force. However, I suspect that those interpretations paradoxically reveal that the external others are not really unearthly beings and that they in fact bear an animosity and a consciousness of inferiority to the white people. As evidence of this, in some of these works, the Western protagonists and the external others deepen their *agon* by being unable to accept each other due to their stagnant consciousness of historical hierarchy. In addition to raising this important issue, I consider that Lawrence has attempted to overcome this deep-rooted consciousness, intertwined with the notion of mastery, by proposing a way of living which has both similarities and differences to Friedrich Nietzsche's argument about aggression. As Greg Garrard puts it, the two writers' post-humanist conceptions do not just express an authoritarian brutality (9); as for Lawrence, I would argue that it is a clue to living in coexistence with the incompatible others in organic and dynamic relation. With this assumption, I will examine to what extent his attempt has succeeded in his works, and the process of the continual destruction and reconstruction which destabilizes the stabilized relationships with the external others.

As the horizon of some of Lawrence's works in his late years returns again to the community inside England, the fourth chapter will return to the internality from the externality which I have focused on in the previous chapter. The texts which I selected in this chapter, 'The Blind Man' (1918), 'Sun' (1926), 'The Last Laugh' (1924), and *Lady Chatterley's Lover* (1928), are filled with insights which focus more closely than ever on the internality of human beings' physicality and nature. They are full of concrete suggestions about how to awaken one's vital energy and live as an active being, through their detailed attack on the consciousness of 'fear' (which is expressed in Clayton's words which I quoted earlier), 'compassion', and 'shame' which hinders the modernized people from releasing the self, and their prescription for regenerating the ability to receive primitive things which human beings fundamentally possess. Furthermore, the notion of animality, which is highlighted in the process of dismantling anthropocentrism, is one of the key terms of this chapter. Lawrence's reference to animality in his later works seems to indicate the reintegration of the motherly land and nature in England with her separated children, that is, the modernized people, by dynamic consciousness. Through this viewpoint, this chapter will reconsider what exactly are the otherness and externality which we have discussed so far. With reference to Jacques Derrida's argument about animals, I will develop a theory which deconstructs the 'imagined' externality and our emotions towards and mental consciousness of the external others. Eventually, I would like to examine Lawrence's own conclusion about the relationship of male and female, which does not maintain the active interchange of physical consciousness merely in a momentary connection. The instruction to become a flexible animal man, a human being who can always be aware of dynamic consciousness, and to sustain the passion between each other in the ongoing future, in spite of the impasse of the mechanized society, will be explored in my later analysis of Lawrence's fiction.

CHAPTER ONE

Unrepresentable Experiences in the Early Works

1. Bridging Social Differential by Dynamic Consciousness

'The great relationship, for humanity, will always be the relation between man and woman. . . . And the relation between man and woman will change forever, and will forever be the new central clue to human life' (*STH* 175) — in many of D. H. Lawrence's novels, which are written in this belief, there appear lovers who fail to understand each other emotionally because of the various conspicuous discrepancies between them. The main factor which hinders their relationships from developing is the social disparity between them, including differences of wealth and education. For example, it is expressed in the miserable end of the love relationship in the first novel, *The White Peacock*: while Lettie Beardsall expects an academic or intellectual mode of life in the city, poorly-educated George Saxton takes pride in the beauty of his physical sturdiness which has been built up in his farm work. In *Sons and Lovers*, the situation seems to be different: the relationship between Paul Morel and Miriam Leivers turns out to be a catastrophe due to the harsh effects of their personal backgrounds. The girl's religious chastity, and the spiritual interference of Paul's mother which causes him to develop a visceral aversion to Miriam by encouraging his sinful conscience, inevitably result in them continuing to resist each other. Still, personal factors such as customs and values are often intertwined with the social distinctions. When

CHAPTER ONE

Paul launches into social life and acquires a new independent character which is unfamiliar to Miriam, who remains in their rural hometown with her static religiousness, the separation of social status has encouraged their emotional breakup. Although the lovers are mutually attracted, they also reject each other due to being unable to tolerate their conflicting views of life which arouse hatred and contempt.

Lawrence's early tales written up to the 1910s are mostly set in the agricultural environment of rural England. They depict the way in which the current of social modernization encroaches upon the communities, carrying the intellect away from physicality and estranging people by giving them discriminatory values. The tales reflect a characteristic feature of the period, in which the families of farmers and colliers from the lower class aspired to rise into the lower-middle class, due to hoping for an increase in their income and greater stability in their lives. This being so, their ambitions bring changes to the relationships of people in the farming village and their attitude toward life. The realism of those tales which handle small romances inside the village is constituted by the historical and socio-cultural conditions of emotion. However, what gives unity to the early tales is the characters' awareness of their love of the region, which flows as a nostalgic *basso continuo*. In *The White Peacock*, meditating on his sister Lettie who forsook George and left for France by marrying Leslie Tempest who can fulfil the aim of her life, Cyril soliloquizes:

> It was time for us all to go, to leave the valley of Nethermere whose waters and whose woods were distilled in the essence of our veins. We were the children of the valley of Nethermere, a small nation with language and blood of our own, and to cast ourselves each one into separate exile was painful for us. (*WP*

237)

All the more because they are aware of their sense of provincial togetherness, the youths are intensely anxious about being unable to stop themselves changing in substance, due to their dispersion to the city. What inclines the youths to the city is their ambition for superiority, which is led by the modern commodified desire for a prosperous lifestyle. It inevitably produces a spiritual discord with the ones who stay in the village. Thus, it was a connection with nature through their flesh that took root in the ground, in contrast with the flight of spirits, which is capable of tying the modernized people to one place, even though they deviate from each other in their mental and bodily consciousness. It reflects the fact that the land of Eastwood where Lawrence himself spent his boyhood, and the fields and birds' nests in Haggs Farm where he nurtured his first love with Jessie Chambers, 'made roots in his blood and curled round his veins. He carried it [the locality] everywhere. His loyalty to it was indestructible. It was what he meant by England' (Callow 40). It is an intuitive togetherness which releases one from the social self and arouses sensory unconsciousness in the depth of the body, that can connect the individuals who are inclined toward emotional separation.

As I have already noted in the Introduction, Lawrence established the notion of an unconscious bodily system and named it in many ways: blood-consciousness, primal consciousness, and dynamic consciousness, all referring to the same specific physical consciousness. It is situated as a counter to mental consciousness which functions solely through the agency of one's mind. This notion which is systematized and expounded in *Fantasia of the Unconscious*, became the foundation of Lawrence's life-long philosophy and writings.

CHAPTER ONE

> The primal consciousness in man is pre-mental, and has nothing to do with cognition. It is the same as in the animals. And this pre-mental consciousness remains as long as we live the powerful root and body of our consciousness. The mind is but the last flower, *the cul de sac.*
>
> The first seat of our primal consciousness is the solar plexus, the great nerve-centre situated in the middle-front of the abdomen. From this centre we are first dynamically conscious. *For the primal consciousness is always dynamic, and never, like mental consciousness, static.* (*PUFU* 79; emphasis added)

Lawrence distinguishes mental cognition from pre-mental physical cognition, and states that the former is the instrument of thoughts and the business of living, while the latter is the root of the existence of human beings. He explains that 'At this main centre of our first-mind we know as we can never mentally know' and it is 'such as cannot be transferred into thought': 'Thought is just a means to action and living. But life and action rise actually at the great centres of dynamic consciousness' (*PUFU* 79). It is the 'first and deepest seat of awareness' (*PUFU* 74) which is the source of our life-activity and physical dynamic, and hence, it has a relation with the sensual mode of human beings' existence which Lawrence collectively calls 'the great affective centre'. Therefore, a vital contact with others without the aid of mental cognition is supported by the abdominal consciousness. By drawing in the gestating mother's blood through the navel cord, the source of consciousness becomes the center of one's life from the time of development in the womb; and 'This is the centre whence the navel-string broke, but where the invisible string of dynamic consciousness, like a dark electric current connecting you with the rest of life, will never break until you die and depart from corporate individuality' (*PUFU* 75). The mother-child ties of 'direct, immediate blood-bonds' (*PUFU* 77) are a pre-mental cardinal interaction. The pre-mental communication which opens the first contact with the 'other' is thus also called blood-consciousness. Therefore, it can be understood as a kind of unconsciousness.

It has to be noted that this dynamic connection is completely different from the excessive emotional connection displayed in Lawrence's self-castigating novels, such as *Sons and Lovers*. Lawrence analyzes the bond of the perverse mother-son relationship in which they console each other by being unduly sympathetic. He criticizes the psychical influence exerted by the consciousness of the upper center, which is the counterpart of the lower nerve center. With the thoracic ganglion, situated in the upper plane, human beings are swayed by intelligence and psychical will so that the fundamental bond with others is deranged. The thoracic ganglion is a ganglion of power and it makes us realize the wonder and the shattering differentness of others (*PUFU* 83). It additionally influences the extravagance of spiritual will — a peculiar will which gives rise to a 'sort of nervous, critical objectivity, the deliberate forcing of sympathy, the play upon pity and tenderness, the plaintive bullying of love, or the benevolent bullying of love' (*PUFU* 84). Lawrence claims that in the domestic realm, due to the vanishing of dynamic connections with her husband, a woman's wandering love is transformed into a mental love for her son, with whom she cannot have a sexual relationship. Once this happens, it becomes a fatal and harmful influence which lasts through the child's formative years and his whole life. The association of sympathetic consciousness with Christian love was an abominable connection for Lawrence, for it takes on a life of its own by ignoring the physical bond, and yields false ties by fettering people to each other through the thrusting of another's will upon themselves.

However, the foremost communication with the other by dynamic consciousness, which begins with the umbilical cord, leads human beings back to the unconscious bond which does not depend on mental consciousness. Lawrence's vision of genuine human relationship starts from the reform of the mother-child relationship, in which one physically separates from and meets one's parent as the 'other' before everything else. Since people are involved in the modernized world and become moral beings to an excessive degree, Lawrence insists that they are enfeebling their dynamic rapport with others. Thus he instructs his readers by recommending a reversal of the hierarchy of body and mind. The most important thing is that the solar plexus inside one's self should regain its presence, and in order for it to do so, one's own physicality has to be recovered. That is, the act of deeply knowing the other person by one's ventral life center is needed: a reemergence of one's primal experience. It can be considered that the experience transcends modernized people's common cognitive behaviour which grasps human relationships with the presupposition of a disparity of intellect and reason. So long as the physical bond with the others is revived, the vital relationship should be restored; the expectation of this possibility is poignant. Instead of mental bonds, what Lawrence continued insisting on was the revival of intrinsic communication by dynamic consciousness. He hopes that the bodily unconsciousness will make a long and uninterrupted bond in relationships ranging from those of lovers and married couples to the social community. It enables human beings to rejoin the rural nature which was the essence of his life. His ideas which originated from physical and organic connection with close relatives in the small farming and coal mining community which he nostalgically recalled, became his dependable means of resisting the mechanisms of psychical modernism throughout his writing career.

Lawrence's physical awareness, which was inseparable from his formative years, was perhaps unpersuasive for George Orwell (1903-1950) who went to Eton College, the elitist school, in spite of putting one of his feet in the democratic socialist camp. Portraying the biased view of social inequity as the barrier between human beings, Orwell criticizes it as follows:

> That was what we were taught — *the lower classes smell*. And here, obviously, you are at an impassable barrier. For no feeling of like or dislike is quite so fundamental as a *physical* feeling. Race-hatred, religious hatred, differences of education, of temperament, of intellect, even differences of moral code, can be got over; but physical repulsion can-not. (*The Road to Wigan Pier*, 112)

Orwell emphasizes that a contempt for the filth which accompanied the working-class people was deeply engraved in the habitual perception of the middle classes and that psychological incompatibilities percolate inside our bodies. Yet, since physical labour was central to Lawrence's collier family, it evokes the image of physical beauty and even demands admiration for the preservation of the privilege of masculinity among married couples. Furthermore, for Lawrence, physical cognition is a phenomenon which is profoundly related to his view of the family in his boyhood, and the development of his own character as a son. As noted earlier, he emphasizes the nightmare of the collapse

CHAPTER ONE

of the dynamic bond between the husband and wife, which changes its direction to focus on the child as a mentally specialized love. In addition, however, the reason why he extremely idealizes the physical cognition is that it has its origin in his strong conviction, as a son, that physicality is exactly what created the sexual union between his father and mother, who are the archetypes of male and female for him. It is mentioned repeatedly in the biographical descriptions of Lawrence's early life that the connection of his father Arthur Lawrence, the working-class collier, and his mother Lydia Beardsall, who came from the middle class before their marriage, has borne fruit, because Arthur's physical attraction had got rid of the social and intellectual differences.[1] However, he describes himself as showing a strong physical rejection towards his father.

> My mother was a clever, ironical delicately moulded woman, of good, old burgher descent. She married below her. My father was dark, ruddy, with a fine laugh. He is a coal miner. He was one of a sanguine temperament, warm and hearty, but unstable: he lacked principle, as my mother would have said. He deceived her and lied to her. She despised him — he drank.
>
> Their marriage life has been one carnal, bloody fight. I was born hating my father: as early as ever I can remember, I shivered with horror when he touched me. (*IL* 190)

The quotation above is from Lawrence's own memorandum in the days when he was composing the manuscript of *Matilda*, the uncompleted novel about his mother's life, which is the precursor of *Sons and Lovers*. Showing the extent of his devotion to his mother, Lawrence's note includes his trembling fear of being touched by his father in his childhood. His position as a son in the relationship with his parents, is thus generally associated by critics with the Oedipal argument. Furthermore, it should be clarified that Lawrence in those times was increasing his aversion to physicality itself, represented by his father whom he disdained by enhancing the emotional bond with his mother. Allied with his mother, his awareness of her social and psychological distinction from his father obliges him to hate the physical contact with him. Nevertheless, although his mother is currently anchored to him, the fact that the physical attraction of his father fascinated her once was an unfathomable mystery to him. The captivation seems to haunt his imagination with the unconquerable impotency that there is no way in which he can give it to his mother. The unbreakable sacredness of physicality which is sustained from his childhood was thus a traumatic though magnetic subject for him.

Lawrence depicts the image of a couple who get over the sense of differentness by physical cognition in *Sons and Lovers* by modeling them on his parents. Before the Morels get married, Gertrude, who is a daughter of an engineer from a 'good old burgher family' (*SL* 15), like Lawrence's mother Lydia, meets Walter Morel, the young coal-miner who dances magnificently. Gertrude encounters his vulgar, non-intellectual, though fresh-looking appearance, unlike her own or her father's, and is strongly attracted by his wildness and hearty laughter.

> Gertrude herself was rather contemptuous of dancing: she had not the slightest inclination towards that accomplishment, and had never learned even a Roger de Coverley. She was a puritan, like her father, high-minded, and really stern. Therefore the dusky, golden softness of this man's *sensuous flame of life, that flowed from off his flesh like the flame from a candle, not baffled*

CHAPTER ONE

and gripped into incandescence by thought and spirit as her life was, seemed to her something wonderful, beyond her. (*SL* 18; emphasis added)

Although she has been making little of the eighteenth-century dances, his dance and the invisible blaze floating from his flesh overwhelm her in a way that is not captured or processed by thought or spirit, and they even overthrow her way of thinking. The flame is used as a simile for his fiery sensuality, and it covers up Gertrude's individuality as a catalyst which burns down the barrier between them. The physicality expresses its potential for getting over the sharp contrast of class distinction and personality, developed by the different circumstances that bore them. The depth of this instant connection was so stupendous that it did not permit her son Paul to take the place of her husband, even though she is bound to him by the indivisible tie of platonic lovers, and however much time has passed.

'. . . [M]y mother, I believe, got *real* joy and satisfaction out of my father at first. . . . That's what one *must have*, I think,' he continued; 'the real, real flame of feeling through another person, once, only once, if it only last three months. . . . And with my father, at first, I'm sure she had the real thing. She knows — she has been there. . . .'

'What has happened, exactly?' asked Miriam.

'It's so hard to say — but the something big and intense that changes you when you really come together with somebody else. . . . — and at the bottom she feels grateful to him for giving it her, even now, though they are miles apart.' (*SL* 361-62)

The vivid imagining of the physical intuitive interchange, which the grown-up Paul discloses as his preoccupation, is bolstered by Lawrence's own domineering primal consciousness. According to the psychoanalytic theory of Melanie Klein, it can be considered that Lawrence's intention to represent this image in his works shows an instinct for repeating his primal wound.

In addition to the practical act of dancing, the sensational and overwhelming experience which Gertrude had felt in relation to Morel, is expressed as an impalpable physical communication. Lawrence presents this as a sudden extraordinary sense which departs from the daily continuity of time and existence. Dancing is 'a sudden bodily tapping into and revelation of what they are at their innermost, unbeknownst to themselves' and it 'becomes a way of breaking through "character" and "social relationship", to reveal something deeper', by releasing the social self into a non-social form of communion (Kinkead-Weeks 59). The transcendent moments of the bodily interaction appear vividly in 'The White Stocking': one of the earliest short stories which Lawrence wrote at the age of twenty-two in his Nottingham University days. In the formless physicality which fills the text, the convulsive energy of freeing one's self and merging with the other, and the various deviations from modernity are presented with surprising vividness. The main character Elsie Whiston, a capricious and somewhat sly woman, is invited to the Christmas party, hosted by her boss at the lace factory, Sam Adams, with her fiancé. The following passage is from a scene in which she accepts Adams' invitation to dance with him, looking askance at her straitlaced fiancé, who cannot dance and plays cards uninterestingly.

At that moment Sam Adams appeared, florid and boisterous,

intoxicated more with himself, with the dancing, than with wine. In his eyes *the curious, impersonal light* gleamed. . . . 'I should never look for you among the ladies,' he said, with a kind of intimate, *animal call* to her. (*PO* 152; emphasis added)

In *The White Peacock*, likewise, Emily Saxton's inability to dance freely is condemned: her being too ashamed and being emotional rather than intuitive make her unable to release herself from excessive self-consciousness (*WP* 97). Compared to Elsie's fiancé's rejection of dancing, Adams' unrestrained and festive physical sensuousness is emphasized here. The 'impersonal' and peculiar gleaming of his eyes, and the animal-like call, which slips out from his subjective will or emotion, entice Elsie to a primitive, collective unconsciousness. The term 'impersonal', which is later expanded into the notion of the 'inhuman', pervades Lawrence's post-war works which focus on the inter-racial communication in the world outside Britain, and also had an important meaning in the context of twentieth-century avant-garde art and aesthetics. Yet, I argue that it is particularly interesting that the notion is found in this early stage of Lawrence's work. Moreover, though Adams is described as a man who has Irish blood, this appears only in the snippets of conversation in a small interrelation inside England.

Returning to the text, Elsie and Adams keep on dancing as follows:

That dance was an intoxication to her. After the first few steps, she felt herself slipping away from herself. She almost knew she was going, she did not even want to go. Yet she must have chosen to go. . . . she seemed to swim away out of contact with the room, into him. She had passed into another, denser element of him, an essential privacy. The room was all vague around her, like an atmosphere, like under sea, with a flow of ghostly, dumb movements. . . . He also was given up, oblivious, concentrated, into the dance. *His eye was unseeing.* . . . His fingers seemed to search into her flesh. Every moment, and every moment, she felt she would give way utterly, and sink molten: the fusion point was coming when she would fuse down into perfect unconsciousness at his feet and knees. But he bore her round the room in the dance, and he seemed to sustain all her body with his limbs, his body, and his warmth seemed to come closer into her, nearer, till it would fuse right through her, and she would be as liquid to him, as an intoxication only.

It was exquisite. When it was over, she was dazed, and was scarcely breathing. She stood with him in the middle of the room as if she were alone in a remote place. . . .

''Twas good, wasn't it, my darling?' he said to her, low and delighted. There was *a strange impersonality about his low, exultant call* that appealed to her irresistibly. Yet why was she aware of some part shut off in her? (*PO* 153; emphasis added)

Although there was no romantic feeling between them from the outset, their relationship is effectively achieved by the flow of vitalistic communication. What Adams shows to Elsie is the means of entering a rapport of physical consciousness which surpasses personal feelings. In the voluminous moment, tempted by Adams who actualizes a liberation, Elsie sets herself free from her earthly personality and 'sink[s]', melts like 'liquid', and 'fuse[s]' into unison with him. The catalyst which conveys the physicality of the other is figured as liquid, while in *Sons and Lovers* it is described as a flame, and I find that the dynamic function of these elemental figures coincide with the new mode of impersonal representation in the twentieth-century novels which Daniel Albright defines as follows: 'there is an abolishing of the demarcation between one character and another; distinct personages are replaced by a single matrix, a fluid sentience endlessly sifting through its perceptions and reflections' (Albright 19).[2]

Moreover, Adams watches nothing consciously with his eyes while dancing: his condition deviates from the quality of modernized human beings' cerebral cognition, which is captivated by eyesight. As the binary theory of body and mind extended by Plato and Descartes and the accompanying emphasis on mind have dominated Western philosophy, the theory of the senses which Aristotle advocates in his *Metaphysics* had a decisive influence in attaching a superior value to vision, leading it to be regarded as noble in the Western tradition, while dismissing the tactile sense as belonging to a lower class due to its being common to all creatures. The theory claims that 'By nature, all men long to know. An indication is their delight in the senses ... through the eyes more than the others. . . . [S]ight is the sense that especially produces cognition in us and reveals many distinguishing features of things' (*Metaphysics*, 4), and it emphasizes the development of cognition in association with visual sensation in the industrial society and anticipates the forthcoming centuries which strengthen this effect. As Mineo Takamura points out, Aristotle's statement that visual sensation enables human beings to become sophisticated not only distinguished human beings from animals, allowing them to live a virtuous life and have intelligence to support it, but also gave an exclusive privilege to visual sensation in a classification of the senses (10-12). As if objecting to Aristotle's account, Lawrence repetitively demonstrates through his works such as the short story 'The Blind Man' that liberation from eyesight is the first step towards reopening the dynamic consciousness. While the affinity of vision with intellectual cognition pervades Western culture in general, Lawrence evokes the radical conversion of values which vision and touch produce. His intention to destroy the hierarchy of senses is explicit in the fact that the source of the transmission of dynamic consciousness in the mother's womb begins with blind unconsciousness.

Furthermore, the impersonality which lurks inside Adams' 'low, exultant call' is another word for his 'animal call'. It is as if it conveys the ferocious ring of a voice with no reserve, that reminds us of something inhuman and uncivilized. The manifestation of animality which is shown to Elsie is a direct experience of being showered with the energy which tears the peaceful regulation of her social self. The liberating energy conveyed from Adams — that is, the abandonment of personal rationality — can be considered as a dissolution of the individual. As we have seen before, the physical communication through dancing exhibits primitive notions which are variously described as impersonality, a reversal of the classification of visual sensation, and animality. Due to the transmission of primitiveness from Adams to Elsie in the ecstatic state, she is led to a sense of the vanishing of the present, which looms from the level of personal time and space; and this experience is linked to antiquity. Interestingly, all of these expressions of primitiveness are essentially the same as those which an English woman, Kate Leslie, experiences in *The Plumed Serpent* when she is involved in the circle of Indian dance in Mexico. It is easily imaginable for us today that the primitivism is preserved in the sound of drums and the wild rhythm of the dance, though in 'The White Stocking', the primeval sense is represented in the small rural town in England. The fact that Lawrence's description of this experience expanded in the actual spot of antiquity after he travelled to Mexico, as compared with his domestic writing of twenty years earlier, suggests that the physicality in Lawrence's works is not an accidental phenomenon.

The physicality in 'The White Stocking' is not presented as a thing which overcomes the gap of social class between individuals. However, its production of pre-modern (or anti-modern) notions such as impersonality or animality promotes a release from modernity, and it possesses an aggressiveness which destroys mental modernity. The physicality breaks the shackles of Elsie's social self, and releases her body from individuality, enabling her interaction with others through dynamic consciousness. The aggression is a vital energy which primitiveness connotes, which psychoanalysis describes as being repressed into the level of unconsciousness. It is also a notion which is defined negatively in the historical and cultural context that constantly gives it exteriority — regardless of its essential immanence. However, the exhibition of aggression as a release of energy manifests itself through a dynamic consciousness that pierces the center of the body, in addition to the idea of the indwelling externality which gnaws its way out of the social self. This aggression, I would argue, brings about changes in the relationships of individuals, and is expressed as a motive power which dynamically reconstructs the human relationships in Lawrence's works. I will return to the aspects of impersonality, the inversion of values in sensory perception, and animality, in the later part of this study, though I would only state here that Lawrence has already displayed his perfect vision of physicality that escapes from modernity in his earliest short stories. It deserves special mention that the issue which he thoroughly questioned in his less than twenty-five years of writing, and which constituted the attraction of his works at the same time, is condensed into this small story, 'The White Stocking'.

As seen above, the physicality which Lawrence depicts is something that comes to fruition in temporality. However, this raises the question of how we should appreciate his idea of temporality in the context of realism, which consists of a linear time axis. The attitude of isolating the events he describes from chronological narrative, as well as the attempt to deviate from modern psychology, can be seen in Lawrence's early writings, due to the representation of a specific aggressive energy which dynamically crushes the static convention by its immanent motion.

2. The Psychodynamics of Affect

As we have already seen, physical cognition in Lawrence's fiction presents lived experience as a form which is opposed to things that are merely intelligible. The sensory experience of bodily activity is so deep and existential that it can remove the distinction between self and other which is based on rational knowledge. At that specific moment, as seen from the standpoint of realism, the experience of an everyday reality, characterized by linear temporality, is defamiliarized. Recent study of modernism has facilitated a theoretical explanation of this experience which escapes from various categorizations and definitions found in modern realist novels. This explanation involves a study of 'affect' that has been flourishing from the late 1990s until now and the definition of its object in comparison with subjective 'emotion'. It was realism that dominated the genre of the novel from the mid-nineteenth century — though critics have discovered the existence of affect as an aesthetic provocation, which deceives realistic narrative by questioning it from within, asking 'What is Real?' and 'Is realism really Real'? This is 'The Affective Turn' which elucidates the frailty of the structure of nineteenth-century fiction by highlighting affect as a resistant energy that lurks inside it. Patricia Clough states that in the aftermath of the death of the subject in poststructuralism and deconstruction, the trend of analyzing the discontinuity of the subject's conscious experience in terms of non-intentional emotion and affect has arisen. Besides, she explains, the turn to affect and emotion urges us to take heed of bodily matter and has thus enriched the study of human beings' immanent dynamism and organic quality (Clough 206-7).

I will firstly explore the concept of affect using a distinction drawn from the description of emotion in the nineteenth-century novel, and then illustrate its position in realism. The modern period in the West, which began with a breakaway from medieval feudalism, brought a dismantling of the semantic world of the previous Christian semiotics. Human beings have obtained individuality apart from God; psychic qualities and emotions as interiority attributed to the subject, and what exists in the exterior can be objectified: that is the constitution of modern psychology ('Affect, Realism, and Utopia' 119-21). With the *récit* of narrating history, a chronologically-determined structuration of the act of representation has been facilitated. As Brian Massumi remarks, emotion participates in society, which is constituted by numerous contracts and conventions, or symbolical meanings and languages. He states that 'Emotion is qualified intensity, the conventional, consensual point of insertion of intensity into semantically and semiotically formed progressions, into narrativizable action-reaction circuits, into function and meaning. It is intensity owned and recognized' (Massumi 28).

The aspect which critics particularly focus on is the subject's proprietorship over emotion. Fredric Jameson states that the description of emotion in realism is arranged under names such as 'love, hatred, anger, fear, disgust, pleasure' and systematized in this way (29). In the same way as colours, emotions can be categorized into types of general perception and positioned in a larger structure of times and cultures. Focusing on the issue of stillness and motion, I would like to elucidate Lawrence's own statement, in the following quotation, that this systematization, or the rigidity of emotion, will invite the adjustment of human relationships.

> All emotions, including love and hate, and rage and tenderness, go to the adjusting of the oscillating, unestablished balance between two people who amount to anything. If the novelist puts his thumb in the pan, for love, tenderness, sweetness, peace, then he commits an immoral act: he *prevents* the possibility of a true relationship, a pure relatedness, the only thing that matters: and he makes inevitable the horrible reaction, when he lets his thumb go, towards hate and brutality, cruelty and destruction. (*STH* 173)

Therefore, it can be shown that Lawrence was pursuing the active experience which can destabilize the subject's consciousness, and expected that it would become a dynamo for activating interpersonal relationships.

Furthermore, Jameson claims that we embody and possess emotions by giving them names and give our intentions and desires an objectified quality by means of emotion. Therefore, emotion has a role similar to that of language, and is captured within the realm of the signifier. Human beings have made the intellect and rational communication with others possible by linguistic activity, and have firmly believed that the world of realistic representation, centered on words and logic, is a remarkable achievement of the civilization and culture of mankind. On the other hand, Lawrence's communication by dynamic consciousness which escapes from the mind and relies on intuition and physical sensations is felt as an unrepresentable, existential and substantial experience. That is, it is a bodily feeling which cannot be named as either happy or sad and is unable to be involved in the framework of emotion. Ultimately, in Lawrence's texts, there exists a line between the representable world of words and symbols and the unrepresentable world of body and sense, which coexist and confront each other. Emotion and affect are critically differentiated in this respect.

However, due to the increasing objectivity of the modernized view, the act of representing objects became inseparable from the structural narrative in ordinary novels. It works in accordance with the birth of the new social meaning, which is not provided by God, and the rearrangement of the older semiotic meaning. Peter Brooks argues that with the coming of the modern age, defined as the end of the eighteenth century with the French Revolution, this independence of representation is 'tied to the rise of the middle classes to cultural influence, and to the rise of the novel as the preeminent form of modernity' and has yielded the value and 'language of ordinary men' and 'the meaning of unexceptional human experience' (7). The mental interiority, which was supposed to be the property of the individual, has come to be expressed in relation to a structured society which categorizes common perceptions and experiences. Thus, it has come to gain the support of the bourgeoisie through their sharing of the general sense of the powerful mass of readers. However, the idea of the 'ordinary' which Brooks uses is worth noting: what becomes the nucleus of modern novels is 'the middle class' and their 'unexceptional human experience' which shapes the new value system. This is traceable, I would argue, in the realistic narrative which virtuously devotes itself to objectivity and restricts the range of representations in texts and connotes the right of control over them.

Jameson singles out the description of the Maison Vauquer in *Le Père Goriot* (1835) by Honoré de Balzac (1799-1850) as a flag-bearer of the nineteenth-century realist novel and discusses the narrator's physical senses which are characteristic of its graphic representation.

> [T]he elaborate descriptions in Balzac do not invalidate the historical proposition I want to advance about the body in literature. For in Balzac everything that looks like a physical sensation — a musty smell, a rancid taste, a greasy fabric always means something, it is a sign or allegory of the moral or social status of a given character: decent poverty, squalor, the pretensions of the parvenu, the true nobility of the old aristocracy, and so on. In short, it is not really a sensation, it is already a meaning, an allegory. By the time of Flaubert, these signs remain, but they have become stereotypical; and *the new descriptions register a density beyond such stereotypical meanings*. (Jameson 33; emphasis added)

Balzac's narrator reflects the privileged viewpoint that naturally conceives class-consciousness in its relation to physical phenomena. Therefore, it is evident that this is not empirically realized by a lived body and exists in the domain of representations, similar to allegory. However, as I have highlighted in the quotation, Jameson explains that there exists a 'density' which transcends stereotypical bourgeois physicality in the novels of Gustave Flaubert (1821-1880), even though they are contemporary realist works as well as Balzac's, and it is expressed with a rare manner of representation, an extra-realism. First, I would like to explore the gloomy supper scene of Emma and Charles in *Madame Bovary* (1857).

> But it was above all the meal-times that were unbearable to her, in the small room on the ground-floor, with its smoking stove, its creaking door, the walls that sweated, the damp flags; all the bitterness of life seemed served up on her plate, and with the steam of the boiled beef rose from her secret soul whiffs of sickliness. (*Madame Bovary*, 62)

Erich Auerbach legitimately points out the stylistic features which should be distinguished from the ordinary rules of realism in this scene in which Emma boils with every possible dissatisfaction. The description in this scene does not allude to any kind of social consciousness and it does not get involved in the categories of existing rhetoric — thus, 'the tone can be tragic, sentimental, idyllic, comical or burlesque' (Auerbach 427). Jameson goes as far as to state that this scene can be relocated regardless of the literary and social era or context, 'from Shakespeare back to medieval fabliaux' (142). If I change this scene to a Lawrentian tone, it is possible to read it as describing the dinner table of a collier and his wife who live on two pounds a week. To sum up, the original mode of narrative in realism has seen its collapse in this scene and faces an unrepresentable reality. It is a way of showing the raw and active experience of Emma that has gained 'a density' which substitutes for telling and representing — 'an intensity' in the psycho-physical term — as a dramatization of the unrepresentable.

Although Auerbach and Jameson lengthily discuss how this scene is de-categorized, I would embark on the definition of the core notion of affect here through the comparison with Balzac. The most notable part is Emma's latent feeling, sickened by insatiable desire which steams with the scent of a meat dish in the last sentence. Through the bodily sensation of smell, the existential inside Emma mingles with the everyday quality outside. It contrasts sharply both with Balzac's physicality which remains redolent of allegories relating to class-distinctions, and with a mere realistic portrait. Several critics argue that this scene in *Madame Bovary* is the first appearance of bodily affect which cannot be enclosed within the frame of emotion or mentality. Here, the material factors do not define Emma's identity in terms of her social status — they evade numerous ramifications of categories and solely and directly embody the autonomy of her sensitive reaction to the depths of life. This disrupts the ordinariness of her life facing Charles, a man she finds boring, and releases her into a limitless dissatisfaction and desire. It is ironically a sort of intensity of temporal replenishment.[3]

The contrast between the perspective of chronology and the disruption of time consciousness is a salient feature in distinguishing realism from the expression of affect. Realism creates a narrative continuity and it describes the chronological temporality moving from past to present and future. On the other hand, Massumi states that 'Intensity is embodied in purely autonomic reactions' (25) and thus a sense of futurity, a 'definite expectation, an imitation of what comes next in a conventional progression' (26) that is registered intellectually, dampens the intensity as I have discussed in the Introduction by quoting Bergson. The expression of affect, which presents non-literary aspects of reality through the incongruity of form and content, yields timeless intensity which cannot be reintegrated into chronological temporality. Expressed in my own words, the non-intellectual event which depends on the degree of the impact of senses that disrupt the expected linear progression, amplifies the suspension of space and time.

    As Nicholas Manning and Geoffrey Baker point out, realism, which achieved sovereignty in the nineteenth century, ignored a kind of experiences that are characterized by 'alterity and heterodoxy, [and] refuse to be integrated into a stable textual apparatus' (Manning, par. 1). It is an attitude of circumventing things that 'resist typical realist values such as formal cohesion, objectivity, totality, and epistemological inclusion (omniscience)' (Manning, par. 1),[4] whereas affect possesses unconfinable intensity and dynamism, although as Fuhito Endo states it cannot be retrieved to discursive sophistication or formal completion ('Affect, Realism, and Utopia', 117). Endo strongly argues that affect expresses itself as a *'negative* constituting power' ('Affect, Realism, and Utopia', 116) and emotion is deconstructed as carrying affect within it, that is, the anti-modern inside the modern. Reflecting on these critiques, I will assert again the connection of Lawrence's aim of expressing physical consciousness to the dynamism of affect. Lawrence is a novelist who aims at reform by craving a resistant energy in what is generally assumed as negative in the modernized worldview. It is not an external force which destroys existing social structures but always a power inside, which is understandable from his trust in the innate dynamic energy which disturbs human beings' superficial intelligence and rationalism from inside their bodies. Developing an affect theory in architecture and aesthetics, Michael Young lucidly describes the process by which the aggressive energy of affect demolishes and restructures the existing representational structure.

> [Flaubert] shifted attention from a narrative whole to the specificity of a detailed scene. This shift implied an attack on the conventions of academic art that stressed certain manners in which art was to be composed. Furthermore, these genre conventions specified the interpretive method for extracting poetic meaning from an artwork. . . . In Flaubert . . . we see the attack on these familiar structures of producing and interpreting meaning. *The resulting void was filled with a new emphasis on the sensations of the body,* or in other words, affect. (Young 59; emphasis added)[5]

The deviation from the linear stream of narrative produces 'the resulting void' which, Young suggests, results from the act of destroying the structure of temporal and phenomenal continuity. Exposed to the a-chronological infinity, the vulnerable body imbued with intensity is exposed to feeling the surge of the senses — the 'waves' (28), as Jameson puts it — and when the annihilating gap is filled, the efficacy of 'emotion' surrenders its place to 'affect'.

Although the concept of affect was not established in Lawrence's time, he ingeniously appreciated this surge, or the motion which is an important feature of affect, and introduced it into his works. It was evidently an aspect of the varied physicality in the several texts which were analyzed in the first section of this study: the quickening of energy which is felt deep-down in one's body beyond the individual perceptive capacity in daily life. For example, in the story 'The Blind Man', discussed earlier, the man rocks every piece of furniture in the room by his extremities without eyesight, and feels an exquisite pleasure in submitting himself to the billow of 'blood-prescience' (*EME*

54), rather than discovering things by guesswork and dead reckoning. This is a case in which affective experience is felt by one person as in *Madame Bovary*.

However, what emphasizes the special quality of the motion and waves of affect even more, is when it is felt intersubjectively among a group of people. It is 'a dissolution, a blurring, an eating away of outline, a loss of the clear division between perceiver, perception, and object perceived' (Albright 20) and I argue that Lawrence has brilliantly realized such an exchange of affect between people in his fiction. The sense of rapture in Lawrence's works discussed in the previous section proves the potential of affect to transcend personality and enables a unification with the other and with exterior things. It is a sense of Gertrude's life enveloped by the flame of young Morel's physique that we see in *Sons and Lovers*, and ultimately, the reduction of individuality to a small mass is meticulously depicted in 'The White Stocking'. In contrast with the people 'all vague around her, like an atmosphere, like under sea, with a flow of ghostly, dumb movements', Elsie 'seemed to swim away out of contact with the room, into him' (*PO* 153). The contrasting motion of the two floods, the slow motion of the reality and the acceleration of affect, are exhibited here. The intoxication produced by the fluid vibration of space, the sense of being wrapped up in the swelling flood, suggests a departure from subjectivity or private speculation: it obviously shows that the quality of affect is transmitted by its motion.

However, Massumi expresses a relatively narrow view of the extent of the power interchanged in the intensity of the magnetic field.

> It is not exactly passivity, because it [the affective space] is filled with motion, vibratory motion, resonation. And it is not

yet activity, because the motion is not of the kind that can be directed (if only symbolically) toward practical ends in a world of constituted objects and aims. . . . (Massumi 26)

Assuming the motion to be more than passivity but less than activity, Massumi's appreciation is mistaken in underestimating its pragmatic function and influence. On the contrary, the differences which exist among individuals are dissolved by the motion of affect in Lawrence's fiction. I would strongly argue that the effect of yielding an intuitive and profound appreciation of other people who belong to another social class is a significant element which distinguishes Lawrence's innovation from Flaubert's. In *Madame Bovary*, affect was not yet sufficiently elastic in terms of unifying the individual with others. What I intend to foreground here again is the idea that the 'dynamic' intersubjectivity of affect in Lawrence's fiction has an effect of overcoming the divisions in human relationships which are in a confrontational situation caused by knowledge or emotion. The evocation of the exchange of existences between different social strata distinguishes Lawrence's text from Flaubert's. The affect in Lawrence's text does not just exist to stress the autonomy of the moment and the senses, but to positively offer the dissipation of differentiating factors by carrying energy between people, as described by Teresa Brennan in her study of the transmission of affect from a sociological and clinical perspective (Ch. 2). The dynamics of its motion display a power of dispelling the reality of social classes by creating an intersubjectivity through the conveyance of affect.

This argument will be supported by specific analysis of a short story named 'Goose Fair', a story on which Lawrence collaborated with Louie Burrows, his fiancé for a short while. It is one of the stories that were written in response to the invitation of Ford Madox Ford, the editor of the *English Review* (launched in 1908), seeking submissions which would boldly depict the true conditions of British labourers.

> Give us, Ford demanded, a picture of life as it is. Enough of rehashed romances and tiresome, hackneyed, historical literature . . . . The Goal of the *Review* would be 'to discover where Great Britain stands, if the discovery can be made.' Where, for example, do the workers stand? Where stand the poor? 'Of knowledge of the lives and aspirations of the poor man how little we have. We are barred off from him by the invisible barriers: we have no records of his views of literature. It is astonishing how little literature has to show of the life of the poor.' (qtd. in Harris 26)

Published in the *English Review* in 1910, Lawrence's contribution thus responded to Ford's 'new young school of realism' project which aimed to pick out an energetic new standard-bearer of proletarian literature. Far from being committed to the proletariat, however, it was finished into a provocative work in which realism and anti-realism are combined. It presents a young lady of the middle class, who is unaware of the realities of the labourers, and who mingles with the intense atmosphere of a different social stratum for the first time in her life through an affective experience.

Set in a destitute suburb which surrounds Sneinton Church, the story portrays the trio of a man and two women belonging to three different social classes. The characters are the young lady Lois Saxton who belongs to an old propertied family who own a lace factory, her lover Will Selby, and a nameless indigent girl who sells geese.

Although Will is also the child of a factory manager, the Selbys are belittled by the Saxtons due to their rootlessness; the factory is said to have 'sprung up in a day' and will 'vanish in a night' (*PO* 137). Andrew Harrison states, 'The Selbys are representative of the *nouveau riche*: they are wealthy, but their wealth is not associated with family tradition or property. The story uses this social background to probe the nature of the feelings which bind Lois to Will' ('The Regional Modernism', 47). The plot is based on the frictional love relationship of the couple who apparently exist on the same social level, though in truth, they are fraught with differences. Lois sees him off to the factory and hears the clamour of the Goose Fair, a customary event in Nottingham in October, far away from her bedside window. Representing 'the girl of superior culture' (*PO* 134), she lives at a distance from the commotion of the public world. Unlike Lois, however, Will knows the nature of labour and understands the industrial downturn and the employees' discontent in the 1870s. At the time when he did not coexist in the same rank with her, he could enter into the lower class through his work. Without her knowledge, he has an active freedom of moving between the social strata.

Apart from the lovers, the goose-girl never gets out of the fair which is the field of her life and work. However, the depressed condition of the regional trade in Nottingham is reported through the portrayal of the girl as ugly and vain, with a dozen unsold geese and a lame one, and through the narrative which seems to be her monologue. It is the girl who secretly maneuvers behind the main plot by indifferently displaying the harsh lives of people in the lowest level of society as a background to the social strife which the emotional friction of the lovers represents. In the background of this tale, there is the fact that the Franco-Prussian War in 1870-71 has been causing a crucial

CHAPTER ONE

disadvantage to Nottingham which is a trading partner of France's market, and the goose-girl represents the problems and struggles which the society experiences. Rather than being merely reportage, she represents the ambience of the market which embodies the locality of Nottingham. She plays the role of portraying aspects of the physical environment such as the collective feverish heat and the skirmish flaring up between vulgar people at a distance from the couple. Labour is an inaccessible world for Lois, who has never felt people's suffering due to trade as a reality, which was as far away from her as the hot bustle of the Goose Fair which is felt obscurely in the distance from her bedroom window.

> She drew the curtains, and stood holding aside a heavy fold, looking out on the night. She could see only the nothingness of the fog: not even the glare of the fair was evident, though the noise clamoured small in the distance. In front of everything she could see her own faint image. (*PO* 136)

The fog veils the forest near her mansion and it symbolizes the lack of substance in her real consciousness which alienates her from her milieu. Even the brightly burning light of the fair in the darkness is dimmed by the fog and she has only seen the world with her misty sight.

However, she wakes in the middle of the night due to the fuss in her house, which is flurried by a disastrous fire at the Selbys' factory. Feeling uneasiness for Will, Lois runs through the fog-dripping trees and heads to the spot with haste. From the manner of talking of her father who was already at the scene, however, a sinister conjecture was passing through her mind that Will had intentionally set fire to the factory to obtain the insurance money. She confronts the glare of the fire in the obscuring fog and then determinedly approaches it.

> With peaked, noble face she watched the fire. Then she looked a little wildly over the fire-reddened faces in the crowd. . . . She looked at the fire, and the tears were quickly dried by fear. The flames roared and struggled upward. *The great wonder of the fire made her forget even her indignation at her father's treatment of her and her lover.* . . . The air became unbreathable; *the fog was swallowed up*: . . . sometimes burning cards of lace went whirling into the gulf of the sky, waving with wings of fire. (*PO* 136-37; emphasis added)

The factory, turned to a deluge of fire, gives off a sensation of unknown heat through the sparks and the blast of hot air. The dense fog, which has been protecting her *naïveté*, is swallowed up by the flames and the disappearance of her hurt emotion is remarkable before the 'The great wonder of the fire'. I would argue that it has a forceful impact which induces the entropy of her emotion, and the undiscovered bodily experience intrudes into the void as a substitute. The heat she felt was an anonymous passion of the labourers that has gone wild. After returning home, Lois washes 'her fire-darkened face' (*PO* 138) and cries, wrapping her body with silk bedclothes. It can be said that her bourgeois physicality has been transfigured and affect has obliged her to experience acculturation. Lawrence seems to have ironically mixed his realism with the affective, evoking a destruction and transformation of bourgeois ideas of physicality through a technique that contradicts the nebulous idea of graphically depicting the workingmen's lives.

The next morning, Lois feels an urgent impulse to go to the scene of the tragedy to overcome the contradiction in herself. Returning to the factory accompanied by her housemaid, Lois happens to encounter Will who has just come back from the Goose Fair and she experiences the heat again that remains from the previous night's fire, the feverish atmosphere of the fair which Will brings with him, and the after-effect of a fervor inside him resulting from the series of events. It was a crucial experience for Lois to meet with the inward passion, the unseen nature in Will, and a solid sense of a confirmation of life hits her. While being anguished by a strong hatred and a feeling that Will's wrongdoing is unforgiveable, she feels a bond between herself and him due to a magnificent rush of affect that deviates from emotion. 'Curiously enough, they walked side by side as if they belonged to each other. She was his conscience-keeper. She was far from forgiving him, but she was still further from letting him go' (*PO* 142). It has created a joint activity between them which surpasses the recognition of his essence through her bodily sensation.

In the tale, in conclusion, the impact of the sensation which surged at her direct confrontation with the fire has de-emotionalized her, and then the heat infiltrated into the space and people evokes an affective interrelation and an appreciation of the others which subdues her anger. Through the motion which affect produces, she experiences an acculturation as if dislodging the social strata. It should be noted that physical interaction is depicted as ascending to the mind which encloses and fetters one's inner self; and the new group affiliation with others in different social strata is achieved by the infectiousness of bodily affect.

The psychodynamics of emotion versus affect has a great affinity to the physical system of mind versus sensation which Lawrence expounds. It is the dynamic consciousness that awakens irrational and intense communication with its autonomous reaction in an organization; and it is completely different from the upper center of the body that governs intellect or rationality. It should be noted that Lawrence called the source of dynamic or blood consciousness 'the great "*affective*" centre': in a mysterious coincidence, as Endo points out (*Jyodo to Modernity*, 60-1), his usage of the idea of affect interestingly resembles the theoretical concept developed in recent years, and displays a potential which anticipates the critics' interests.

3. Transmitting Epiphany by Affect: The Effect of Ecstasy

In the previous two sections, we have seen how Lawrence's early works contain evocations of affect and how the characters escape from emotions that have been socially and conventionally determined. By dramatizing the revitalization of physical perception, an intense temporality is created which suspends the influence of worldliness and minimizes emotion, and it overturns the consciousness that discriminates between the self and the other. This literary innovation was virtually an attempt to escape from traditional novelistic style, as Lawrence declares in describing his aim in a well-known letter to Edward Garnett written in 1914.

> I don't care so much about what the woman *feels* — in the ordinary usage of the word. That presumes an *ego* to feel with. I only care about what the woman *is* — what she *is* — inhumanly, physiologically, materially . . . instead of what she feels according to the human conception. . . . You mustn't look in my novel for the old stable ego of the character. There is another *ego*, according to whose action the individual is unrecognisable, and passes through, as it were, allotropic states which it needs a

deeper sense than any we've been used to exercise, to discover are states of the same single radically-unchanged element. (Like as diamond and coal are the same pure element of carbon. The ordinary novel would trace the history of the diamond — but I say, 'diamond what! This is carbon.' And my diamond might be coal or soot, and my theme is carbon.) (*2L* 183)

Since this letter had the purpose of defending the sale of the prohibited novel *The Rainbow*, Lawrence's fiction is thought to be distinguishable into that written prior to and after this letter or *The Rainbow*. The proclamation of depicting the profound reality of carbon, not minerals like diamond and coal, is called the 'carbon identity letter' among Lawrence scholars and has attracted extraordinary attention and been frequently quoted in recent years. The statement that 'The ordinary novel would trace the history of the diamond' describes the conventional novels that adhere to the subject's personality which is moulded by its historical context and the passage of time. Here, Lawrence's usage of the motifs of 'diamond and coal' and 'carbon' seems to be convincing: coal and diamond, I argue, imply the adamant ego which is defined by writers and novels themselves in multilayered ways that are predetermined by historical, cultural, social, and sexual patterns. The carbon, a metaphor which reflects Lawrence's own connection with the world of collieries, stands out in relief by removing 'the human conception' which is the property of the subject. The existential new identity shows itself by activating physicality or intuition simultaneously with the entropy of modern human beings' conceptions and emotions. Patrick J. Whiteley rephrases Lawrence's intention, stating that 'Beneath the "stable ego" — the individuated self — is the "other ego" that cannot be recognized by individual actions because this ego — a transindividual selfhood — passes beyond the boundaries between individuals' (125). Stressing the idea of continuity or the collective identity, Whiteley's statement directs us towards the interpretation of Lawrence's works from the perspective of affect.

Although I agree with Whiteley's summary, I would also argue that the true motive for Lawrence's words has been conveniently distorted by critics to stress the view of Lawrence as a dictatorial idea-based writer rather than a story-based author. The critics accept his polemical statement that we should not look in his novels for the old stable ego at face value and interpret this letter as implying that Lawrence has completely relinquished depicting human beings' emotions and superficial relationships — an attitude which is also evident in Whiteley's statement that 'In Lawrence the self is a sham exactly because there is a more rudimentary self that is mingled with other selves in a collective unity' (126-27). Additionally, Gaku Iwai suggests that at that time, around the period of the First World War, Lawrence was expressing a disdainful attitude toward both the writers and the readers of over-sentimental mass-market fiction (210).[6] Therefore, the critics judge that this 'carbon identity letter' insists on the negation of romantic novels and bids farewell to over-emotional fiction. Raising an opposing view to the arguments of these critics, I would ask how the self or individuality could be deliberately reduced to a sham in Lawrence's works, which brilliantly depict the conflicts of the individual's emotions toward others, and the succeeding agony. I would argue that Lawrence had not even dreamed of the possibility of completely eradicating the old self, since he was aware of the transient duration of affect and its disappointing failure through his mother's (and we should also say Paul's mother's) married life with her labouring class, drinking husband.

Moreover, the 'carbon identity letter' does not mark a watershed in his literary style; Lawrence's oeuvre has a consistent quality. As I have argued so far, the affective moments in works earlier than *The Rainbow* explicitly draw our attention to their intensity by the characters' interaction within the de-emotionalized depths of their physico-mental being. On the other hand, it cannot be said that Lawrence stopped depicting the persistence and collisions of the old selfhood in subsequent works through the failure of his characters' romances, which I will analyze in the later chapters. As long as he illustrates frictional human relationships that are swayed by emotional forces, in parallel with the continuous collective identity, he keeps highlighting the differentiating factors between people which cause rejection. My view is thus analogous to Giuseppina Gregorio's observation regarding Lawrence's fluid creativity that he delineates characters who 'cannot be described according to old patterns, because they are inconsistent, ephemeral traces of ever evolving identities' (par. 7). Therefore, his purpose is to depict the essential element, 'an impersonal identity, something that lies under the epidermis, a region where true actions take place — the unconscious' (Gregorio, par. 7).

As I have stated earlier, Lawrence believed in the novelistic possibility of the rejection of time schemes as a way to depict the unconscious ego which is undetermined by social conventions. In a passage which Gregorio quotes from *Study of Thomas Hardy*, Lawrence favourably evaluates the unpredictability of the actions of characters and the aggressive energy in the novels of Thomas Hardy (1840-1928) — 'he refers to their actions using the adjective *explosive* and the adverb *suddenly*, in order to highlight the lack of possibilities to foresee their actions or to determine the reasons behind them' (Gregorio, par. 9).

> [In Hardy's novels there is the] slightest development of personal action in the characters: it is all explosive. . . The rest explode out of the convention. They are people each with a real, vital, potential self, . . . and this self suddenly bursts the shell of manner and convention and commonplace opinion, and acts independently, absurdly, without mental knowledge or acquiescence. (*STH* 20)

In the Introduction to this study, I have used Bergson's discussion to suggest that the subject's intellectual pleasure has to do with his or her dominion over the object. In contrast, with regard to the specific words on which Gregorio focuses, and especially the verb 'bursts', Lawrence admires the strength of Hardy's fiction in depicting the unpredictable quality which is not regulated by the social self.

By giving a sharp intensity to the present moment, in many of his experimental short stories Lawrence manages to produce experience which is distinctive for its suddenness more than for the affect which it involves. It is a phenomenon called 'epiphany', a sensation of unexpectedly reaching the unknown reality, which is produced in the moment of the sudden disruption of the permanently repeated routine of daily life.[7] The etymological origin of the word 'epiphany' is a manifestation of Christ to the Gentiles, though its meaning has been extended in the realm of literature to include the depiction of 'spots of time' by William Wordsworth (1770-1850) as an experience of momentarily deviating from chronological time, and the innovative use of moments of revelation or enlightenment as a modernistic technique of expression by James Joyce (1882-1941). Thus, not only confined to religious experience, 'the term is today loosely applied to any moment of sudden and great revelation in which a character gains a special insight into his life' (A. Harrison *Selected Short Stories*, 78).⁸ Generally, there is a reason for people's awareness and a motivation for a change. However, epiphany is a mystical incident in which one's cognition and values change into their opposites through receiving a revelation which is disconnected from one's consciousness of reality. Whereas the 'stream of consciousness' of Joyce and also Virginia Woolf presents epiphany mostly as a negative feeling for the characters, Lawrence's epiphany is a positive and 'enthusiastic type' that 'renders a certain optimism through its preoccupation with providing a world of discontinuities with its opposite — ways of ensuring continuities, means of survival from both existential dead-ends and formal exhaustion' (Camelia 80). Lawrence actively introduces epiphanic awakening into his works as an illogical experience which brings about a transformation of the self, and I argue that it consequently has the potential to bridge wrecked relationships with others in an entirely new way by the intervention of intuition. However, it must be said that the unrepresentable, intuitive experience in Lawrence's texts tends to be misunderstood by critics as a mixture of elements, despite his heightened attention to physical theories, and I would argue that the distinction between affect and epiphany has not even clearly been made in studies of Lawrence.

The biggest difference between the two notions is in the epistemological quality of epiphany. Ashton Nichols comments that 'In Joyce it is the mind of the observer that is responsible for this adjustment' and also that '[Robert] Browning clearly suggests that an operation of mind is the cause of the epiphany' (82). In addition, he states that 'What is clear is that *a process of self-definition* is the result [of the final formulation]: "I am named and known by that moment's feat." The moment elevates the percipient and leads to *a new awareness of the self's place in the world*' (Nichols 92; emphasis added). This epistemological and ontological renewal of selfhood cannot be seen in the intersubjective nature of affect. In the final phase of *The Rainbow*, Ursula suddenly obtains a luminous vision by seeing a magnificent cosmos in one drop of water through the microscope lens. She casts off her troubled love relationship and its earthly complications, and attains an experience of unity with sheer knowledge.

> Suddenly in her mind the world gleamed strangely, with an intense light, like the nucleus of the creature under the microscope. Suddenly she had passed away into an intensely-gleaming light of knowledge. . . . Self was a oneness with the infinite. To be oneself was a supreme, gleaming triumph of infinity. (*R* 408-9)

The aspect of escaping one's individual self and 'pass[ing] away into' the object is similar to affect in terms of involving a sense of unity. However, it can be suggested that being reassured of one's subjectivity by the contact with a new and grand knowledge is characteristic of epiphany. I strongly agree with Garrard's view on this scene of 'scientific epiphany' that the experience involves 'the integration of the intellect and the sensual self' (16) — that is, the mysterious unification of mind and body which Lawrence frequently seeks to express. From this point of view, the novel provides Ursula with a turning point to reassure her of her vital, potential self as an independent new woman through being awakened to a whole new reality. Accordingly, I would conclude that epiphany is a remarkably private experience of the sublime. Although it is similar to affect in terms of their being cut off from time and space,⁹ the private phenomenon of epiphany can be compared to a form of affect which can be extended to the dynamics of intersubjectivity: epiphany is a shock-like sensation which is felt as if the character is directly joined to an eternal verity, and is generated by a strong one-to-one connection between the self and truth, and makes one self-sufficient in one's own transformation.

Lawrence wrote a tale which expresses the privacy of epiphany: as its original title 'You Touched Me' shows, the story 'Hadrian' depicts the tactile sense as bringing about a sharp alteration in the person's consciousness. Hadrian, the boy who was taken from the charity school, gets on his sister-in-laws' nerves with his defensive and shrewd attitude. However, after he leaves home to find a job and comes back from five years' absence, they are impressed by his maturity and the elder sister Matilda 'blushed deep with mortification' and 'felt her disadvantage' (*EME* 95). Nevertheless, they become filled with hostility towards him, supposing that he has returned to snatch their sick father's property. One night, feeling pity, Matilda visits her father's sickbed and touches the lying man's face without noticing that it is Hadrian instead of her father, and the fresh and smooth texture stirs a surprise and a trance in her. However, regaining rational consciousness from Hadrian's murmur, she gets furiously nervous at her indiscretion; feeling as if she has injured her hand, she even harbors a hatred towards the young man.

On the other hand, Hadrian, who has been touched, experiences a powerful sense of epiphany, unlike his sister-in-law, who has been perplexed with shame and revulsion, for he 'was a charity boy, aloof and more or less at bay. The fragile exquisiteness of her caress startled him most, revealed unknown things to him' (*EME* 100). It is such a drastic change for his unconscious and essential part as suddenly to awaken his affection for Matilda. The next morning, although Matilda determinedly puts on an appearance of composure, she is unable to control his inner change.

> But she could not control him as she thought she could. He had a keen memory stinging his mind, a new set of sensations working in his consciousness. Something new was alert in him. At the back of his reticent, guarded mind he kept his secret alive and vivid. She was at his mercy, for he was unscrupulous, his standard was not her standard. (*EME* 100)

Due to his awakening, Hadrian plans to marry Matilda to secure the touch forever. Therefore, the story is considered as a kind of sleeping-beauty story, in which the gender roles are reversed. However, although his awakening has evoked a dramatic change inside him, the epiphany cannot get them further in sharing their consciousness and binding them to each other with their mutual consent.

As a comprehensive explanation of this, my argument is that Lawrence exerts his ingenuity by combining the *personal* revelatory moment of epiphany with the *impersonal* solidarity of affect. The short story, 'Second-Best', is a narrative which renders the acceptance of the other possible by linking the personal experience of epiphany to the collective experience of affect. A young lady, Frances, returns to her home village from Liverpool due to the loss of her love with Jimmy Barrass, an intelligent gentleman who is a Doctor of Chemistry. She confesses the story to her younger sister Anne, yet the way she talks is self-protective and she hides her inner ruefulness. Then, Anne finds a mole and kills it, regarding it as an unsacred animal that is harmful to the farm; however, Frances cannot even touch it, and suddenly

CHAPTER ONE

something dies inside her, and her despondent heart freezes with indifference and isolation either from others or from nature. After some time, the sisters encounter a youth with a provincial accent, Tom Smedley, whom Frances had been keeping as a second prospective lover. The discrepancies of rural against urban and 'The vulgar speech [which] jarred on her as a rule' (*PO* 119), have been creating a gap between them which is hard to overcome. Meeting Frances after her long absence he gets excited, though he mildly banters that she cannot kill a mole — that is, she is a city girl who has lost her bond with the wilderness. As if incited by his words, Frances is prompted to a sudden and intense idea that she too can kill one; simultaneously, she is assailed by the idea that the act of killing a mole decisively will make him appreciate her real worth and it becomes a rite of passage which allows her to rejoin the rural community. The next day, she kills a mole by herself and goes to see him to show it to him. The depiction of Frances, triumphant and over-excited, and Tom, watching her with an astonishment which gradually turns into an ardent thrill, emphasizes the intensity of their transforming encounter.

'Did you think I couldn't?' she asked, her face very near his.
'Nay, I didn't know.'
She laughed in his face, a strange little laugh that caught her breath, all agitation and tears and recklessness of desire. He looked frightened and upset. She put her hand to his arm.
'Shall you go out wi' me?' he asked, in a difficult, troubled tone.
She turned her face away, with a shaky laugh. The blood came up in him, strong, overmastering. He resisted it. But it drove him down, and he was carried away. Seeing the winsome, frail nape

of her neck, fierce love came upon him for her, and tenderness. (*PO* 120)

As Frances' inner transformation is conveyed by strong agitation and overwhelms him, a violent change occurs inside Tom's body and mind. Emotions such as surprise and perplexity are absorbed by the power of blood which surges beyond his control, in a way which suggests the embodiment of a strong blood feeling in dynamic consciousness. The transmission of the unearthly affect can be observed here, and the couple are liberated from the friction of mutually discriminatory consciousness as a sophisticated townswoman and an unrefined countryman, and enabled to communicate.

Although it is a cliché in studies of Lawrence that focus on physical cognition that Lawrentian liberation never occurs without actual touch, interestingly, it is not the case in this tale. In lieu of physical contact, what is characteristic here is the description of the rush of tears as a bodily phenomenon which is not attended by general emotions such as sorrow or joy. Tears are frequently used in Lawrence's fiction as a motif of women's sexuality which induce the male's compassionate affection by showing the feebleness of heroines who have been equipped with the armour of haughty egos. However, I would argue that the quality which tears have of producing an inner change and creating a bridge between body and mind is effectively used here: the physiological phenomenon whose gushing releases the psychological tension is an outward manifestation of an inner alteration. For instance, the flush of cheeks and the contrasting pallor, the movements of eyebrows, the trembling of lips and facial muscles, have a similar effect, though tears have an additional function as a way of revealing the self-liberation by proving ecstasy. The affect is conveyed by tears from the young woman and the youth and it can be said that the couple are sharing rapture with unconscious harmony.

The point which is often focused on in this story is that Frances experiences the abolition of her modernized self which has been fostered in the city, and the rebirth of her new self which lives with Tom at the farm. It is a standard interpretation to suggest that the girl's ritualistic experience overlaps with the killing of the mole; however, Janis H. Harris overly simplifies the vividness of the couple's ecstasy by her prosaic assessment:

> She must face life as it comes: moles must die . . . ; and she must redirect her own life away from the man who could have been a pioneer to her soul toward good-humored, easy Tom. A day later she seals her pact with Tom and the view he represents by taking him a mole she herself has killed. (40)

The awkwardness between Frances and Tom in no way reflects her reluctance about or mild resignation to a second choice (as the languid title of the tale may suggest), but the pursuit of an opening to unknown communication. The epiphany and affect which Frances experiences are linked with the event that represents metaphorical death and resurrection for her, and through his being led by Frances, elevates Tom too from ordinariness to the height of ecstasy. As a consequence of their affective communication, they promise each other a hasty marriage and the story ends with 'a thrill of pleasure in this death [in the tone of her voice]' (*PO* 120). Although Frances has acquired a new self and been reborn, the phrase hints at her rather strong awareness of the death. One might observe that it expresses Frances' submission as a female to Tom, associating this with Lawrence's reputation for misogyny. However, I would argue that there is no submission in the triumph of Frances, who has succeeded in breaking down the obstacle between herself and Tom. When we focus on the roles of sending and receiving inspiration in the affective space, her dynamic and aggressive energy even seems to challenge and master Tom. The 'thrill of pleasure in this death' can be understood as a feeling associated with freedom from the restrictions of mind, and the exhaustion of the old stable ego in the face of the power of epiphany and affect. As we have seen, Lawrence's strategy is to develop a connection of the epiphanic inspiration and the affective communion. The next section will further explore the relation of these experiences to the symbolical moment of death and resurrection, with the help of Bataille's theory of 'inner experience'.

4. The Symbolical Gap between Death and Resurrection

In Lawrence's fiction, the death and rebirth of one's self often appears as a significant rite of passage and the short story 'The Horse-Dealer's Daughter' 'is perhaps Lawrence's best-known tale of resurrection' (Harris 125). It is a cross-class romance between Mabel Pervin, the woman referred to in the title, and Jack Fergusson, the doctor of the village, which involves the gulf between their social positions. Although they are acquaintances, they have no intimacy; their lives do not seem to be connected and the insuperable difference of their circumstances is accentuated. However, their consciousnesses are led to a bold transformation by an epiphanic experience, and an unknown communication opens and strangely unites them. The phenomenon of awakening does not conclude with the subject and involves the possibility of actively accepting or approaching the other person. It fascinates the object and triggers him to experience the same striking change or more than that, in consequence of the transmission, and thus allows each to receive the other.

Although we have already seen this process in 'Second-Best', I will argue in this section that a special meaning can be discovered in this story, in that the couple both undergo the turning point of substantial or metaphorical death and restoration to life. The transition is developed in the abyss of the forces of death and rebirth experienced by both characters and it can be analyzed alongside the idea of Georges Bataille. As Masashi Asai argues, both Lawrence and Bataille had an eye on human relationships which are 'split between the conflicting tendencies towards the fulfilment of the ego and the union with the other', and Bataille finds the solution 'by proclaiming the importance of eroticism, which is "assenting to life up to the point of death"' (qtd. in Asai 'Lawrence, Sade, Bataille', 12). This Bataillian way of transcending the possible limits of union with the other, I argue, is somewhat similar to Lawrence's thoughts about seeking 'a new relatedness' (*STH* 174). He writes:

> Each time we strive to a new relation, with anyone or anything, it is bound to hurt somewhat. Because it means the struggle with and the displacing of old connections, and this is never pleasant. And moreover, between living things at least, an adjustment means also a fight; for each party, inevitably, must 'seek its own' in the other, and be denied. When, in the two parties, each of them seeks his own, her own, absolutely, then it is a fight to the death. And this is true of the thing called 'passion.' On the other hand, when, of the two parties, one yields utterly to the other, this is called sacrifice, and it also means death. (*STH* 174)

Lawrence's thoughts about the hurt, the pursuit of unity, and the obliteration of one's life to an extreme point, which happen when the self-and-other relationship aims at a new adjustment from stagnancy, have important features in common with those of Bataille. Moreover, it can be considered that these common traits suggest important ideas about the active mingling of the self and other in the moment of epiphany and affect in Lawrence's stories. Taking this presupposition into account, I will survey the story in detail.

One morning, the Pervin brothers, who are doomed to separation because of bankruptcy, are discussing what to do with their lives. In contrast with the flippant brothers, their sister Mabel does not have any attachment in life and remains tongue-tied however persistently the brothers ask about her future prospects. Since she keeps mourning her mother's death and frequently visits her tomb, she has a gloomy yearning for death. Doctor Fergusson, who is on close terms with the brothers, stops by and breaks into the conversation, though Mabel does not care to answer his words and her 'steady, dangerous eyes' make 'him uncomfortable, unsettling his superficial ease' (*EME* 141). After his patients' house calls, Fergusson witnesses her sinking unconsciously into the pond near the cemetery; being all in a flurry and due to his vocational mission, he rescues her and takes her back to her house, takes off her wet clothes, and lays her down. Mabel comes to her senses, and from the moment when she notices that he has removed her clothes, she repeatedly confirms that he loves her. Fergusson feels shocked by this outrageous leap in logic, and the more he thinks about the difference in their social status, the more he feels repulsion at her sudden falling in love with him and tries to resist. However, while he touches her body and gazes at the tears shading her cheeks, he feels her rapture, and inexplicably, he madly loves her. And despite the fact that

Mabel contrastingly regains her objective consciousness, Fergusson proposes marriage to her in a delirious manner. It is unmistakable that it is Fergusson who was truly awakened and the story ends in the midst of his intoxication.

I have proposed in the last section that not every Lawrentian affective communion is accompanied by an actual physical touch, though attention should be drawn to this point again here; for the traditional belief in the power of the touch of skin is extremely deep-rooted in the studies of this tale. Regarding the fact that the touch is a keyword in the lifesaving treatments in Lawrence's fiction, the tale has conventionally been seen as in the lineage of sleeping-beauty tales, even more than 'Hadrian', as Martin F. Kearny presents the chronological summary of the studies of this tale. Mabel's arousal from sleep and physical contact with a man who has saved her life has been considered as inducing an erotic awakening; however, this story does not end with a female's sexual rite of passage. In accordance with the fact that the communication does not rely on words in this story, critics seem to share a preconception that the action is a necessary requirement as the substitute for logos in order to solve the incomprehensibleness of the events.[10] For instance, Kazuo Ueda comments that 'In the moment when his hand touches her shoulders, everything is solved. The touch explodes his unconscious desire, revives the deathlike girl, and also revives the young doctor who was sinking in his dull life' (496; my translation). Although the physical contact assures the awakening of Fergusson's new consciousness which is not mediated by realistic thought, it is impossible to jump to the conclusion that it holds the clue to everything. The critics' excessive emphasis on Lawrence's belief in touch has established the theory that the act of touch proceeds from consciousness by betraying human beings' recognition or self-awareness. However, I suspect that this puts an incorrect interpretation on the transmission of real dynamic consciousness in Lawrence's works.[11] Rather, I propose that the infectious affect transmitted from Mabel to Fergusson in the crucial life and death situation has aroused him profoundly. The vital event which this story traces is that Fergusson receives a far stronger revelation than Mabel, who is touched, and thus yearns for the lower-class girl who has been living in a different social group from his.

When Mabel asks him whether she is out of her mind now, he tells her that she is not, though nevertheless, he gets afraid 'because he felt dazed, and felt dimly that her power was stronger than his, in this issue' (*EME* 147). Although he wishes to change his clothes which became filthy from the water in the pond, Mabel's emboldened aura is stronger than that desire and makes his body heat up from inside as if it surpasses the cutaneous displeasure.

> He very much wanted to go upstairs to get into dry clothing. But there was another desire in him. And she seemed to hold him. His will seemed to have gone to sleep, and left him, standing there slack before her. But he felt warm inside himself. He did not shudder at all, though his clothes were sodden on him. (*EME* 147)

We can introduce here again the theme of affect which connects alien social groups. De-emotionalization has been described in my study as a sign of the generation of affect; supporting this claim, as Fergusson physically perceives Mabel's aura, his rational will is tempted into a hazy drowsiness which makes it inert. The two of them communicate in this gap, incautiously and uncomfortably severed from daily life.

CHAPTER ONE

Bataille envisaged 'inner experience' in the 1940s as one's special experience of an ecstatic apex which can be attained by the sacrifice of reason and intelligence. Bataille writes, 'we reach ecstasy by a contestation of knowledge' (*Inner Experience*, 12) when we fling off what constitutes and maintains our general identity in some way and then 'non-knowledge communicates ecstasy' (*Inner Experience*, 58). Notwithstanding the dogmatic realm of religion which focuses on the goal of obtaining knowledge, for Bataille's inner experience, the 'Preestablished religious systems and frameworks of interpretation tame the intensity of the experience' (Irwin 108). When the 'projective-discursive thought is left behind', the experience gains authority of its own and 'the subject approaches, enters, becomes the state Bataille terms "the extreme limit of the possible"', that is, 'the way toward unknowing (*non-savoir*)' (Irwin 110). Therefore, I would suggest that the spiritual transmission envisaged by Bataille resembles the form of communion which Lawrence tried to evoke by epiphany and affect, thus replacing the orthodox novel. The extremity of the unknowing experience is expressed in Ursula Brangwen's thoughts in *Women in Love* (1920):

> To speak, to see, was nothing. It was a travesty to look and to comprehend the man there. Darkness and silence must fall perfectly on her, then she could know mystically, in unrevealed touch. She must lightly, mindlessly connect with him, have the knowledge which is death of knowledge, the reality of surety in not-knowing. (*WL* 319)

Moving back to the story, the crevice between death and resuscitation gathers weight here. Whereas it is evident that Mabel was experiencing a self-abandonment in this space, there is an implication in Ueda's expression, previously quoted, that the event 'revives the young doctor who was sinking in his dull life'. Like Mabel who was living in a half deathlike condition, Fergusson also has been feeling the lack of stability in his life. Despite having a profession as a doctor, he was actually worn out by being employed by and providing a service to the local population like a 'slave to the countryside' (*EME* 143). However, it is vividly illustrated that encountering the life of the working class and being involved in its roughness was secretly the source of a dark excitement and stimulation to him.

> Another resource would be lost to him, another place gone: the only company he cared for in the alien, ugly little town, he was losing. Nothing but work, drudgery, constant hastening from dwelling to dwelling among the colliers and the iron-workers. It wore him out, but at the same time he had a craving for it. It was a stimulant to him to be in the homes of the working people, *moving, as it were, through the innermost body of their life.* His nerves were excited and gratified. He could come so near, into the very lives of the rough, inarticulate, powerfully emotional men and women. He grumbled, he said he hated the hellish hole. But as a matter of fact it excited him, the contact with the rough, strongly-feeling people was *a stimulant applied direct to his nerves.* (*EME* 144; emphasis added)

In Fergusson's consciousness, there exists a perverse desire for exile from daily emotion which is remote from charitable sympathy for the labourers' lives and circumstances. Physically, in actuality, he was craving to mingle with them; hence the separation of the

Pervin brothers and Mabel's attempted suicide meant Fergusson's disconnection from the little town: he was in danger of losing a solid sense of his life. In a way that is inconsistent with his discriminatory emotion toward them, it is revealed that Fergusson was desperately craving for existential contact with the lower-class people who directly stir his nerves. Moreover, as a definite portent of his later experience, he was arrested by Mabel's gaze at him and gained a sense of being released from earthly ego through her grasping of his existence.

> It *was* portentous, her face. It seemed to mesmerize him. There was a heavy power in her eyes which laid hold of his whole being, as if he had drunk some powerful drug. He had been feeling weak and done before. Now the life came back into him, he felt delivered from his own fretted, daily self. (*EME* 144)

It is precisely an affective moment — the inexpressible delivery of consciousness has already occurred at this moment, instead of narratable communication.

Contrasting it with sustainable time, Bataille also gives a meaning to the 'moment' which involves the laceration of the general notion of life time. It is an experience of being temporarily severed from one's social self and leaves one in a space released from one's fixed perception of reality. Moreover, in contrast to our notion of time, Bataille considers that we are fundamentally discontinuous beings and we can gain the lost continuity with the assistance of this transcendent experience. Asai regards the idea as 'strikingly Lawrentian' ('Lawrence, Sade, Bataille', 26). Quoting Bataille's thought that either dying or bursting through our barriers is unavoidable for us, Asai remarks that what the two writers have in common is that they both consider that the specific experiences are equally effectual for solving our ontological insecurity and thus can reveal the 'primeval oneness', which is strange and unfamiliar to modernized people ('Lawrence, Sade, Bataille', 26). Therefore, I will add that in the extraordinary moment in which the presence of the social self is destroyed, an affective interaction occurs and creates the impersonal wholeness between people.

After he rescues Mabel and takes her home, Fergusson nurses a dread of the powerful force in her, when she has been warmed by the fire and awakened. Although her agitating condition, deviating from morality and overly sexually released, is horrible to him, he cannot take his eyes off her, and tears bring a sensational change again in this tale. Due to witnessing the tears which Mabel sheds, a change inside Fergusson has obviously been induced:

> With an inward groan he gave way, and let his heart yield towards her. A sudden gentle smile came on his face. . . . He watched the strange water rise in her eyes, like some slow fountain coming up. And his heart seemed to burn and melt away in his breast. (*EME* 149)

This is when the tears appear for the first time and it demonstrates the reason why their physical contact is not the immediate cause of the evocation of his tenderness. Being mentally confused, her tears dripping on 'the hollows of his neck, . . . he remained motionless, suspended through one of man's eternities. . . . He wanted to remain like that forever, with his heart hurting him in a pain that was also life to him' (*EME* 149), and Fergusson becomes aware of his own inner experience coming over him. Accordingly, tears work both as tools for expressing one's ecstasy and as a means of stimulating communication.

Bataille discusses this as follows:

> If we didn't know how to dramatize, we wouldn't be able to leave ourselves. We would live isolated and turned in on our selves. But a sort of rupture — in anguish — leaves us at the limit of tears: in such a case we lose ourselves, we forget ourselves and communicate with an elusive beyond. (*Inner Experience*, 11)

Although it was Mabel who was first led to inner experience through her recovery, her ecstasy was not completed personally, but was wafted from her and transferred to Fergusson. As I have already suggested, Bataille argues that a gift of ecstasy between people inside the laceration between life and death is precisely what renders communion possible. In response to Maurice Blanchot's question about why he should not pursue his own inner experience, Bataille argues that 'inner experience is conquest [for one's self] and as such *for others*' (*Inner Experience*, 61; emphasis added). In a way that corresponds to his argument, Mabel's inner experience did not conclude in herself: it was not her property, like emotion, but had a motive power to open the way for communicating with *the other*, that is, Fergusson. Her inner experience involved an attraction and a conquest *for him*. For people who depend on knowledge, encountering others who have abandoned rationality shocks them and causes them to become unstable; therefore, the subject's experience is filled with remote force which can also liberate the object's ego. The significance of tears in the two stories hints at the possibility that the act of touching does not have supreme importance in Lawrence's fiction. It dramatizes the releasing of one's self to the other, more quickly and intensely than intelligence and actions.

However, a discrepancy is caused in the final part of the story. Mabel's epiphany does not endure and her consciousness of reality rapidly returns in a cruel manner: she notices that she smells so horrible and breaks into bitter, heart-broken sobbing that she is too awful to be loved by him. Yet, Fergusson still remains intoxicated: '"No, I want you, I want you," was all he answered, blindly, with that terrible intonation which frightened her almost more than her horror lest he should *not* want her' (*EME* 152). Although Orwell insisted that people cannot get over the physical quality of their class-consciousness — the foul smell in particular — Lawrence proposes the reverse idea. At first it was Fergusson who 'could not bear the smell of the dead, clayey water, and he was mortally afraid for his own health' and it can be understood as his socially-orientated physical perception. His consciousness was at first closely entangled with the external reality, and the sense of shame originating from his vocational pride agonized him due to the possibility that people would jeer at him if they knew that the doctor should love the horse-dealer's daughter (*EME* 150). However, when both senses disappear at the same time, he gets filled with life due to his irrational will to accept her instead; 'He never intended to love her. But now it was over. He had crossed over *the gulf* to her, and all that he had left behind had shriveled and become *void*' (*EME* 150; emphasis added). The story ends with Mabel still being frightened that the doctor's illusion may return, and his urgent manner of loving her which seems never to tire.

Lawrence was interested in liberating modernized people, who cannot live except by depending on their awareness of social indices and the power of representation expressed in realistic narratives, by providing them with a space in which their egos could be extinguished and revive. Nevertheless, their forgetting of interpersonal incompatibilities which seemed to have been erased by the emancipating effect of passionate physicality is not sustained forever, and they arise again as a barrier.[12] The commotion of the Morels' married life proves that the dispelling of the difference does not last on a long-term basis and Mabel's epiphany reveals its impermanence. As long as he is a preacher of liberation, Lawrence deeply recognizes the difficulty of freeing the self from one's social ego, so that he does not devote himself to idealistic outcomes and depicts the tragedy of modernized people's pettiness that is recurrently haunted by empirical consciousness. While depicting the strife of human relationships, Lawrence must have gathered the existential angst of people in the leisured, upper social classes. Thus, he must have been thinking of how to enable them to have a profound life experience through interaction with the lower class, which contains the writer's own physical identity, apart from their intellectual and emotional experience. Putting this in a different way, it is an exile from 'the old stable ego' that Lawrence pursued the most. A limitless possibility of the internal renovation of one's life by communication with the other is evoked in the cleavage of anxiety which opens up in daily life.

The distinctive features of unrepresentable experience which appear in the texts which I have analyzed in this chapter have verified Endo's statement that 'The "experience" in the early works of Lawrence exhibits a novelistic intensity which lives (experiences) a paradox of the simultaneity of separation (individuality) and aggregate (society)' (*Jyodo to Modernity*, 112; my translation). I would additionally argue that while the immobile human relationships and the hardened social ego are supplied with motion and transformed, the existence of the individual is recovered through his or her exile from mundane life. Destroying the old personal boundaries, Lawrence's characters are released from the diseased modernized human relationships, from which they have been aggressively seeking liberation.

However, like other typical modernists, Lawrence was troubled by the binary opposition between the anomie of 'aggression' issuing from the age of war, and the self-protective instinct of 'stillness'. Lawrence was still interested in human relationships; but does the aggressive power toward self and others still have validity as a resolution in his works? Or, to what extent does the mode of stillness affect the characters? In the next chapter, I will explore the theme of the escape from active force and the self-defensive inclination to stillness which show the peculiarity of the middle period of Lawrence's texts, and will diagnose how the writer's conflicting views act and react in the texts.

CHAPTER TWO

The Ambiguity of 'Stillness' and Finding a Remedy in 'Aggression'

1. Conflicting Texts — Desirable or Undesirable Inertia?

In the first chapter of this study, I showed how physicality combined with techniques of anti-realistic expression facilitated an escape from the current of modernity which forces the mental and physical consciousness to confront each other. Through the tales examined so far, I have investigated the process by which the old consciousness is regenerated into the new, and the symbolic death and rebirth of the self is accompanied by disconnected temporality and spatiality. Mental and physical consciousness are regenerated and reintegrated, producing a strong sense of repletion and the energy which directly affects life. The focus of my observation in the previous chapter is that Lawrence finds a remedy in the active energy of our psychodynamics which is generated by an explosive reactivation of the relationship with others.

However, a change takes place in the middle period of Lawrence's career, which corresponds to the First World War period. A predilection for a physically immobile and static condition, with no undulations of consciousness or emotions, starts to appear in his fictionalized world. The change becomes salient chiefly in his long novels around the period of *The Rainbow*, which sanctifies the respite following the consummation of a dynamic bond with the other, and narrates it at length. What naturally results from the consumption of power and motion is stillness — it is a requirement for organisms, including human beings, to have a rest after lively motion, and sleep is a time to restore energy for the metabolism or the next activity. Both body and spirit feel exhaustion particularly after hard exercise and need the pleasure of serenity which the exuberance of stillness produces. It is a quality exclusively of organisms, which differ from machines that continue consumption and movement until they stop functioning. There is no doubt whatsoever that this perspective fits the agitated situation of England as it launched into the First World War period. Lawrence became increasingly skeptical about the contribution of mechanical industry toward warfare and the insatiable pursuit of energy which led to the excessive and devastating expenditure.

Bergson contrasts the two rival systems, mechanism and the dynamism of nature. He argues that mechanism 'never gets out of the narrow circle of necessity [in which the result is predictable and calculable] within which it at first shut itself up' (*Time and Free Will*, 140). In contrast, dynamism is free from the shackles of various laws and it 'starts from the idea of voluntary activity, given by consciousness, and comes to represent *inertia* by gradually emptying this idea' (*Time and Free Will*, 140; emphasis added). Dynamism can loosen the strength of the will-to-motion and Bergson suggests that inertia occurs when one is released from will. These statements remind us of the frequency with which Lawrence relates the persistence of human beings' will to the motion of machines and harshly criticizes it.

Andrew Kalaidjian's discussion which focuses on the term 'inertia' and its generative potential in Lawrence's works has taken on increasing importance in recent studies. He argues that the inertia extolled in Lawrence's works is a counterbalance to the obsession with mechanism which aims at limitless production and infinite consumption.

Kalaidjian suggests that since it is what is required by the human body, which intrinsically does not have inexhaustible energy, the inertia is positive as a means of regeneration for the body and the existence of the individual (42). Whereas the unnatural mechanical power arbitrarily directs life to the worst attrition of war in the end, Kalaidjian argues that Lawrence places an emphasis on 'positive inertia' which leads to the growth of human generations. Thus, it can be said that the ultimate difference between the restless, profit-seeking, and callous industrial mechanism and the dynamism of animate things is expressed in the requirement of stillness.

Due to his contempt for mechanical will, Lawrence's works are connected by 'a rhythmic form that is not pseudoscientific or mechanical' but '*a kinetic movement like a living thing*' (66; emphasis added), as Thomas H. McCabe argues, and the subtle modulations of energy inside individual bodies and human relationships are depicted in a way which has an affinity to the ebbs and flows of nature. Besides, in the affinity of life energy with nature in Lawrence's works, Thomas Jeffers states that one sees the anxiety about 'the following century's death-in-life' which accompanies the progression of industry from handcrafts to mechanization (150). When in harmony with the rhythms of nature, human beings can return to a non-human mode like that of 'preliterate societies' (Jeffers 150). The societies 'have always known the experience of strong physiological sensations which . . . is universally human, universally organic: we apprehend the world, we know what's going on within ourselves, just as the plants and animals do'; and the people of the first generation in *The Rainbow* could do this without ceremony (Jeffers 150). However, for the sake of the succeeding generations which are burdened with the predicaments of modernization, Lawrence developed a substitute method.

CHAPTER TWO

As Kalaidjian also notes, the completion of motionlessness is overly idealized in *The Rainbow*. Accomplishing a perfect unity by marriage, Anna's and Will Brangwen's honeymoon in the cottage is an unmoving, wasteful, and idle inertia in a self-contained world which shuts out other people.

> [H]e was with her, as remote from the world as if the two of them were buried like a seed in darkness. Suddenly, like a chestnut falling out of a burr, he was shed naked and glistening on to a soft, fecund earth, leaving behind him the hard rind of worldly knowledge and experience. . . .
> Inside the room was a great steadiness, a core of living eternity. Only far outside, at the rim, went on the noise and the distraction. Here at the centre the great wheel was motionless, centred upon itself. Here was a poised, unflawed stillness that was beyond time, because it remained the same, inexhaustible, unchanging, unexhausted. (*R* 135)

The metaphor of the buried seed makes us imagine the notion of germination. Will hallucinates a condition in which the pleasure of inactivity in the stillness, withdrawn from external knowledge and experience, is the ataraxia of absolute and peaceful truth. The core of 'living eternity' is strikingly similar to the 'perpetual present' which Jameson describes affective space and time as involving. Because the inertia of physical energy echoes the density of space, it can be considered that this location metaphysically exists in the final point of Anna and Will's affective communication.

As they lay close together, complete and beyond the touch of

> time or change, it was as if they were at the very centre of all the slow wheeling of space and the rapid agitation of life, deep, deep inside them all, at the centre where there is utter radiance, and eternal being, and the silence absorbed in praise: the steady core of all movements, the unawakened sleep of all wakefulness. They found themselves there, and they lay still, in each other's arms; for their moment they were at the heart of eternity, whilst time roared far off, forever far off, towards the rim. (*R* 135)

The calmed condition of the life energy is overstated and the sense of repose is repeatedly foregrounded against the background of movement. The quality of regeneration is highlighted in stillness, due to the slow pace of the dissolution of social consciousness. As this shows, the reverence for the closed utopia in which one takes pleasure by escaping from volatile contact with outsiders, is given prominence in the middle period of Lawrence's works. Daniel J. Schneider sheds light on Lawrence's self-examination and his evolution from the early works to his middle period, commenting that he 'had captured "something of the eternal stillness that lies under all movement, under all life, like a source, incorruptible and inexhaustible" — "the great impersonal which never changes and out of which all change comes" (Cambridge *Letters* 2: 137-38)' (40).[1] Hence, in this period of his career, *the great impersonal* meant *eternal stillness* for Lawrence and was a state which was everlastingly undisturbed. It can be said that Lawrence himself was imagining that the state which we finally reach at the end of the violent motion of affect is an enclosed area of space and time achieved by cutting our connection with the outer reality. Accordingly, I would point out that we can see a continuum between the space of affect and stillness: this view is supported by the fact that the intensity of affect is continuously connected in Lawrence's works with the intensity of the space of stillness.

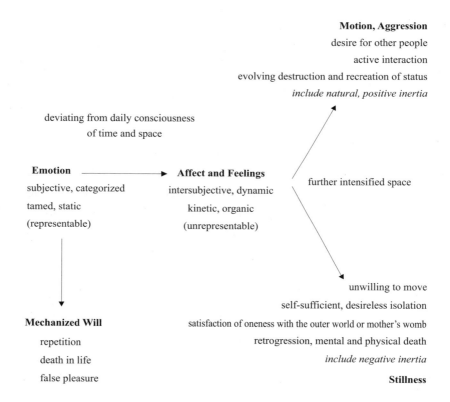

Illustration of Psychodynamics in Lawrence's Fiction (Oyama)

This perspective has much in common with Lawrence's uniqueness in expressing differences in the quantity of space. Moving back slightly earlier in the novel, after Tom Brangwen eventually succeeds in creating an enriched mingling with his wife, from whom he had been feeling a bitter distance, the atmosphere which covers his family bears a sense of intensity: 'There was over the house a kind of dark silence and intensity, in which passion worked its inevitable conclusions. There was in the house a sort of richness, a deep, inarticulate interchange which made other places seem thin and unsatisfying' (*R* 98). The presence of the family is insidious and 'was powerful, sustaining. The whole intercourse was wordless, intense and close' (*R* 98). The dark stillness and intensity which fills the Brangwen family who have succeeded in isolating themselves by creating a strange, tense condition, compresses the separated exterior world into a thin and worthless space. Even though the theme of non-knowledge or the affective communication is unchanged from the early works, the spatial limitations begin to cover up the secretive interchange, such as in Ursula's perception in *Women in Love* which I examined in the previous chapter. The still, though strained mystery of space gains intensity and is self-sufficient through its connection with bodily consciousness.

Therefore, the devotion to stillness undergoes an important transformation in Lawrence's fiction. The effects which the social affairs of the war period wrought upon individuals brought about a mental shift in Lawrence's life and artistic career, though he had formerly believed in provincial togetherness. Various modernists had both an eager hope to be isolated from the mechanized England and the chaos of the resulting anomie and commotion of people, and a terror of being cut off from the continuity of the current of events and the world. In the case of Lawrence, he was yearning for the perfection of a sheltered life as an imaginary protection from the agitation of the societal mutation. However, had Lawrence truly rejected the efficacy and potential of motive energy? Had he downplayed the aggression for which physical consciousness craves, in favour of the glorification of stillness? It seems to be paradoxical that it is the immobile state which Lawrence seeks to achieve, notwithstanding his encouragement of escaping from a fixed personality.

A negative answer to this question emerges from the texts themselves. The paradisiacal mental island is a terminus for the escape from an aversion to mechanized will; yet, the mental numbness annuls the desire to contact others, which has to be the root of life energy. Lawrence does not conceal his anxiety about losing the aggression which his body autonomously requires and also the contact with the external world. As we have seen in the last chapter, while an intuitive sense of the moment is particularly associated with Ursula in *The Rainbow*, Michael Bell suggests that the 'ordinary time becomes merely empty and mortal' (Bell, par. 15) for her. The sense of the past is no longer a saving resource as it was for her predecessors, Tom, Anna, and Will, and Bell observes that this implies a revolt against the mechanization of the solemn system of producing each generation by the repetition of the past (pars. 13-5). Although Anna and Will yield themselves to the 'living eternity', it is part of a cycle of germination. For Ursula, this cycle is also mechanized. The sense of the moment which she desires does not involve feeling oneself involved in the cycle but, rather, actively extricating oneself from all time durations.

Lawrence himself writes in recommendation of aggressively breaking out of human beings' limited ethical notions and mechanical activities:

> [T]he vast, unexplored morality of life itself, what we call the immorality of nature, surrounds us in its eternal incomprehensibility, and in its midst goes on the little

human morality play, with its queer frame of morality and its mechanized movement; seriously, portentously, till some one of the protagonists chance to look out of the charmed circle, weary of the stage, to look into the wilderness raging out. (*STH* 29; emphasis added)

As for Lawrence, I would argue, the mechanized will does not only literally represent the industrial world; it also expresses his satirical point of view towards the mechanization of organisms due to the automatized will which results from an absence of desire for change. Therefore, it can be said that Ursula's epiphanic awakening and sloughing off of the past is a paroxysmal departure from the inertia as unchanging utopia which the generations preceding her have exemplified. At the same time, Lawrence expresses his thoughts which straightforwardly contest the aestheticism of stillness.

> If the one I love remains unchanged and unchanging, I shall cease to love her. It is only because she changes and *startles me into change and defies my inertia, and is herself staggered in her inertia by my changing*, that I can continue to love her. If she stayed put, I might as well love the pepper pot. (*STH* 196-97; emphasis added)

A constant mutation of one's self and also of one's lover must threaten their mutual inertia: I would argue that this makes us recognize anew the will for perpetual change and a desire for motion to stir the negative inertia which creates stagnation in human relationships. Kalaidjian's survey of a long-term generative inertia cannot wholly accept the dynamic energy which is the basis of creating the relationship of a nuclear couple, as suggested by McCabe, who argues that 'Lawrence saw a static perfection as essentially dead — the constantly changing relationships of his characters, becomes the highest good; and usually he seeks no final resolution of tensions' (65).

Meanwhile, in his unique criticism of poetry, Lawrence expresses his ambiguous attitudes towards motion and stillness and elaborates the view that human beings consist half of pure will-to-motion and half of positive inertia. He writes, 'Since there is never to be found a perfect balance or accord of the two Wills . . . so must the human effort be always to recover balance, to symbolise and so to possess that which is missing' (*STH* 59). The two wills between them 'cause the whole of life, from the ebb and flow of a wave, to the stable equilibrium of the whole universe . . . .' (qtd. in Granofsky 186). Even here, it can be surmised that the subtle flux of bodily energy is accompanied by the waves and tide of natural phenomena, in contrast with Lawrence's detestation of mechanized movement (Granofsky 186).[2]

If so, could it not be considered that the excessive predilection for stillness, shown in a considerable number of his works, is patently damaging the physiological balance and ability to maintain one's self? Nancy Hayles argues that Lawrence's dualistic metaphysics itself is driven by a 'tense, dynamic interplay' that leads to 'the instability of its dialectic, its continual defeat of that toward which it is striving' (90). She continues that 'If the favored term prevails, the dialectic collapses into unity, leading, in Lawrence's terminology, to "rigidity." The incipient collapse can be prevented only if the two terms are subsumed into a larger unity which then becomes the favored term of a new dialectic' (Hayles 90). It is therefore essential that the balance of motion and stillness should not cease to show the tidal range. As Franks argues, 'all of Lawrence's works address two competing psychic drives, one for connection, the other for isolation' (121); they put the characters in alternative vicissitudes of active connection with others and the undisturbed state produced by isolation. Centering on the dialectic of motion and stillness, which is the crux for every animated thing, several binary themes expand like the growth rings of a tree, such as mechanical motion versus the unpredictability and indeterminableness of natural impulse, and the issue of humanity and nonhumanity, which I will focus on in the subsequent sections. Focusing on this point, I will examine some of the texts which beautify the immersion in stillness, presenting a paradoxical situation by causing the dynamic energy to decline and finally stopping it from functioning. Behind the eloquent insistence on stillness, the characters are tragically ruined, due to the restraint of their energy. To what extent and how, as a consequence, the remedy is found in active desire will be explored later in this chapter.

2. Stillness in Islands: The Abandonment of External Desire

The tendency to retreat from other people into a reclusive life coordinates with Lawrence's own weakened mental condition in the wartime. He was in fact tormented by misfortunes in the mid-1910s: from his political stance towards Germany and his interest in Italian futurism, it seems that Lawrence in his early years showed an approving attitude towards war, though he was exempted from military service because of his health problem. Moreover, the system of socialist revolution which Lawrence was zealously proposing to his friend Bertrand Russell was judged to be unfeasible, and being in poverty due to the banning of the sale of *The Rainbow*, his misanthropy was aggravated and his human relationships narrowed. It resulted in him becoming dispirited about his incipient aim in his fiction, which was to depict active interaction with others as the means to a drastic reform of the ego. Therefore, it can be hypothesized that the theme of finding repose in a tranquil and static world, rather than the pursuit of motive power, has a close connection with the writer's limited interpersonal world in this period. Since there is no doubt that his closedness was prompted by a wish to escape from the society to which he failed to adapt, the inertia is not only related to the problem of energy or motion but also to the exclusion of other people.

This inclination led him to harbour a strong interest in the space of islands which geographically fits best with his concern. Lawrence had a vague vision for many years of emigrating to an island and constituting a community with companions to whom he could give trust. This was in a sense a fanciful artists' colony like the Bloomsbury Group, but with Lawrence at its center, and he called the utopia 'Rananim'.[3] Lawrence harboured a wish that if only the communal harmony in England could be moved intact from one's native soil to another land, a peaceful quietude would be secured. However, although he made an effort to realize the project 'Rananim' with his friends, it eventually failed because of their frequent disagreements. Therefore, the repeated trial and error of his exploration of small degrees of exile can be seen in Lawrence's various tales of fictitious islands as sites of seclusion — while an island was a paradisiacal ideal in which one aimed to live with strictly selected comrades and a lover, the place also involved a gloomy prospect due to being occupied by a protagonist who has forsaken his human relationships.

Lawrence's second novel, *The Trespasser*, can be described as a tale which illustrates a character who withdraws into stillness throughout the novel. The novel depicts the five-day elopement of Siegmund, a middle aged musician, and his mistress Helena, in the Isle of Wight. It is based on the real-life experience of Helen Corke, who was an acquaintance of Lawrence in the days when he worked as a teacher. The reason why this novel is rarely taken up by scholars may be that it is not entirely Lawrence's fictional creation, or the tiresomeness of the insulated lovers' excessive lack of movement. The text, which depicts the intensity of the lovers' honeymoon, recalls the aforementioned case of Anna and Will; however, it presents the beautiful and somber life of the protagonist, gradually crumpled to death because of wanting stillness rather than motion. Although it also has a non-fiction aspect, the novel seems to have significance as the dawning of a series of island narratives by Lawrence which overwrite the theme of self-imprisonment and misanthropy onto the space of an island. Here, I will point out that the text turns out to present an alarming commentary on the prejudice in favour of stillness. The death of the social self in the excursion, which is not accompanied by rebirth, does not restore the energy for the regeneration of motion. In *The Trespasser*, the dynamic bond between Siegmund and Helena becomes loose, and a discrepancy of ecstasy occurs between them. In consequence, he is solely inclined to inertia, becomes reluctant to interact with her again or even move his own body, and achieves complete solitude.

> 'I can't get hold of them,' he said distractedly to himself. He felt detached from the earth, from all the near, concrete, beloved things; as if these had melted away from him, and left him, sick and unsupported, somewhere alone on the edge of an enormous space. He wanted to lie down again, to relieve himself of the sickening effort of supporting and controlling his body. If he could lie down again perfectly still, he need not struggle to animate the cumbersome matter of his body, and then he would

not feel thus sick and outside himself. (*T* 104)

A resistance to moving and a growing sense of the cumbersomeness of his body are obviously depicted in the above passage. This phenomenon, which encourages both physical and mental retrogradation, can be expressed by the oxymoron of '*progressive retirement* from the world, from the promise of prosperity, of love, of family' (Camelia 76; emphasis added). Lawrence sought dynamic construction of human relationships as a necessary development. Therefore, the loss of outgoing desire 'turn[s] out to be the source of a dangerous loss of contact with the outside world, besides being [a] serious [obstacle] to the protagonists' *Bildung*, for the achievement of which the confrontation with otherness and with difference is — anthropologically and culturally — an essential step' (Michelucci, par. 5). The sites in the island novels thus exorcize the otherness, and make the islander's physicality dull, and the island turns into a treacherous place which forces human beings into paranoiac self-entrapment.

'To have no want, no desire: that is death to begin with.' (*T* 181) — The memorable monologue of Siegmund is an aphorism which condenses the theme of the entire novel. Although the motivation of the couple's excursion to the isle was originally a guilty though provocative elopement, he gradually loses his sexual, interpersonal desire for the relationship with Helena, as well as his ruined family, and moreover, his desire for life activity. After the short stay in the island, he chooses a lonely suicide. Generally, the meaning of his death is interpreted as a failure to return from his unworldly journey to the old and responsible daily life. However, the weariness which makes it impossible to restore the broken family cannot be attributed to his guilty conscience or wish to avoid publicity. He is in a state of ennui, unable to recover the vitality needed for him to be reconciled with his family, who are filled with scorn for him. What made him so, is a forfeiture of the desire to deal with others, caused by the retreat into the enclosed space — yet, I will insist that the eclipse of the subject by external nature, and the loss of his purpose in living, can be determined as the cause. Following Siegmund's sensory world, we can decipher the change in his movement by degrees, which include his great melancholy that causes him to lose desire for material and physical satisfaction, and his unwillingness to have affective interaction with Helena, rather than seeking to achieve unity with the surrounding natural world.

Through the five days in the island, the disharmony of Helena and Siegmund widens. Helena is censured to some extent for not believing in Lawrentian blood-consciousness and going astray by fettering her man with her mental power. Whereas Siegmund physically merges and releases himself into the world of nature, she keeps her firm selfhood.

> His dreams were the flowers of his blood. Hers were more detached and inhuman. For centuries, a certain type of woman has been rejecting the 'animal' in humanity, till now her dreams are abstract, and full of fantasy, and her blood runs in bondage, and her kindness is full of cruelty. (*T* 64)

The estrangement in body and psyche is shown in the detachment of the couple: while Siegmund's blood and dream, which correspond to his body and mind, match each other, for Helena, the mental force has ascendancy over physicality. She is remote from the substantial sense of nature and only appreciates it through the veil of religious imagery.

One might find it incomprehensible that the term 'inhuman' is applied to Helena, who discerns things with intellectual consciousness, and here I find it necessary to clarify our understanding of the notions of the 'inhuman' and the 'impersonal' in Lawrence's fiction. In the early part of this study, I simply noted that Lawrence used the figurative expressions 'impersonal' and 'inhuman' throughout his works and suggested that they refer to an unknown self which enables a dynamic connection with the other in the phase of their communication that transcends a humanistic quality. However, Midori Tagata plausibly points out that there are other implications in these terms which are inseparable from Lawrence's speculation, by arranging them into three schemes.[4] She writes that inhuman and impersonal are 'terms which basically arise from Lawrence's attitude of opposing the limitations and problems which lurk in modern humanity and searching for a new form of existence for humanity' (Tagata 38; my translation).

One of the three divided realms of the inhuman and impersonal world is 'the phase in which the chaotic life, squirming in the darkness of the bodily unconscious, is depicted. It deviates from the established humanity or personality' so that it conforms to the elements which I have discussed so far. The second one is 'the natural world or cosmos other than human beings' (Tagata 38; my translation), and is expressed in Lawrence's use of various images of animals to qualify human beings and in the intermediation of real animals and plants and the interplay of sexual intercourse and the cosmic image. It is an expression of Lawrence's attitude of 'regarding [living organisms] as impersonal forms of existence to the utmost, an individual life with its flesh which floats in the stream of the natural world and cosmos' (Tagata 40; my translation), in contrast with Wordsworth who celebrates pantheism by personifying animals and plants. It can be said that the two notions of impersonality are ideas which express Lawrence's optimistic prospect of 'existing in connection with nature and the cosmos' (Tagata 39; my translation).

However, the last remaining element contains Lawrence's grudging indignation toward modern people. It is the 'inhumanness of the mechanical system in the modern society of mechanical industry' (Tagata 38; my translation): it draws a clear distinction between the richness of the image which the two former images have and thus makes it difficult for the readers to construe the meaning of the term 'inhuman' and troubles their readings. Ambiguously, although the opposite sense is included in the usage of the word, Tagata does not give any profound consideration to this last point. However, a sharp criticism of modern people is insinuated here, since they are implied to have lost the flexibility to return to a connection with nature and to the unconscious state instead of having a stubborn and mechanical will. As I have commented in the previous section, the significance of the divergence between natural dynamics and mechanical dynamics lies in the tides of energy of the former which include stillness. Therefore, I would argue that the insurmountable enstrangement between Siegmund and Helena is due to the fact that he has the first two kinds of inhumanness and is able to have a physical contact with nature, while Helena corresponds to the third inhumanness — or, I will call this case 'dehumanisation' — in terms of automatically following her mechanical mind.

Returning to the topic of the couple on the island, she feels that Siegmund's preoccupation is 'an unreasonable, an incomprehensible obsession' (*T* 101), and on the other hand, he finds companionship with the moon and universal nature as a replacement for Helena. 'One of the novel's remarkable aspects is this transferred lovemaking', Leo Gurko remarks; and 'Recoiling, each seeks comfort and assuagement in the third party to their love affair, nature' (31). Their way of finding companionship in natural surroundings is just the same as their mutual contact. Being materialistic, Helena keeps objects at a distance:

> The sea played by itself, intent on its own game. Its aloofness, its self-sufficiency, are its great charm. The sea does not give and take, like the land and the sky. It had no traffic with the world. It spends its passions upon itself. Helena was something like the sea, self-sufficient and careless of the rest. (*T* 76)

Meanwhile, Siegmund loses sight of the boundary between the moon and the sea and nurtures a sense that the differences between things are removed in his environment. '"I can hardly tell the one from the other," he replied, simply. "The sea seems to be poured out of the moon, and rocking in the hands of the coast. They are all one, just as your eyes and hands and what you say, are all you"' (*T* 70). Deepening the connection with nature rather than his companion, Helena, Siegmund exposes his impersonal aspect. Being hurt by sensing that he 'was beyond her now and did not need her' (*T* 70), she hates him due to perceiving the harshness of nature like 'the brute sea' (*T* 83) inside him. A wild brutality shows its face where his acquired personality becomes vacant: the non-human quality which Helena does not admit. Abandoning any vital contact with her, he experiences a significant loss of desire to bridge the gulf and of the will to have a dynamic rapport. Ironically, however, it is not recognized as a loss by Siegmund himself. He departs from the world of representation, which is the phase of an active involvement with human beings, using symbols and languages, and shuts himself up in the self-sufficient world of inertia involving a sense of fusion with nature. His existential angst of selfhood thus dissipates in a complacent sense of melting into the natural surroundings, depicted as an impressionistic vision of the world. As Endo states, 'the imaginary and aesthetic confusion [by which we overcome] the ideological dualism of the external / internal, confirms a security from the angst of the modernized self, and a unification with the outside world and nature' (*Jyodo to Modernity*, 32; my translation). This state involves the organic oneness of one's interiority with nature, and thus, there is no need for a modern human craving to find one's importance in relationship with other people. The relationship with Helena which requires a search for the unity of ecstasy and an effort to achieve reconciliation, generates an irksomeness of motion which disrupts Siegmund's comfortable fatigue. However, this situation implies an alarming extinction of the subject, since Lawrence insists on the relative position of individuals in the cosmos:

> I am I, in distinction from a whole universe, which is not as I am. This is the first tremendous flash of knowledge of singleness and separate identity [from the parent nuclei]. I am I, not because I am at one with all the universe, but . . . [b]ecause I am set utterly apart and distinguished from all that is the rest of the universe, therefore *I am I*. (*PUFU* 80)

Lawrence claims that this root of knowledge, which is the center of separate identity, is at the lumbar ganglion of one's body, which human beings need along with the solar plexus in order to establish their presence in the universe. Not only do we know ourselves by the solar plexus, but we also instinctively know our independence and difference from others by the lumbar ganglion. While the solar plexus makes one blood-bound to one's progenitor, the lumbar is an organ that obliges one to exist independently in the universe, *not by intellectual thought but physically*. Therefore, losing this knowledge of the separateness of the self and failing to live independently, Siegmund has gone beyond maintaining his 'dynamic psychic existence' (*PUFU* 80).

The problem of the unification of nature and individual existence deepens the incompatibility between the lovers. The world which Siegmund perceives involves the unity of himself with exterior nature, not only psychologically but also physically. Furthermore, taking into account his transition from motion to stillness, his life comes to be in danger. The act of sloughing off everyday consciousness is expressed by the loss of time, while lying on the ground and facing the natural surroundings for long hours in his insular life.

> 'But really,' she insisted, 'I would not have believed the labels could have fallen off everything like this.'
>
> He laughed again. She still leaned towards him, her weight on her hand stopping the flow in the artery down his thigh.
>
> 'The days used to walk in procession like seven marionettes, each in order and costume, going endlessly round— —'. . .
>
> 'You have torn the labels off things, and they are so different. . . . Why should I be parcelled up into mornings and evenings and nights? *I* am not made up of sections of time. Now, nights and days go racing over us like cloud-shadows and sunshine over the sea, and all the time we take no notice.'
>
> She put her arms round his neck. He was reminded by a sudden pain in his leg how much her hand had been pressing on him. He held his breath from pain. (*T* 98)

The first thing we notice is the perilous sign of death in Siegmund's body. He thanks Helena for removing the labels from the universe and freeing him from everyday consciousness and bathing him in a superficial romance for a while. Suddenly, however, he realizes that her body, pressed against his leg, was intercepting the flow of his blood and he abruptly remembers his physical pain. His body gets violently pulled back from deadness to liveliness at that moment, and he sharply remembers the dynamic force of blood which has been interrupted. I would suggest that the stopping of the life flow, suggested twice in the quotation, shows that the existence of the other person is necessary in order to realize one's life energy. Although Helena's and Siegmund's feelings are not fundamentally in agreement, the touch of her flesh gives his body a palpitation of life energy which he cannot feel in isolation. This point recalls Lawrence's idea of the strong need for physical contact. The existence of Helena, which directly forced his body to remember pain, represents a caution against his degeneration, exceeding the bodily need for rest, and ultimately vanishing from the world.

The harmful effects which dissolving in nature brings are hinted at again here. Although the days used to seem to march mechanically for Siegmund, now he feels free from being determined by time, and night and day fuse into one — the sensory world he observes is smoothed from movement into stillness, similarly to the change in himself. The disappearance of the contours of night and day corresponds to the dissolving perception. It grows out of the general laws of sensation according to which the impressionist artists argued that 'all of our habits retreat into the area of the unconsciously automatic' (Shklovsky 11). This decline of Siegmund's visionary and representational ability draws our attention to Lawrence's aim of highlighting physical consciousness by breaking away from depicting things from the point of view of a privileged visual sensation. However, the discrepancy between the perceptions of the lovers implies that they have already lost their dynamic nexus. What makes matters worse, Siegmund's unity with nature ruthlessly severs it. In the first chapter, I have drawn a parallel between the representable phase of realism and the unrepresentable phase of 'affect' and argued that descending to the latter makes possible a dynamic rapport with the other. Yet, we are able to communicate in the affective phase just because there exist other people, the targets of our communication and desire. If the others are absent, the subject reaches a stalemate in the intensified space due to being unable to gain the object of his affective energy. With the help of physical inertia, human beings degrade themselves by being unable to adapt and regenerate their lives. It seems that in this paradoxical way Lawrence presents to his readers the defective aspect of stillness.

3. Islands and Regression

When we investigate the relation between regression and the attitude of being indifferent to the distinctions between things, it is appropriate to mention another of Lawrence's notable island stories. 'The Man Who Loved Islands' — a fable which was written in the latter part of his career — includes the portrayal of a hopeless bad end as a final comment on his concern about islands and human beings. The main character possesses three islands, and tries to form ideal worlds of 'community, the sexual Other, himself' (Franks 129) on each island in succession. However, he repeatedly makes blunders and gives up making any effort to change the collapsed human (including sexual) relationships for the better. He takes his misanthropy to extremes and relinquishes the unsatisfactory island to move to an even smaller one. Here again, the man forsakes the other people, animals, and even the words and labels on objects. The way in which he does so is expressed as being an aberration even more than in the case of Siegmund in *The Trespasser*.

In the first island, he lives a luxurious life with lavish expenditure of money and is called a Master by the other inhabitants who worship him excessively and support his life like servants. However, what was actually whirling under the fake good-will of their relationships was a derisive, insulting, and malicious attitude towards the Master. The man's ideal community in fact depended on a balance of power involving a mercenary emphasis on money and egoism and the community eventually breaks down, while the man becomes bankrupt. The man horrifyingly moves to the second, smaller island with a handful of servants whom he can trust. Disheartened in the new dwelling, he is surprised by his own change: 'The strange stillness from all desire was a kind of wonder to the islander. He didn't want anything' (*WWRA* 162-63). However, having sexual intercourse with a woman who is one of the inhabitants, the man feels horror at the relationship again. The woman fetters him with her unspoken mental will and 'Automatic sex shattered him, and filled him with a sort of death. He thought he had come through, to a new stillness of desirelessness' (*WWRA* 164). Again, he flees by deserting the woman, his island, and his new-born baby. However, the terminus he reaches is a final land where there is nothing but the man himself and the harsh natural surroundings, in which he has reduced the annoying sense of otherness to its utmost minimum.

> He was soon almost startled when he perceived the steamer on the near horizon, and his heart contracted with fear, lest it were going to pause and molest him. . . . The tension of waiting for human approach was cruel. He did not want to be approached.

> He did not want to hear voices. He was shocked by the sound of his own voice, if he inadvertently spoke to his cat. *He rebuked himself for having broken the great silence.* (*WWRA* 167; emphasis added)

Not only fearing the disturbance of silence by the voices of humans and animals, the man hysterically gets irritated even by written words. He frantically tries to take the labels off the furniture and even his own name off the letters he receives: these acts represent his discarding of the signs which may possibly relate him to other people. He feels 'as if he were dissolving, as if dissolution had already set in inside him' (*WWRA* 169), which extinguishes the individuality that distinguishes him from the rest of the world. In the approaching end, the man watches a seagull flying, and gazing at the shape and the pattern of its feathers, he wonders why it should distinguish itself with its alien importance from the far, cold seas. He gets attracted somehow to the otherness of the pattern and movement which give portentous meaning to the seagull, contrasting with the vastness of nature. Nevertheless, the bird leaves him at last.

The enfeebled man becomes united with nature in the tragic end by being absorbed into the heavy snow, which tortures him. Although the season changes, the activity of the living things does not restart and the islet becomes transfigured by the accumulated snow and turns into an 'unrecognizable island' (*WWRA* 173). The man and the island itself lose the sense of difference between the parts of nature, and they are buried in the winter in a way that implies his death. Not only in *The Trespasser* but also in 'The Man Who Loved Islands', the affinity with the enclosed space and stillness, the escape from representation, and the unification with nature act in concert and lead human beings to a collapse.

Ben Stoltzfus applies Jacques Lacan's 'Theory of Three Orders' to the three islands of the story. The theory is a psychoanalytic model which stages individual development in terms of the Orders of the Symbolic, the Imaginary, and the Real (*Ecrits: A Selection*, 217-19). Stoltzfus presumes that the islander belonged to the Symbolic in the first island, where he had maintained an active contact with other people. Then the man follows the steps which Lacan hypothesizes by declining to the Imaginary in the second island, and the Real in the last; though I should note that the Symbolic and the Real are particularly helpful in explaining Lawrence's concept and are also in conformity with the intention of my study.

Lacan calls the original state of the neo-natal baby the order of the Real, which preserves the secure, unfractured satisfaction inside the mother's womb. The only thing is the primal need of fullness in which the subject, or the baby, has an integrated relationship with the external world and it does not even have a need to objectify and represent the exterior as otherness. This, I would argue, precisely matches Lawrence's nascent idea of the contact of blood-consciousness: the blind and absolute fullness which does not need verbal communication, and has originated from the primal mother-child bond through the umbilical cord.

However, the connection with the mother becomes insubstantial in the process of growth, and a dissatisfaction of desire results from the anxiety about this absence. Subsequently, the entrance into linguistic activity occurs in order to compensate for the absence, which Lacan theorizes as the Order of the Symbolic. The connection among people in the Symbolic which is conducted by language and representations, is called the shared, 'big Other', and participation in this realm authorizes the subject to participate in civilized and rationalized human relationships. While Lacan himself envisages that experiencing the Real is impossible as far as modern life is concerned, I would argue that Lawrence's ideal was to extricate one's self from the realm of the Symbolic by resuscitating the blood-consciousness, and to reenter into the Real which enables individuals to experience the unrepresentable, existential reality. Recalling the comparison between emotion and affect which I made in the previous chapter, it can be further argued that emotion belongs to the Order of the Symbolic, and affect contrastingly exists in the Order of the Real as something unrepresentable. Since they are not captured in the Symbolic, which is the world that is representable by language, the physical and intuitive experience remain in the Real.

This curiously coincides with the ideas of Jean-François Lyotard, who was one of the leading post-humanist critics in the twentieth century. Similar to Lawrence's usage of the notion of the inhuman (or impersonal), Lyotard also distinguishes 'common humanity' and 'the nonhuman' by defining the latter as the infant's undifferentiated condition, before the former becomes second nature to it (*Inhuman: Reflections on Time*, 3). It is a slightly more macroscopic way of gathering the dynamic condition, intimate with natural surroundings, before one is involved in the Symbolic and schooled to meet the norms of humanity. Therefore, the deviation from common humanity in order to redeem the primitive, inhuman state has an effect on the restoration of modern human relationships. It can be said that Lawrence's oeuvre overall aims at introducing the transition from the Symbolic to the Real — in other words, from the realm of humanity to an inhuman communion.

However, in his island tales, it is obviously shown that a

transition opposite to this model of individual development satirically pursues its way to an irretrievable failure, and the negativity of the retrogression is highlighted. David Lowenthal analyzes in detail how the relation of the sequestered island and its degeneracy has been defined in disparaging ways throughout the nineteenth and twentieth centuries, not only in literature but in socio-political contexts, in comparison with continental progress. Arguing that 'Islands feature as prelapsarian infancy in today's appetite for heritage . . . they often physically embody desired pasts in personal memory or in collective fancy' (Lowenthal 208), he suggests that there is a tendency for human beings' unconscious infantile dreams to be reflected in the island's insularity.

As already mentioned, Stoltzfus draws a figurative comparison between the islander's switching his dwellings and his psychological retrogression from the Symbolic to the Real. He interprets this tale as a metaphor of returning to the mother's womb:

> The islander's death is the result of his longing to return to the nest where he can, once again, be whole (like Humpty Dumpty before the fall), not the cracked egg of misrecognition (méconnaissance). According to Lacan, the infant's misperception of self pursues it into adulthood where the voice of the Other (the unconscious), in this case the language of Lawrence's man who loved islands, dictates the reasons for returning to the mother — the egg — white entity of an impossible perfection. (Stoltzfus 28)

The allegory of the cracked egg follows Lacan's concept of 'the splitting of the self when the infant accedes to language' (Stoltzfus

29). The regression to the sense of wholeness in the world of fetal satisfaction is expressed in the ultimate integration with nature in the story. Stoltzfus describes the way the man wishes to go back to the comfort before the primal cleavage as a return to the 'womb / tomb' (29).[5] As I have already noted, the obsessive idea of avoiding other people and returning solely to an integration with that wholeness, changes one's pursuit of desire into a pursuit of death.

In *The Trespasser*, Siegmund's self-abandoning oneness with the natural surroundings seems to correspond to the 'oceanic feeling' which Romain Rolland has envisaged. It is an exquisite sense of losing oneself in the infinitude of the wholeness of objective nature when one faces, for example, stunning scenery. Whereas Rolland conceived that this specific, aesthetic experience is the aim of the religious mind and art, Sigmund Freud fiercely argued that it is like a condition of regressing towards the mother's womb in which one cannot tell the difference between the interior and the exterior (*SE21*, 64-68, 72). In other words, it is a state of pure narcissistic love of the mother's body. Since, as I have pointed out, Siegmund is devoid of the function of the lumbar ganglion, the organ which originally establishes one's identity, his attitude brings to our mind the oceanic feeling which dissolves the firmness of his own presence but also his motivation to live.

Hence, rather than 'The Man Who Loved Islands', which has no single reference to the motherly image, I would argue that this concept becomes more interesting when it is applied to *The Trespasser*. In *The Trespasser*, the way in which Siegmund traces the gradual progression from human contact to the devotion to nature, is parallel to the transition from the Symbolic to the Real. Since, as Gurko implies, the couple's ruptured love and desire are both transferred to their relationship with nature, it can be said that the interpersonal connection, which evokes discord and discomfort, precisely gives way to the pleasure of integration with the natural environment. Furthermore, in the middle of the declining process, there is a scene in which Siegmund is seized by a hallucination of his young lover, Helena, resembling a mother.

> Without touching him, she seemed to be yearning over him like a mother. Her compassion, her benignity, seemed so different from his little Helena. This woman tall and pale, drooping with the strength of her compassion, seemed stable, immortal, not a fragile human being, but a personification of the great motherhood of woman. 'I am her child, too,' he dreamed, as a child murmurs unconscious in sleep. (*T* 103)

The way he sees a huge and somehow hideous incarnation of a Great Mother in Helena in his half-conscious mind is associated with the typical image of a mother, who mentally aligns herself with her child and finally destroys her loving child. This image can be attributed to Siegmund's anxiety about being mentally fettered by Helena due to the discrepancy between them in the realm of the Symbolic. His hazy but neurotic fantasy represents the floating of his displeasing desire, and implies that he is half way to being ultimately confined in the Real with the motherly nature. Helena, on the other hand, fails to descend to the Real, or the realm of blood-conscious contact, in company with Siegmund.

To summarize the argument so far, Lawrence's island tales are suitable to be analyzed by the 'Theory of Three Orders'. The blindness of the affective, intuitive communication would presumably have been desirable for Lawrence, who aimed to attain a satisfactory bond by a means beyond words and representation. However, the undifferentiated state before mental recognition is related to degradation and death in these tales. What surfaces here as the reason for this is the issue of stillness, and the risk of the lack of desire. The desireless, self-effacing fusion with nature presents a peril of annulling subjectivity, both mentally and physically, and also the energetic will to live. While the order of the Real provides a profound fusion with the object, unimaginable in the moral consciousness within social conventions, it could turn into a womb / tomb if the subject remains unmoved in inertia while getting soaked up into the wholeness of the outer world — this is the respect in which Lawrence's island tales seem to sound the alarm. As David Gordon states, 'the human heart must remain in conflict, a conflict between nature and culture or between competing instincts. There is no return to a wordless, undifferentiated state in the Edenic womb' (374). The dynamic consciousness, primarily inherited from a dyadic relation with the mother, has to be exerted towards other people as a substitute for the womb experience.

The Lawrentian affect or supreme experience in the Real, I would argue, becomes substantial for the first time when it takes place in the space of active interaction with other people. As Siegmund's monologue says that to have no desire means death, human beings have no alternative but to forsake their vital activity if they lose active desire and confine themselves to the intensity of inertia. Whereas the island tales propose a beautiful sense of unification, they allegorically imply that the inert intensity of space distances the characters from direct physical communication with others, and that such circumscription tends to kill one's vital energy.

4. The Introversion of Aggression and Necessity of the Other

'The Prussian Officer' is famous among Lawrence's electrifying fiction in terms of its image of homosexual desire in the bottled-up circumstance of the masculine and homosocial army. However, the story reflects a more significant meaning for this study in that it formulates the crucial theme that the lives of human beings are maintained and driven by desire for the other. Although the tale is not set on an island, the themes which I have focused on in this chapter recur in the text — when the desire to contact the other fades, it turns into introversion, and the transition from movement to stillness yields a tragic ending.

The middle-aged Prussian officer takes offence at the young orderly's innate 'blind, instinctive sureness of movement of an unhampered young animal' (*PO* 3). The orderly's unconcerned and impersonal nature provokes the officer's violent rage and he forces his staunch military discipline on the youth's lithe and elusive physicality. However, the officer gets even more carried away by a fiery passion because the orderly does not even entertain a definite hatred towards him. Because he wants to stimulate the personal part of the attendant, the officer demonstrates his sadistic desire by a morbid power and violence in controlling him and it turns into a homoerotic passion at the same time. The youth gets hurt both physically and mentally; ironically, however, the bully fills the orderly with emotion and personality to some extent as the officer had wished to. José Santos argues that this relationship is produced by the compulsion of 'mimetic desire': it occurs due to the officer's recognition that the other possesses the quality which he lacks, so that he desires the other as both his model and his rival (93-4).[6] Using a class-oriented theory, Santos observes that although the two men's contrasting dispositions have created an inviolable contract between them, the 'mimetic desire' trespasses on their harmony and 'threatens social order' (101) by impelling them to violence. However, Santos fails to note that the destruction of social hierarchy is an essential desire in Lawrence's fiction, as I have shown so far. The orderly's hot blood seethes with animosity and also attraction in his body as if in response to the captain's passion, and he feels his nerves revive like an electric shock when he sees the elder man's figure. The orderly secretly craves his mate's existence with his physical intuition. Their stable, vertical relationship of social rank has turned into a convulsive relationship through desire on a physical level.

The officer feels excitement and satisfaction at the definite change he detects in the orderly. On the other hand, however, the youth lives by completely subduing his inner agitation. He does not openly express his aggression to the officer or even reveal his own heart, either to the other soldiers or his heterosexual lover: 'No one should ever know. It was between him and the captain. There were only the two people in the world now — himself and the captain' (*PO* 10). Therefore, he gradually gets enfeebled and loses his will to live. He spends nights in a condition of stupefaction, and in the morning and when the time to make coffee for the officer comes, 'At last, after heaving at himself, for he seemed to be a mass of inertia, he got up. But he had to force every one of his movements from behind, with his will' (*PO* 9-10). Although he used to glory in his unconscious and lithe movement, now he has deteriorated so much that it has become painful for him to exert his will to escape from the inertia. Ironically, it can be said that he is mentally afflicted by directing his drive for aggression to himself, so that it has nowhere to go and has no target, and the orderly's body is precipitating into a state of stupor, which is reminiscent of the state of being discussed in earlier sections of this study.

This actively self-inflicting phenomenon has to do with the Death Instinct, which Freud discussed: according to his idea, organisms feel displeasure at the world filled with stimuli and possess an instinct to conservatively return to the pre-life condition with no unpleasant incentive, and thus to return to an inanimate state (*SE 18*, 37-8). According to this principle, organisms continually aim at a motionless state, and Freud in his later years called this notion the 'nirvana principle'. Needless to say, it is a lethargic, motionless state which causes caution and a movement towards death. In order to live and avoid the self-destructive instinct, human beings turn its trajectory towards other animate beings, as Freud says: 'It really seems as though it is necessary for us to destroy some other thing or person in order not to destroy ourselves' (*SE 22*, 105). However, the orderly's object-less aggression has nothing to do but to turn back to himself and put him into inertia. On one occasion, he clings to a feeling that if only the officer did not exist — which means, if he extinguished the officer's existence — all the displeasure would be eradicated and he would continue to live healthily. However, 'when he saw the officer's hand tremble as he took the coffee [which the orderly made], he felt everything falling shattered. And he went away, feeling as if he himself were coming to pieces, disintegrated' (*PO* 10). What can be noted from this description is that when the orderly appreciates the officer's passionate awareness of the orderly's existence, he seems to feel an indescribable existential pleasure; his will to break off this relationship is shattered and he chooses to keep absorbing himself in this suffering.

Holding his suffering inside himself, not only in the night time but also in the day, he perceives the march of his army unit as like a lazy slumber: 'he was going mad with fever and thirst. He plodded on, uncomplaining. He did not want to speak, not to anybody. . . .

And the march continued, monotonously, almost like a bad sleep' and 'It was only the long agony of marching with a parched throat that filled him with one single, sleep-heavy intention: to save himself' (*PO* 10). The inertia of the file of soldiers which absorbs all into the same movement, has a major significance in this story. The death drive and its logic of repetition can enable us to understand the condition which it symbolizes. What is suggested by the repetition of the unvarying pace of the military is a mechanical inhuman movement which has no natural dynamism. It is ostensibly a movement, though it involves a torpor, a negative inertia which increases apathy.[7] This stillness inside motion becomes prominent as one of the most harmful things for human beings in Lawrence's works from his middle period onwards. Since there is no object towards which its energy can emanate, the imposed movement merely afflicts the subject by the inward repetition. Leo Bersani claims that finding the pleasure of stillness in repetitive movement can represent the impulse of the 'nirvana principle' and gives a false pleasure, and he uses the term 'activity of inertia' to describe this effect (181). Theoretically, it is a paralyzing repetition motivated by the wish to escape real death; and moreover, it expresses a death instinct which directs the aggressive instinct towards the self, produced as a constant force from within the organism. The orderly's restrained body, losing its freedom by persistently obeying his repressed will, wears out his life. This kind of Freudian unconsciousness is of course unhealthy and disapproved of by Lawrence, since the Lawrentian unconscious expands its organic and dynamic reaction within the relationship with others, though it can be said that Lawrence makes use of the group unconsciousness through repetitive movement as an unfavorable example. As a matter of course, the unconscious repetition is linked with the automatic movement of machines and censured as divesting organisms of their natural instinct by human oppression.

In the latter stage of *The Trespasser*, the ex-lovers, who respectively perceive their total separation, return to London by train. After being soaked in the impressionistic sensory world and brought back to real life from the island, Siegmund gets intimidated by his bodily feeling of the mechanical movement of the train. The fear of the monotonous vibration of the train is connected with his uneasiness about leaving the self-sufficient island.

> The heavy train settled down to an easy, unbroken stroke, swinging like a greyhound over the level, northwards. All the time Siegmund was mechanically thinking the well-known movement from the Valkyrie Ride, his whole self beating to the rhythm. It seemed to him there was a certain grandeur in this flight, but it hurt him with its heavy insistence of catastrophe. . . . Then a dullness came over him, when his thoughts were stupid, and he merely submitted to the rhythm of the train, which stamped him deeper and deeper with a brand of catastrophe. (*T* 165)

Being led inexorably by the fixed rhythm and being deprived of his own resistant energy, Siegmund has nothing to do but to submit to the mechanical throb. The inertia of being helplessly taken back to the real world by the movement of the train, leads to the anticipated finale of the tragedy, that is, his suicide. As this shows, the dichotomy of motion and stillness which is central to the psychological dynamics evoked in the text, introduces a new form of negativity involving an underlying stillness in mechanical motion.

CHAPTER TWO

Returning to 'The Prussian Officer', the sound and odour of the natural surroundings turns into a burden for the orderly in his dim consciousness during the procession of the troops. As in the island novels, nature violates his body and exhausts his energy to live. He was even actually sleeping while having lunch during break time. Watching the flock of domestic sheep on the hill in the distance under the radiant daylight, the youth projects his self-awareness onto the sheep. He feels uncomfortable with the unconscious movement of the group and its automatic quality, though he too becomes powerless due to being unable to protest about his own condition. Hazily recognizing the loss of his solid sense of life, 'He felt as in a blackish dream: as if all the other things were there and had form, but he himself was only a consciousness, a gap that could think and perceive' (*PO* 11). The sudden intuition of one's self being cut off from one's environment is a kind of negative epiphany which also appears in Virginia Woolf (1882-1941). As noted in Naomi Toth's study, since the passive self is too delicate to resist the dominant effect of the experience, Woolf's epiphany disturbs the subject by inducing 'a peculiar horror and a physical collapse' (par. 8). Woolf's fiction thus suggests that epiphanies not only bring self-approval but can produce intense pathos for a passive subject; it can be said that negative epiphany has an affinity with the sense which separates the subject from companionship and material connection by fusing the subject with the outside world.[8] Anna Grmelová focuses on the relationship of the terrain in the natural surroundings of 'The Prussian Officer' with the inner quality of the character. As the story progresses, the orderly's sense of serious disintegration leads to his identification with the landscape of the mountains. The mountains which link the earth and heaven, 'represent an ideal of integration as they stand for what is missing . . . "He stared till his eyes went black and the mountains as they stood in their beauty, so clean and cool, seemed to have it, that which was lost in him" (PO, 20)' (Grmelová 146). Becoming a substitute for what is absent in him, the mountain comes to complement the orderly's inner state; adding to Grmelová's view, a sense of unity has developed between the individual and the landscape in the background, in lieu of the loss of the bond with the human community.

However, the doomsday comes as a consequence of this. The orderly reaches the limit of his physical and mental tolerance for patiently enduring the captain's assaults and finally, when he parts from his army unit, he throttles and breaks the detestable officer's neck on impulse, causing his death. His nightmare is over and it seems that his security is guaranteed. However, a mysterious thing happens: although 'In his heart he was satisfied', sitting by the dead body of the officer, 'Here his own life also ended' (*PO* 15). The orderly tries to leave, though due to the defeat of his precious Other, he falls off his horse as if he had lost the meaning of life. As he lets the saddle go from his hand, the moment 'was his last connection with the rest of things' (*PO* 16) in the material world. With 'an ache of exhaustion' and 'inability to move' (*PO* 18), he lies on the ground, wearing out his whole energy by the temporary explosion. In contrast with his immobile body, burnt by the dry heat, his consciousness was 'too busy, too tearingly active in the incoherent race of delirium', and it 'went racing on without him. A big pulse of sickness beat in him as if it throbbed through the whole earth' (*PO* 17). The description suggests a dangerous somatization in which the orderly's overexcited mind, having lost its object, changes the direction of its aggression towards his body — it lets the sunstroke ravish his motionless body and destroys it from inside.[9] It corresponds with a scene of *The Trespasser* in which Siegmund feels himself

CHAPTER TWO

pushed to a deadlock of sexual relationship, both with his wife and with Helena. Feeling that he has gone beyond his strength to get back to his previous footing, Siegmund notices that his thought-activity is killed by the scorching sunlight and he self-inflictingly submits his body to the killing incandescence:

> The sun was burning deeper into his face and head.
> 'I feel as if it were burning into me,' thought Siegmund abstractedly. 'It is certainly consuming some part of me. Perhaps it is making me ill.' — Meanwhile, perversely, he gave his face and his hot black hair to the sun. (*T* 147)

In accordance with the orderly's case, it can be considered that Siegmund's desire misses its object by losing the connection with people and targets himself through the mediation of the fierce natural phenomena. Lawrence's later fiction includes a story of resurrection called 'The Sun', in which the heroine stupendously retrieves her inner strength to live from sunbathing, though the case of Siegmund and the orderly are abnormally self-sacrificial in their relation to nature. Through his finally executing the officer, the half-abhorred and half-loved greatest Other, the physical and mental necessity of the other is shown through the young man's frailty.

> It was peace. But now he had got beyond himself. He had never been here before. Was it life, or not-life? He was by himself. They were in a big, bright place, those others, and he was outside. The town, all the country, a big-bright place of light: and he was outside, here, in the darkened open beyond, where each thing existed alone. But they would all have to come out

there sometime, those others. Little, and left behind him, they all were. There had been father and mother and sweetheart. What did they all matter. This was the open land. (*PO* 18)

Being satisfied by reaching the space about which he is uncertain whether it is life or not life, the orderly takes pleasure in staying in the friendless stillness. The intensity of the space is the same solitary stillness in which the central characters of the island stories meet their fate. In this development of the story, I would argue, the orderly curiously shares the fate of those characters who have spent their desireless life in the womb / tomb.

Finally, the story ends with a shocking denouement in which the orderly's power to live lapses and he naturally dies. The cause of his death is the infinite loss of the officer, for certain. It is as if it allegorically implies that the orderly's impulsive decision to murder the captain suggests the cessation of his own repetitive death instinct and causes him to lapse into a final inanimate state. The dead bodies, lying side by side in the mortuary, are perhaps at peace: 'the one white and slender, but laid rigidly at rest, the other looking as if every moment it must rouse into life again, so young and unused, from a slumber' (*PO* 21). John Haegert incisively argues that the fact that it is unclear from the description of the two corpses 'Who is the "one," and who is the "other"' and 'which body belongs to which man', shows that the differences which had been emphasized between the men earlier in the story are terminated here at last; 'Antithetical beings to the very end, the officer and the orderly are nonetheless bound by a transgressive logic that blurs and "obliterates" their opposing natures, that relativizes their essential differences' (3).

However, it is obvious that the extinction of the differences by death due to the temporary, fatal violence is not an ideal terminus of human relationships. Depending on momentary means which lead to death or to the recurrence of the consciousness of reality, is a drastic means of dealing with the ingrained animosity and difference between individuals. Hence the text paradoxically suggests the necessity of maintaining a dynamic bond, evolving on a long-term basis, by transcending the hostility on the surface. Lawrence's psychodynamics encourage his characters to maintain the dynamic relationship, the struggle to overcome barriers and relapse into the stillness of unity, instead of distorting it on either side. As I have already argued, if one side of the binominal stillness and motion is suffocated, the subject consumes his vital energy to an excessive degree. It is the same as in the relationship of self and other — that is, it is necessary for both sides of the binary opposition to function, and to keep the dynamism of the dichotomies spreading, rather than that their conflict should efface each of them.

This study has provided so far an analysis of the affective intuition involved in receiving others, achieved in the context of temporality and it has also explored the importance of the aggressive energy involved in activating the dynamic consciousness, due to the anticipation of persistent inertia. Furthermore, the issue of the vitality of human beings is introduced into Lawrence's postcolonial texts after the 1920s. It is an aggression which organically ties and develops the fluid relationship of the self and the other, together with the maintenance of one's life and it is what the relative power of the captain and the orderly lacks. The next chapter will investigate those of Lawrence's protagonists who explore the reestablishment of the relationship with the racial others, showing how the process of exchanging vitality is needed in a wider context.

CHAPTER THREE

Facing the 'External' Other in the Late Works

1. The Heroines' Quests and the Mystic Figure of the External Other

Lawrence's writings became dogged by misanthropy which worsened in the wartime period; still, he kept seeking active interaction with people, and also with animals in the world outside England where heterogeneous species coexisted. After he obtained an exit permit with a great deal of trouble, he traveled overseas and encountered cultures outside the modernized perspective which predominated in England. Fleeing to the outside world, Lawrence exerted himself further in exploring his concern about how civilized people should bring out their suppressed dynamic consciousness, and thus he started to introduce phenomena which exist outside modernity by various adventurous methods.[1] Travelling to countries such as Mexico and Australia which had a history as colonized lands increased his creativity and he sought not only friendly communication but also dynamic interrelation with racial others and endeavored to achieve an unremitting renovation of relationships with them. The late works reflect Lawrence's own lively experience abroad; though I would argue that they cannot be read independently from his earlier fiction. They follow the traits of the previous works which changed the emotional class-conflict in his homeland into organic and affective relationships; and besides, they extensively explore the various kinds of emotional race-conflict.

CHAPTER THREE

However, the external differences between the characters are so massive that the late fictions expose the triviality of the battle arising from social differences in the earlier works.

The stories make the European beholders, who are dissatisfied with their homelands, actively travel to foreign countries and face the racial minorities, who differ from English people in terms of history, religion, culture, or customs. The protagonists interact with people they perceive as exotic who enshrine the anti-modern way of life, uninfected by the vice of civilization. As Fiona Fleming argues, the modernized people are losing the 'capacity to feel through the senses and instinct, losing the primitive, vital flow of the "blood-consciousness," still to be found in some populations on the globe' (par. 11) and thus the encounter is a drastic treatment to revitalize them. Fleming claims that 'Those forgotten chords are parts of the primitive self that had been lost under the effects of mechanisation and encroaching mental consciousness, but the encounter with blood-conscious people and an alien, unspoiled spirit of place stimulates the senses and brings the traveler closer to the pre-civilised instinctive self' (par. 11). Being influenced by the alien others, they become aware of the existence of dissimilar lives and mingle with the others on a level of physical consciousness which surpasses their biased view.

The peoples whom they encounter appear as topoi which are metonymically imbued with the foreignness of the landscape and the spirit of the land. They display their otherness to the protagonists in terms of their indifference to the reasonable, civilized lifestyle. What is additionally highlighted is their impersonality and also inhumanity as outsiders to modern rationality: for example, in *The Virgin and the Gipsy* (1930), the dark stare of a Spanish gipsy man who gazes at the gang of English youths including the heroine Yvette from the caravan steps is depicted as follows:

> [The gipsy man] stood imperturbable, without any expression at all. . . . It was a peculiar look, in the eyes that belonged to the tribe of the humble: the pride of the pariah, the half-sneering challenge of the outcast, who sneered at the law-abiding men, and went his own way. All the time, the gipsy man stood there, holding his child in his arms, looking on without being concerned. (*VG* 45)

His unemotional expression is that of an 'outcast' from the 'law-abiding' Western values, though it makes Yvette aware of the powerful male pride deriving from remote ages by transfusing the unknown mode of life into contemporary Britain. It is expressed that it is a mode of life which can only be accessed by the abyssal blood-consciousness that cannot be deciphered by a modernized Western mode of thought.

As I suggested in the first chapter, the aspects of 'impersonality', 'the inversion of the customary hierarchy of values in sensory perception', and 'animality' appear as principal elements when interacting with others through blood-consciousness. These aspects are emphasized more in Lawrence's late works in which the contacts lead to a greater emphasis on the primitiveness. They particularly reappear in *The Plumed Serpent*, when the white heroine Kate bashfully gets involved in the circle of the wild dance of Mexican peons and women.

> She seemed to feel the strange dark glow of them [men] upon her back. Men, dark, collective men, nonindividual. . . . Men and women alike danced with faces lowered and expressionless, abstract, gone in the deep absorption of men into the greater

manhood, women into the greater womanhood. It was sex, but the greater, not the lesser sex. The waters over the earth wheeling upon the waters under the earth, like an eagle silently wheeling above its own shadow. (*PS* 131)

The lesser sex is a personal sex which we are constantly aware of in our minds and the greater sex is rephrased as 'greater womanhood' and 'greater manhood' (*PS* 131), suggesting a domain which transcends the knowledge of who am I and who the other person is. 'She felt her sex and her womanhood caught up and identified in the slowly revolving ocean of nascent life' (*PS* 131), Lawrence writes; and the individuals metaphorically whirl above the ocean that is male and female like birds, beautifully likened to the relationship of animals and the physical world. As a matter of course, the overthrowing of the modernized protagonist's old ego again becomes the key factor in enabling her to understand the racial others. As it is described as follows — 'She did not know the face of the man whose fingers she held. Her personal eyes had gone blind, his face was the face of dark heaven, only the touch of his fingers a star that was both hers and his' (*PS* 131) — the physical communication, for which eyesight is unnecessary, teaches Kate to access the inhuman world with the flow of affective blood-consciousness through an inversion of values in which sensation takes precedence over other forms of perception. Gradually, her egoism fades and she devotes herself to it.

Through the dance which was effective as a medium that bridges the class difference, the three principal elements, mentioned earlier, deprive Kate of her personal identity. However, these primitive elements spur the emphasis on alterity or heterogeneity by arousing *fear* when they are introduced as qualities which the external others possess. The others' primitiveness and the protagonists' abandonment of personal identity are well-balanced in the reciprocal communication in the dancing scene in *The Plumed Serpent*. However, in the other scenes, the savageness seems to be over-emphasized as jeopardizing the protagonists. Lawrence often obscures the distinctions between the individuals whom he regards as external to Western life by briefly calling them 'the dark races' (*PS* 148). Although they range from Mexicans, European Gypsies, and Italians to Australians, since Lawrence valorizes the aboriginal pre-Christian peoples who cherish the old values of their respective regions, left behind by civilization, they all have the same role of threatening the Western hierarchy. Kelley Swarthout argues that 'In Lawrence's work, indigenous characters rarely receive individual recognition. Generally, Lawrence refers to all Indians collectively as "columns of dark blood," (47) who possess an "unconscious, heavy, reptilian indifference" (151)' (133). The way in which Lawrence groups them by blurring their respective emotions in some of his fiction, has driven many critics to assume, somewhat simplistically, that Lawrence is a racist, pointing out that the inhumane characteristics are emphatically described as barbarous and horrific.

In particular, the individuality of the Chilchui Indians in 'The Woman Who Rode Away' is almost erased, and they appear as a cluster of intimidating others with no faces, forming a sinister existence. On the other hand, they do not recognize the Western heroine as an individual, and maintain an indifference to her distinctive qualities or sex, as noted by Marijane Osborn, who states that 'She is as non-human to them as they, with their glittering "snakes's eye[s]" (13), are to her' (64). In this idiosyncratic short story, this complete indifference is the way in which the racial others forcefully and cruelly obliterate the heroine's personal sex, in contrast with the scene of the dance in *The*

CHAPTER THREE

Plumed Serpent. Describing the eyes of one of the Indians, Lawrence writes that:

> They were black and of extraordinary piercing strength, without a qualm of misgiving in their demonish, dauntless power. He looked into the eyes of the white woman with a long, piercing look, seeking she knew not what. She summoned all her strength to meet his eyes and keep up her guard. But it was no good. *He was not looking at her as one human being looks at another. He never even perceived her resistance or her challenge*, but looked past them both, into she knew not what.
>
> She could see it was hopeless to expect any human communication with this old being. (*WWRA* 51; emphasis added)

The Indians are unconcerned with her life force or power to resist and she dispiritedly realizes the impossibility of exchanging sympathy with them. Moreover, 'Always they treated her with this curious impersonal solicitude, this utterly impersonal gentleness, as an old man treats a child' (*WWRA* 57), and they do not respect the white heroine's sensual uniqueness. Even the young Indian man who is attached to her communicates 'without ever making her self-conscious, or sex-conscious' (*WWRA* 58). Neglected by the Indians as a personal being and as an appealing Western woman, the heroine loses her will to maintain her old identity. Watching their ancient dancing, the heroine feels a 'trance of agony' (*WWRA* 60) due to their anonymous resistance and negation of the female, modern, and Western quality she puts on.

> Her kind of womanhood, intensely personal and individual, was to be obliterated again, and the great primeval symbols were

to tower once more over the fallen individual independence of woman. The sharpness and the quivering nervous consciousness of the highly-bred white woman was to be destroyed again, womanhood was to be cast once more into the great stream of impersonal sex and impersonal passion. Strangely, as if clairvoyant, she saw the immense sacrifice prepared. (*WWRA* 60)

Differently from Kate, who feels the mutual physical communication with men who are racial others by proactively joining in the dance, this woman endures her selfhood being disrespected and subsumed under the greater sex and greater passion. The Western mentality and mode of thought are violently denied in a way which is associated with the otherworldly values that the Europeans encounter. This forceful negation of the subject's value involves a postcolonial intensity which did not exist in the process of flattening the class-consciousness in the early fiction. Moreover, they present a sinister schema of the women in the master race being required or compelled to give themselves up to the otherworldly religion. Even when she dedicates herself to their ritual as a sacrifice, being enchanted by its marvelous mystery, she is deprived of her self-defensive will and even feels pleasure in destructively proffering her body to the pagan god. This controversial way of describing the others and associating the Westerners with them has provoked antipathy from the viewpoints of feminism and post-colonialism.[2]

However, it is notable that the heroines who appear in these narratives similarly bear a sense of emptiness and of discontent with their old life. Yvette is one of the members of the adolescent group who possess a defiant spirit of opposition to the banal conventional society of England, though wandering in obscurity due to being uncertain as to what they should direct their frustration at and what it will lead to. The woman who rode away is also in an impasse in the situation of her married life and child-rearing so that she needs a change of climate. The heroines are thus eagerly awaiting someone to change them and something to arouse their physical instinct which replaces 'the quivering nervous consciousness' (*WWRA* 60). As soon as the woman encounters the Indians lurking in the mountains, she goes through a transforming experience as if she had been looking forward to it:

> [She was] feeling like a woman who has died and passed beyond. She was not sure that she had not heard, during the night, a great crash at the centre of herself, which was the crash of her own death. Or else it was a crash at the centre of the earth, and meant something big and mysterious. (*WWRA* 44)

Marina Ragachewskaya suggests that the exuberance of the death images in these narratives 'indicate[s] absolute immobility, time frozen and conserved' and that 'the Woman consents to becoming a victim in order to conquer time, in order to fill in the gap in her deadness produced by industrialization [of her former environment]' ('Turning a Moment into Eternity', par. 15). In this sense, it is possible to read these references to the death of the self as an extension of the context of Lawrence's earlier fiction. The distressed condition of the loss of emotion and the qualities of humanity is favourable to drawing out the inner unconscious which is prior to mentality. Therefore, the heroines hospitably receive the overcoming of their old selves in the subsequent experience. Presumably, the alterations in the white heroines' recognition have a similarity to the epiphanic transformation discussed in my first chapter. If the stories were set inside England, the transformation of the women would not cause repercussions. Ironically, however, the orthodox reading interprets the heroines within the postcolonial context and the author's anti-feminism. To make matters worse, stretching the interpretation of Lawrence's 'carbon statement' that he would not depict human beings' old personalities, many scholars imagine the stereotype of the white women being deprived of their personalities by the ferocious others who do not even have personalities to lose, and this interpretation has developed in such a way as to sully Lawrence's artistic reputation. However, it must be mentioned that the case of 'The Woman Who Rode Away' is fable-like and Lawrence does not compose unambiguously self-sacrificial stories in most of his other works. Although this tale is literally a dead-end, in other fictions, in order to avoid the same denouement, the English women's attachment to their identity and their emotional turmoil are depicted more realistically. Fleming points out that Lawrence himself declared his personal grief in the foreign land at not having been identified as a singular being by ethnological others.

> Worse still than being deposed from a pre-supposed pedestal is to be altogether ignored on the grounds of one's lack of importance, which the woman experiences [in 'The Woman Who Rode Away'] . . . and the narrator of *Twilight in Italy* deplores at length. He repeatedly fails in his attempt to communicate with an old Italian woman, gradually perceiving that he is of no interest to her: "In her universe I was a stranger, a foreign *signore*. That I had a world of my own, other than her own, was not conceived by her. She did not care." The realization comes rather as a shock because he is used to attracting the inhabitants'

attention and because he never expected that his curiosity for the foreign other could go unanswered. (Fleming, par. 14)

In the narrative based on Lawrence's experience, the Englishman reacts dejectedly to others' making light of his identity, and finds it nearly impractical to discard his personality in an off-hand manner in the foreign place. It seems to suggest Lawrence's awareness of the difficulty of dissolving the self-consciousness for nationality and identity.

On the other hand, I would argue that the fact that descriptions of the personalities of the racial others and their private desires are omitted in 'The Woman Who Rode Away', implies that the erasure is an artificial scheme. Their inhuman indifference is faked in order to emphasize the goal of the completion of the metamorphosis of the heroine who is thoroughly attracted to them. As a proof, with the exception of the specific story, Lawrence's fiction is filled with battles between the egos of characters on both sides of the racial division. In addition to the turbulence of the emotions of Western characters which occurs through their self-renewal, he minutely describes the complex feelings which the racial others bear. Therefore, it can be argued that the contrasting perspectives and emotions of both parties cannot be reconciled by the one-time-only nature of epiphany, and Lawrence has directed his attention to the continuous emotional conflict. Lawrence displays diverse patterns of this battle through the respective plots of each of his narratives. Focusing on both white women's desire and that of the ethnological others, the relationships move on dynamically, and do not stay in the predicament of stagnant inertia. In most cases, their desires do not coincide and the relationships fail to gel. However, I argue that we can see Lawrence's deep insight and respect from the depictions of the others' complex personalities which covertly pulse inside their unearthly personae. The next section will explore the way in which Lawrence tried to set forth the desires and personalities of the racial others and their confrontations with willful white characters.

2. Conflicting Desires and Identities between Racial Others

The difference between the central protagonists and the racial others in Lawrence's fiction was originally based on the historically-determined power relationship. However, the relationship changes by degrees: with the encounter with the others, the external point of view is thrust upon the protagonist's sense of value which has seemed reasonable in her past life. Through the negation of the value of her past life by the encounter, the protagonist becomes aware of the vulnerability of the enmeshed hierarchies for the first time. Then she discovers through her emotional conflict that the external aspects enshrine an unfathomable power, and her reaction to it includes an irresistible attraction towards the differentness. The inscrutability of the racial others, which is accentuated, appears as a fetishized form of quasi-textual being to the modernized Western character, and she is agitated to discover and understand them. Therefore, her devouring will to know the others and the desire to control and possess their foreignness, encroaches upon the others and thus makes them reproach her and shrink even more from the predator.

The novella, *St. Mawr*, presents an example of the friction. In the story, there appear a variety of alien others: Lewis, the Welsh groom, Phoenix, another groom partly of American Indian origin, and St. Mawr, the grand and restive stallion. The central characters are the white mother, Mrs. Witt, and her daughter, Lou, who are inclined to make contact with the others' mysterious quality which contrasts with modernity — though the fact that alien beings of three different origins are mixed up and confused in a uniform otherness has to be overlooked. Moreover, it should be mentioned firstly that St. Mawr is a horse belonging to Lou's husband and there is a grave accident in the story in which the baronet is thrown off his rampaging horse and fatally injured. The story is thus haunted by an inauspicious sign of the upsetting of the social class structure in the way that the being of inferior status inflicts harm on the superior.

Mrs. Witt is a widowed mother who celebrates her freedom, independence, and vigorous youthfulness. She perceives the blood of an old savage England in Lewis, and is troubled when 'his pale grey eyes met hers, and they looked so non-human and uncommunicative, so without connection, and inaccessible' (*StM* 72). Lewis is from Wales, though in Keith Brown's reading of *St. Mawr* as a story in which the concepts of the Celt and the Indian in the south-west of the U.S.A are blended, his appearance resembles that of a Celtic Briton (181). He seems to belong to an aboriginal world which is closed and preserved intact, and Mrs.Witt feels a vivid curiosity and envy of him for living indifferently, externally to what is real in her world. She becomes enchanted with the undiscovered nature which underlies the social and cultural difference between them, and grows tense due to being unable to domesticate him.

> There was something about this little man . . . that irritated her and made her want to taunt him. His peculiar little inaccessibility . . . his way of looking at her as if he had looked from out of another country, a country of which he was an inhabitant, and where she had never been: this touched her strangely. . . . In spite of the fact that in actual life, in her world, he was only a

groom, almost chétif, with his legs a little bit horsey and bowed; and of no education, saying *Yes Mam*! and *No Mam*! And accomplishing nothing, simply nothing at all on the face of the earth. Strictly a non entity.

And yet, what made him perhaps the only real entity to her, his seeming to inhabit another world than hers. A world dark and still, where language never ruffled the growing leaves, and seared their edges like a bad wind. (*StM* 103-4)

The hatred mixed with attraction disturbs the hierarchy between Lewis and Mrs. Witt as in 'The Prussian Officer'. Every time she perceives his unapproachableness, she cannot help taking a fiendish delight in railing at him, though 'his face was blank and stony, with a stony, distant look of pride that made him inaccessible *to her emotions*' (*StM* 105; emphasis added), which is reminiscent of the invalidity of emotion in the primeval affective interaction, which I have discussed in the first chapter. Lewis's attitude towards his employer is inscrutable due to his lack of verbal expression. Language is the means of expression in the Western world and utilizes intelligence, and thus his incapability or refusal of verbal expression is a rejection of any compromise with the world in which Mrs. Witt exists. However, one could discern his determination not to accept her in his attitude of refusal. Although she tries to understand him by disrupting their fixed relationship and trespassing on the mystery of the world he lives in, Lewis silently commits himself to the relationship of employer and employee and conveys his enmity towards her controlling desire, and this indicates that his impenetrable, strained will frictionally opposes her will. Although trying to break down the barrier between herself and the groom, Mrs. Witt is only exploiting the other world he represents by being filled with the vanity of her *Herrenmoral* authority.

However, as a consequence of her fruitless approach, on one occasion Lewis cheerfully recounts the story of the god he has believed in from his boyhood, and Mrs. Witt grasps that 'he, in an odd way, was in love with her. She had known it by the odd, uncanny merriment in him, and his unexpected loquacity' (*StM* 112). It was the first self-disclosure in which Lewis uttered his past memory using the means of the ruling world, language. Moved by his reconciliation, Mrs. Witt daringly asks him to marry her. At this very moment, however, Lewis shuts his heart to her again and exhaustively refuses to physically interact with her. He insists on the need for his male body to be respected and never to be insulted: that is, he keeps himself on guard by his principle that he would never defile his body by touching a woman who has once been in a patronizing relationship with him, and Mrs. Witt can do nothing but get hurt and retreat. It was possible for Lewis to move to the plane on which Mrs. Witt remains, though he could not admit her descending — or rising — to his plane. The Westerners often fail to achieve a dynamic contact with the racial others, impeded by their fear and discriminating awareness of them. However, I would suggest that here, it is revealed by Lewis's repulsion that the racial others are *also* deterred from further associating themselves with the masters' race by being mentally captured in relationships of governance. It betrays his own textual role as an enigmatic being, who elusively lives in an inhuman world, which is characteristic of Lawrence's portrayal of the others of Western class-hegemony.

Moreover, as already noted, Lewis once chose Mrs. Witt as a listener and exposed his personal desire for her to understand his own history. Apart from an indifference to time — the quality that has been figuratively associated with the external others — it shows that he is actually not a timeless being. However, he strongly resists exposing his male body to an inferior consciousness and self-protectively winces back again into the inhuman shell. In this text, I would argue, Lawrence dismantles the imaginariness of the monolithic impersonality which he previously lets the colonized people put on, and discloses their gesture of being unable to contact the master's race, due to being tinged with hierarchical consciousness. Hence, Lawrence distinctly indicates that the racial others are also confined by egoism, similarly to the Western characters.

Meanwhile, Lou becomes fed up with the mestizo Phoenix's frivolous appetite for commercialization, and disillusioned with the fact that he 'risks losing his real Indian credentials' (Snyder 675) by being superficially modernized and assimilated with American men. She brushes him off, saying that there is nothing respectful in men, either in her race or in the other. Moreover, she loses her interest in St. Mawr, who instantly reduced his dignity by obediently following after a mare by wagging his tail, and the mystery of the otherness is debunked in the end. It surreptitiously expresses both irony and a significant meaning in Lou's reluctant recognition that the 'supposed' other men were in fact dogged by personality, and differed little from the English men she knows. What makes Lou ultimately find the meaning of life is neither human beings nor animals, but the power of the landscape of South America, and the story is concluded by her anti-climactic recognition.

Lawrence attempts in an experimental way to represent the power relationship of a white woman and a Mexican man as convincingly as possible in various of his narratives, and it was also an experiment in how far he could develop the personalities of the characters of the exotic races. In the short story 'The Princess', a peculiar way of portraying the progress of the relationship with an indigenous man is demonstrated.³ The conspicuous thing is that the usual inhumanness of a Mexican man is depicted in the first half of the story, and the humanness — that is, the explosion of his emotion and desire — is contrastingly illustrated in the latter half. In contrast to Lewis, who bigotedly declined Mrs. Witt's dominance of his male physicality, the story emphasizes the aggressive but sentimental craving of a Mexican man towards an English woman. Romero, an owner of haciendas, taciturn and unselfish at first, and the heroine Dollie have been feeling inward intimacy with each other. One day, they visit a mountain to grant her wish to see the wild animals, and as events turn out, she insincerely makes love with Romero. His joy and inflamed passion surges up at having got her; however, she sexually rejects him from the following day and Romero gets ferocious at her unreasonable and cruel blow and astounds the readers by exposing his sensual desire for possession by sheer brute force. Yet, the essence of this story by no means identifies him only with an immoral and lustful violence: it was a request for her to admit her need of him. Having been told bluntly by Dollie that he can never conquer her in that way, the signs of human emotion flicker in him: 'He stood arrested, looking back at her, with many emotions conflicting in his face: wonder, surprise, a touch of horror, and an unconscious pain that crumpled his face' (*StM* 192). The personal emotion of the characters who take on the role of racial others had never been so meticulously depicted.

  This time, it is not the Westerner who exerts her will over the other and restrains him, but Romero — the description highlights the reversible relation between the qualities of the Westerners and the racial others. Furthermore, while he tries to get her under his will, he struggles to be loved and reiterates his heart-breaking order, compelling Dollie to express her need for him, and repeatedly cries, '"you've got to say you want to be with me'" (*StM* 192). Although Romero was hotly waiting for some sign of affection and of warmth from her, he could try to solve the problem of the dissociation between himself and Dollie by resorting to violence. Besides, it is notable that he tried to obtain his self-affirmation by linguistic expression and that he incongruously tries to secure his existence by the consolation of words. However, due to her thorough 'lack of compassion' (Squires 93), she steadily rejects him. The explosion of his desire, unstoppable in rushing to his disastrous end, is full of grief: Romero is finally shot to death, too soon and too indifferently, by white men who come to rescue Dollie. Neil Roberts writes that 'Cultural difference manifests itself in a wholly destructive way' through the characterization of Romero; 'Although his plight is portrayed sympathetically', he is 'something of a stereotype' and 'effectively *stand[s] for* the otherness that Dollie ['s white consciousness] so self-destructively tries to break through to' (115-16). As Roberts states, the typical underprivileged situation of the racial inferiors is mingled with Romero's death. However, the portrayal of the desire to be loved is undetectable in 'The Woman Who Rode Away' or in *St. Mawr*: the desire of the others, who were superficially covered in a veil of impersonality, is given a concrete form through the portrayal of Romero's carnal desire and his wish to confirm his existence. In compensation for evading Romero's earnest request or her own unconscious desire to free herself, Dollie lives a blank life, losing her strength to live forever. In both 'The Woman Who Rode Away' and 'The Princess', we can find the conflict between characters deriving from contrasting cultures, though it is prevented from fully achieving the destabilization of the social status of each by their mental defences. I would argue that it is undeniable that both Lewis and Romero believed that their unprivileged status would be recompensed: for Lewis, it is

CHAPTER THREE

the reason for not violating his male body by the consciousness of inferiority, and for Romero, it is the reason for making the white female admit his sexual presence.

Here, I would raise a crucial issue which Lou proposes in *St. Mawr*. Lou aspires to elucidate the true nature of the evilness of the unwieldy St. Mawr, who threw his rider and almost killed the man. She ruminates, 'Was it *the natural wild thing* in him which caused these disasters? Or was it *the slave*, asserting himself for vengeance? If the latter, let him be shot. It would be a great satisfaction to see him dead. But if the former —' (*StM* 82; emphasis added). It is the question of the intrinsic quality of the others' aggression: on the one hand, it is an inhuman unconsciousness that involves a natural evilness which is not interfered with by any kinds of personality; on the other hand, it is the consciousness of *Ressentiment*, which Friedrich Nietzsche defined as servile feelings, that watches for a chance to overthrow the power relationship from the inferior point of view. Lou's sharp tone of regarding the consciousness characterized by slave morality as despicable, seems to be fuelled by a euro-supremacist and authoritarian point of view. However, by what means do we tell the difference between the personal aggression of *Ressentiment* and pure, impersonal aggression in the related context of race?

It is well known that there is a similarity between Nietzsche's and Lawrence's ideas, and it can be said that their vitalistic ways of viewing the life-demands of people with different statuses is the respect in which they coincide most closely. Just as Lawrence presents a hypothetical proposition in *St. Mawr* that both personal aggression and impersonal aggression exist, Nietzsche gives an acute observation of the difference between the *Ressentiment* of the inferiors and aggression as an original instinct of organisms. The point at issue is the presence or absence of the *pre-emotional, intrinsic vitality* in the aggression. Nietzsche discusses the uneasiness with which aggression as a healthy instinct has become contorted into an unhealthy vice in modern civilization. He argues that moral civilization has defended itself from the natural urge of human beings by political organization and Christian rationality or conscience. Those bulwarks made 'all those instincts of wild, free, roving man [turn] backwards, *against man himself.* Animosity, cruelty, the pleasure of pursuing, raiding, changing and destroying — all this was pitted against the person who had such instincts: *that* is the origin of "bad conscience"' (*On the Genealogy of Morals*, 57). This 'bad conscience' or guilty conscience is what the servile spirit represents. Nietzsche's argument that although aggression is an old vital feeling inherent in organisms, it is deformed as an enmity and directed towards others, corresponds with the depiction, in Lawrence's fiction, of the discriminative intention stagnantly preserved in the class hierarchy. Therefore, the natural aggression which is spontaneously produced in the individual's unconscious mind becomes emotionalized and mentalized, and has a rebounding effect on the superior class or one's self by preserving servility.

In 'The Princess', both Dollie and Romero are responsible for wearing out their emotions and wills. The conflict, remaining on a purely personal level and ending in the collapse of their relationship, shows that the aggression has not yet achieved a vital energy. We have seen the consciousness of *Ressentiment* in the relationship which ends up in personal friction: Lewis is mentally entrapped by the problem of his physical humiliation and Romero 'seeks to win back his pride by keeping her [Dollie] hostage and forcing her to repeat the [sexual] experience' (A. Harrison *The Life of D. H. Lawrence*, 285) and eventually commits a sinful act. I would argue that their consciousness thus does not cause a sense of the affirmation of life and does not have a productive effect of destroying and recreating relationships with the English women. In this respect, it can be shown that the racial others are neither idealized as inhuman beings nor despised as savage ones in Lawrence's post-colonial fiction. Rather, the others are depicted as equal to the English characters in having historically affected emotions and personal desires. Realizing this, Lou becomes disappointed with the common quality she finds in the idealized others. Hence, the issue of the aggression remains unsolved in *St. Mawr* because of her loss of interest in the company of contemporary people, and in the end, Lou has become attracted to the spirit of the land instead. However, as if making a suggestion on this issue, we see a healthy aggression — not a depressed twist of personality — in the struggle of the Indian maid, Juana, against her white employer, Kate in *The Plumed Serpent*. The analysis of the motive for Juana's aggression should reveal the dialectical relation between the two variants of the quality of aggression.

3. *Ressentiment* or the Natural Life Competition

In *The Plumed Serpent*, Kate experiences two patterns of the reform of her old egoism. Firstly, she participates in the Indian dance and experiences an affective and pre-emotional mingling with the Indians at the ceremonial occasion. She experiences a greater self through the ritual awakening and feels as if she is returning to being a young and innocent virgin during the Quetzalcoatl ceremony. The ritual dance and ceremony involve an extraordinary experience of affective affiliation with the ethnological others, and make not only the difference of the social strata but also the races of Kate and the uncultivated men seem insignificant. It is the transitional stage of extinguishing her old self in order to displace the old connections with the other, and this is the sacrificial change in Kate which has been generally recognized in studies of the novel.

However, Lawrence hints in his essay at another possible way of having a real living relationship 'which is neither sacrifice nor fight to the death' (*STH* 174). It needs 'Courage to accept the life-thrust from within oneself, and from the other person' and 'to accept the fact and not whine about it' (*STH* 174-75). Although Lawrence does not specifically clarify in his essay what exactly is the unsacrificial way of having a new connection with the other, I would suggest that it is expressed in the second type of experience Kate has. Kate feels another sense of the reform of her ego in the contact with her maid Juana in her everyday life through the other woman's persistent attacks on her Western quality. The characteristic of this experience is *to emphasize the contrast* between the two women's lives: in this respect, it is a different matter from affective experience. While the racial and social differences between the two are strongly emphasized, both women are impressed and influenced by each other through the contest between their individual lives.

The struggle for interracial and social supremacy between the women is vividly depicted through the way 'Juana challenges Kate with her difference' (Carpenter 123). Juana feels occasional delight when her family's standard of living is improved by Kate's mercy and when she receives her share of the modern life which Kate has worn out. Yet, it should be said that she is not grateful or obliged to Kate for her courteousness in a real sense. It was a derisive 'Fun!' (*PS* 141) for Juana to come into contact with the unknown, methodical way of living: Kate 'was a source of wonder and amusement to them. *But she was never a class superior.* She was a half-incomprehensible, half-amusing wonder-being' (*PS* 141; emphasis added). With an exceptional duality of loyalty and excitement in their rivalry with Kate, Juana and her family are kindled to a destructive joy by offending Kate's Western and aristocratic sensibility. Humiliating their snobbish employer, the act of dragging her down and forcing out her undeserved superiority, gives them enormous existential pleasure. When Kate tries to teach Juana's daughters how to write and sew, 'They would press upon her, trespassing upon her privacy, and with a queer effrontery, doing all they could' (*PS* 147) to reject Kate's benevolence and insult her. They show her their laziness and depravity in a way which is hard for Kate to bear and they get intoxicated with a pleasant sensation by continuing to do this until she gives up teaching them. When Kate is hosting her guests, Juana and her daughters and niece appear close to the Europeans, and display themselves plucking lice out of each others' hair. 'They wanted the basic fact of lice to be thrust under the noses of those white people' (*PS* 147) and whereas it seems to be a cruel trick to disgrace Kate who belongs to the white group, 'It was as if it were a meritorious public act' (*PS* 152) for them. When Kate scolds them and gets rid of them, trembling with fury, 'One instant, Juana's black inchoate eyes gleamed with a malevolent ridicule, meeting with Kate's. The next instant, humble and abject, the four with their black hair down their backs slunk into the recess out of sight' (*PS* 147-48). By performing uneducated and irrational acts, and intentionally showing no awareness of the situation, they pride themselves on their ability to face unclean reality, in contrast with the Europeans who put on elegant and clean airs. Besides, it is nothing but a natural and crude mode of life for them, involving no effort to keep up their appearances.

In accordance with the Mexican sociological theory which has marginalized women, Rebecca Carpenter thinks that Juana 'must be deferential in order to maintain employment, yet she can only express herself through reactive behavior' (120). Keiichi Okano positions Juana as a 'woman who is compelled to live a self-defensive and nasty life' and he claims that she 'insults Kate and shows an attitude of kicking her out' (526; my translation). The family's harassment can be seen as involving low, preposterous and irrational actions and it seems to be appropriate to consider this onslaught as showing an undisguised offensive desire towards the master. However, I would argue that it is remarkable in not involving an emotion of subservience: rather, the root of the aggression is in the deep fountain of natural instinct. As the following passage shows, we can read Juana's positive craving for Kate and her effort to change it to an energy of life, and therefore Carpenter's observation towards Juana that she 'cannot help but display her resentment of their unequal positions' (120) and Okano's interpretation of her as wishing to expel Kate are both unconvincing.

> But it pleased Juana that she had been able to make Kate's eyes blaze with anger. It pleased her. She felt a certain low power in herself. True, she was a little afraid of that anger. But that was what she wanted. She would have no use for a Niña [madam] of whom she was not a bit afraid. And she wanted to be able to provoke that anger, of which she felt a certain abject twinge of fear. (*PS* 148)

It can be inferred that Juana's aggression is not a mere servile feeling or fervent antagonism toward white people. This is a rapture, and an innocent craving for Juana.[4] She does not feel hatred for Kate on an emotional level nor even want her to get out — rather, it would be a bore if she were really to leave and escape from their heated contest.

Her aim is gratified by manifesting her definite power and existence to Kate, and she fulfills herself by giving herself confidence that at any time she can overturn the transient ascendant power which Kate believes herself to possess naturally. It is the same as the case of her daughters who flatly reject Kate's benevolent offer to let them acquire skills. Making their lives collide with that of Kate signifies the positive appeal of their lives which involve an unreservedly powerful affirmation, rather than resistant acts. Facing the vigor of Juana's contrasting mode of life, Kate reflects on her own way of living, while emotionally trembling with anger and disgrace. No compassion flows between the two women and they are both influenced by each other by constantly fighting for triumph over the other. However, in this process conducted by life competition, we see the disarming of the English woman's egoism through her being impressed by the vividness of the other's life. Although neither of them tries to deprive her counterpart of her identity, the fresh experience replaces their old ideas in this different method.

What is the most eminent differentiating factor between Juana and male characters in the stories discussed earlier? I would argue that her release of animosity and her act of subverting the social order is not a logical or defensive action, like taking precautions against hurting one's pride as Lewis and Romero do, but a more intuitive action. Juana craves the presence of Kate and the proactive, vigorous communication with her in her deep physical consciousness. It is an unreflectively manifested act of seeking to earn the affirmation and energy that is necessary for life and is linked to an existential triumph. In Juana's attitude to life, I would argue that the binary opposition between two forms of aggression between organisms — that is, *Ressentiment* and natural instinct — in *St. Mawr*, is invalidated: the personal and impersonal aggression are not entirely separated but it is hinted that they have a continuity. Although Juana's harassment of Kate looks like a despicable and ignoble insubordination, she is not haunted by an introspective, self-deprecating mind like the characters in the other tales. While she takes her inferiority into account, I consider that her aggressiveness is fuelled by the energy of destroying and ridiculing her own humble position, and the friction she generates is immediately connected to her own agitating life energy. Consequently, the issue highlighted in *St. Mawr* cannot be resolved merely by explaining it as a binary opposition of *Ressentiment* and natural instinct. As Nietzsche argues, the instinctive, natural aggression has been converted to an emotional aggression targeting the self and others, due to being subjected to an historical and political aggression. Yet, the aggression we see in Juana's displays is one in which the socio-politically determined inferior consciousness returns once again to a natural instinct; and it does much for the revival of human relationships by active and healthy interaction.

Here, I would look at Lawrence's own point of view on social Darwinism which has some similarity to the way Lou in *St. Mawr* shows loathing towards the consciousness of *Ressentiment*. Lawrence argues that in terrestrial forms of life, including animals and vegetation, there is a natural hierarchy among species in the degree of their ability to survive and it should not be ignored or disregarded.

> Life moves in circles of power and of vividness, and each circle of life only maintains its orbit upon the subjection of some lower circle. If the lower cycles of life are not *mastered*, there can be no higher cycle.
>
> In nature, one creature devours another, and this is an essential

> part of all existence and of all being. It is not something to lament over, nor something to try to reform. . . . And if we see that the whole of creation is established upon the fact that one life devours another life, . . . then what is the good of trying to pretend that it is not so? The only thing to do is to realise, what is higher, and what is lower, in the cycles of existence. (*RDP* 356)

Lawrence claims that the selection should occur naturally with regard to 'species', as human beings can trample on or pluck flowers. Accordingly, the exercise of servile will in subverting the power relationship through hatred is contrary to natural law and should not be admitted. However, Lawrence continues in his essay that his aforementioned notion, which is a kind of imperialistic social Darwinism, concerns the contest of 'species', which are ruled by the dispensation of nature; and this rule is not applicable to the life force which the individual 'beings' enshrine.

> [W]e are talking now of existence, of species, of types, of races, of nations, not of single individuals, nor of *beings*. The dandelion in full flower, a little sun bristling with sun-rays on the green earth, is a nonpareil, a non-such. Foolish, foolish, foolish to compare it to anything else on earth. It is itself incomparable and unique. (*RDP* 358)

Therefore, it is highly probable that *the individual life force*, independent of the relativity of mastery, occasionally overwhelms the other beings. In brief, according to Lawrence's argument it is absurd to try to disguise the differences of power between species in the coexistence of animated things in the gladiatorial, natural world. However, on the level of individual vitality, power is unique and even has the potential to be subverted. Akinobu Okuma writes as follows,

> [When] lives are experienced as beings which are not manipulated by the consciousness of mankind, . . . the other animals and plants also emerge as inscrutable others for human beings. . . . Although the other creatures have hitherto been given their appropriate positions by the values of mankind, they get apart from the anthropocentric ways. This reveals that human beings are also forms of life which are equivalent to other creatures. (240; my translation)

For that reason, the individuals can overpower their opponents by expressing their natural vigor. Okuma continues:

> [When] the living organisms, except human beings, emerge as others which exceed our recognition, it is a situation which simply gives a relative viewpoint to mankind's self-insistence and teaches us the lesson of the vacuity of our egoisms. At that moment, we humans have nothing to do but to abandon not only our ego but also our consciousness as mankind and intently endure the solemn existence of the unknown, living activity. . . . By confronting the primordial, living perspective which is "now and here" with the reality [which is interpreted from the viewpoint of imperial social Darwinism and that of harsh naturalism], Lawrence tries to resist the reality by creating a new form of life. (240-41; my translation)

CHAPTER THREE

In his real life, for instance, Lawrence sees the natural force inside his pet cat, Timsy: 'She looked at me with the vacant, feline glare of her hunting eyes. It is not even ferocity. It is the dilation of the strange, vacant arrogance of power. The power is in her' (*RDP* 356). Although it is unnecessary to mention that human beings have a dominant power over domestic cats, Timsy can win a victory over her master by attracting him in terms of her life force. It reminds us of Kate's wincing at Juana's eyes and acknowledging in the depth of her consciousness that Juana's vital force has temporarily defeated her. After Christianity has been rescinded by Don Ramón Carrasco and when the barbarous rhythm of the drum of Quetzalcoatl resonates instead of the mechanical sound of the Catholic church bell, Juana's and Kate's eyes encounter each other; then, a question instantaneously and madly rushes about inside Kate.

> Kate caught the other woman's black, reptilian eyes unexpectedly. Usually, she forgot that Juana was dark, and different. . . . Till suddenly she met that black, void look with the glint in it, and she started inwardly, involuntarily asking herself: Does she hate me? Or was it only the unspeakable difference in blood? Now, in the dark glitter which Juana showed her for one moment, Kate read fear, and triumph, and a slow, savage, nonchalant defiance. Something very inhuman. . . . Then again she glanced up, and the eyes of the two women met for a moment. 'See the Niña's [madam's] eyes of the sun!' cried Juana, laying her hand on Kate's arm. Kate's eyes were a sort of hazel, changing, grey-gold, flickering at the moment with wonder, and a touch of fear and dismay. Juana sounded triumphant. (*PS* 334)

Through her letting the 'Niña' know her ignominious defeat due to the death of Christianity, Juana's offensiveness achieves a glorious culmination. It is not just a brutality which is inside her black eyes — as is hinted in the text, what is depicted as a beautiful contrast with Kate's eyes that resemble the sunshine is the gleam of the Indians' reptilian eyes, deriving from the preconquest days. Its mystical beauty hidden under menace thrusts her triumph towards Kate; and here, the eyes of the sun and the eyes of the reptile express both their strong presence and their difference by not denying each other. Thus Lawrence ventures to employ unconventional means of highlighting otherness in his interracial writings, in order to combat the dominant vividness of life in individual 'beings'. Although Kate is not compelled to ritually discard her identity, she is being challenged to a duel through the exchange of living force with Juana in her daily life. As before, Lawrence conveys the influence which the intensity of experience produces by naturally surmounting and revising the old perspective. The possessor of power is thus both frightened and attracted by the experience of the destabilization of the basis of her life, and the relationship dissolves and reforms by repeating the destruction and transmutation through actively challenging the other existence.

As Colin Milton points out, since Nietzsche greatly values the impulse of life, he flatly objects to the theory of the generative and responsive behaviour of organisms which Darwinians have argued for. Milton states that Nietzsche thought that the biological theorists 'had mistakenly concluded that the fundamental life instinct is an "instinct of self-preservation" or "will-to-live" and that this goal was typically reached by adaptation' (29). For Nietzsche, on the other hand, 'aggression and exploitation of what is around are the basic impulses of living things — typically, the healthy organism does not wait to be acted on but takes the initiative to change the environment, working not just to maintain itself, but to grow and increase' (Milton 29) — an opinion which resembles that of Lawrence. To put the "instinct of self-preservation" or "will-to-live" in another way, it could also be described in terms of the notion of Eros, though this cannot fully explain the vicissitudes of life and the nature of organisms. As I have noted in the second chapter, Lawrence combines the ideas of will-to-motion and will-to-inertia: accordingly, he expresses distaste for the act of blindly repeating the same movement of repelling the stimulating change merely for the sake of self-preservation. I would therefore argue that, like that of Nietzsche, Lawrence's ontological theory also recommends actively approaching the others and one's environment and continuing to overturn the static or familiar elements and increase one's vitality at the same time. However, the difference between the ideas of the two thinkers, I suspect, is that exploitation is not what Lawrence really intends through the depiction of Juana. Milton writes that Nietzsche's ideology is indicative of the way in which 'the aggressor struggles to overwhelm, to reshape . . . while the victim seeks to maintain independence and integrity' (30). However, as far as Juana is concerned, I argue that her attitude towards the other on the level of individuality is not founded on the will to grow or the will to power as in Nietzsche. When she takes a lively part as an aggressor, she does not seize Kate as a victim. This is what distinguishes her from the other characters who are restricted by servile consciousness. She does not need a victim to justify her will to gain power; while she accepts the circumstance of coexisting with her Niña and that she is employed under her, she craves a good opponent, whom it is worthwhile to combat. She has an attitude of respecting otherness, not exploiting the other or striving to erase the differentness of the other.

In the opening chapter of his essays about Mexico, named 'Corasmin and the Parrots', Lawrence presumes that Rosalino, the *mozo* or Indian servant, Corasmin the terrier, two unnamed parrots, and himself from the white man's land, are living things which exist on different planes of life, and he observes the jovial exchange of enmity between all of them. Andrew Harrison observes that this skirmish reflects 'the tides of conflict and revolution in Mexico' (*The Life of D. H. Lawrence*, 289);[5] nevertheless, I would argue that the spectacle does not represent a world entangled with that kind of bitter feeling. Lawrence's focus on their life competition is warm and gentle and what is saliently depicted is the parrots' mean but merry attitude towards life. The birds screech and imitate the words of the human beings in a way that is even more than life-like and they even mockingly represent the rolling sound of the Spanish 'r' with their highly talented performance.

> 'Perro! Oh, Perro! Perr-rro! Oh, Perr-rro! Perro!'
> They are imitating somebody calling the dog. . . . But that any creature should be able to pour such a suave, prussic-acid sarcasm over the voice of a human being calling a dog, is incredible. One's diaphragm chuckles involuntarily. And one thinks: *Is it possible?* Is it possible that we are so absolutely, so innocently, so *ab ovo* ridiculous? (*MM* 2)

By showing off all their abilities, the parrots attack the human beings with their satisfactory manifestation of life. On the other hand, due to being imitated unceremoniously and with intuitive cruelty by them, people realize their own objective appearance and become astonished to find that they were funny indeed — here we meet Lawrence's idea of receiving organic influence from the other beings. Furthermore, the demonic birds mimic the whistling of Rosalino, who indifferently sweeps the patio, though their exaggerated way of doing so is 'extremely sardonically funny' (*MM* 2) for the listeners. We hear the hysterically rejoicing parrots: 'Up goes the wild, sliding Indian whistle in the morning, very powerful, with an immense energy seeming to drive behind it' (*MM* 2). This is precisely the best example to show the way in which natural aggression is directly linked with one's vital energy. The parrots' tentacles are extended to the dog Corasmin, and hearing the mimicry of his own yapping repeated continually, with a look of annoyance, the dog permits their act. Grinning with his sidelong glances at the dog, Lawrence meditates: 'Poor old Corasmin's clear yellow eyes! He is going to be master of his own soul, under all the vitriol those parrots pour over him. *But he's not going to throw out his chest in a real lust of self-pity.* That belongs to the next cycle of evolution' (*MM* 4; emphasis added). This is just the reason why Lawrence does not accept the pessimism of the *Ressentiment*-oriented mind. As Edward Engelberg notes, Nietzschean self-deprecating decadence is the 'inversion of vindictive man who needs to sublimate his lust for masochism by creating a system of "payment"; the strong have always had a clear conscience' (qtd. in Rose 80). However, Lawrence is impressed that Corasmin, who silently forgives the parrots' wicked act, has not fallen into masochistic self-contentment — 'Invictus! The still-unconquered Corasmin!' (*MM* 4), he calls out. Lawrence writes that there is an 'invisible gulf' between the respective planes on which the variety of creatures live, and the passage includes a condensed expression of the author's viewpoint towards the notion of the external other itself.

> If you come to think of it, when you look at the monkey, you are looking straight into the other dimension. He's got length and breadth and height all right, and he's in the same universe of Space and Time as you are. But there's another dimension. He's different. . . .
>
> He mocks at you and gibes at you and imitates you. Sometimes he is even more *like* you than you are yourself. It's funny, and you laugh just a bit on the wrong side of your face. . . .
>
> 'Perro! Oh, Perr-rro!' shrieks the parrot.
>
> Corasmin looks up at me, as much as to say:
>
> 'It's the other dimension. There's no help for it. Let us agree about it.' (*MM* 7-8)

The essence of this example can patently be applied to the relationship of Juana and Kate as well. Lawrence further speculates that Rosalino also repudiatingly gazes at Lawrence with his black eyes which the master does not possess, and he also sometimes feels pleasure in deliberately annoying him. However, they both consent to this in the knowledge that they are prohibited from trespassing on the invisible gulf between the two tribes in the earthly realm of nature.

> But he [Rosalino] can imitate me, even more than life-like. As the parrot can him. And I have to laugh at his *me*, a bit on the wrong side of my face, as he has to grin on the wrong side of his face when I catch his eye as the parrot is whistling *him*. With a grin, with a laugh we pay tribute to the other dimension. (*MM* 8)

In the interracial context, Lawrence encourages his readers to understand that others are others. The way in which people live in the land of Mexico, which Lawrence experienced in his everyday life, expresses a coexistence with natural aggression, and a deference to the disparity of otherness. There is a purpose in making a bilateral agreement not to infringe the otherness by their mutual exploiting wills, and then in aggressively upsetting the individual relationship, so as not to fall into the condition of stagnant inertia.

This conclusion is incompatible with that of *St. Mawr*, in which the central character is disappointed with the attitude of modernized and standardized Mexicans who have lost their singular otherness in terms of history and culture. The only existence which kept its keen otherness in relation to human beings in *St. Mawr* is *nature*. The natural animosity of the spirit of the land towards human beings appears to be a kind of aggressive power which should not be forgotten in the primeval coexisting space which Lawrence depicts. Kenneth Inniss suggests that the aggression which nature itself bears is the vitality to attack mankind and our civilization (171), and writes: 'the natural ecology itself imposes harsh limits on their endless generation, the mysterious malevolence refusing to allow a single principle to triumph' (172). Therefore, I would argue that in this universe, nature changes stagnant things into a movement of contestation by showing its vital force, in order not to let a single power or dictatorship remain unchallenged. The way in which Lou gets attracted to the malice of the primitive nature can thus be explained by her admiration for 'the otherness' which the pluralistic space originally respects, and also for the elastic relationship nurtured by the mutual active interaction.

4. Friction and Reconciliation in *The Plumed Serpent*

As Alfie Bown repeatedly states, the act of rejecting otherness, which is widespread in Western societies, creates the exterior identity of the other (263). Therefore, the civilized consciousness not only intensifies the discontinuity between others but recoils from its unstable condition that is vulnerable to the unknown. Hence also, the European protagonists' and the racial others' will for self-approval and the reaction against accepting the other cause a continual struggle between them. In the previous section, I have drawn close attention to the mutually influential relationship between females of different races, Kate and Juana, though the text of *The Plumed Serpent* is still so complicated that it has bred many points of dispute.[6] The main plot challenges Kate to pin down her wilful and independent character and compels her to enter into the death of her old ego. Numerous critics have been misled by this, such as Kingsley Widmer, who wrongly concludes that Kate 'must finally learn to make "submission absolute" to the male, including forgoing usual sexual orgasm . . . and become subordinate partner to a military-sectarian thug and his utopian-reactionary ideology' (145). However, the complexity of the novel has been attributed to Kate's fierce resistance and her conflicting feelings which are depicted against the background of the plot.

As in the other stories I have discussed in this chapter, Kate is also strongly inspired by the Mexican ethnicity and feels the death of her will and a silent reaching for stillness whenever she experiences the overturning of the values she holds dear. The Mexican men, Don Ramón and Don Cipriano Viedma, who judge her independence and the disposition of her ruling will as unsavoury Western qualities, try to implant the virtue of stillness in Kate. It means to her becoming restrained, passive, and dependent like a local woman: 'These men wanted to take her *will* away from her, as if they wanted to deny her the light of day' (*PS* 185). In some scenes, Kate feels pleasure in the experience of stillness in which she completely evacuates her old selfhood and meanwhile she is depicted as if she has become a selfless woman who has lost aggression. However, she gets disillusioned again with the aim of receiving satisfaction from the stillness they teach and soon regains her fierce emotions and finds her way back to the agitating state of further desire and her need of stimuli. She keeps provoking her violent conflict and vacillates in indecision over whether she should preserve her active self or not. Here, the vehement struggle has been launched between the male's will which promotes the Quetzalcoatl religion which tries to deprive Kate of her modernized womanhood and soak her in stillness, and Kate, who partly gets fascinated by the constraining power, though she does not allow her own submission and keeps feeling the bliss of the triumph of her will.

In the retaliation of healthy enmity with Juana, Kate has been incessantly reviewing and renewing her self through the other's existence. However, it was perhaps accomplished due to the female relationship: it is in the problem of her sexuality through relationships with men that Kate's egoism gets complicated. The modernized female quality which the Quetzalcoatl men refuse in Kate is cognate with the quality which Lewis declines in Mrs. Witt in *St. Mawr*. It can be said that it is a characteristic of the ruling women in Lawrence's works which is driven by avarice, making use of money and freedom, and making little of male physical power and exploiting men by their desire. Moreover, they desire the admiration of their womanhood by the exchange of looks and words, which are given a hierarchical value by being attached to power and domination. It is the 'sex in the head' (*PUFU* 148), the phrase which Lawrence himself uses, which constitutes the modernized gender that has put too much weight on mental sex rather than physical. Since Kate exceedingly retains her persistence in this identity, interlaced with sexuality, I argue that her relationship with men does not work in the same way as the exchange of sheer vitality with Juana. Therefore, she experiences intense conflict before accepting her unknown self which is obliged to be awakened.

At the beginning when Kate visited Mexico, in mourning for her husband's death, she was making herself believe that her 'yearning for companionship and sympathy and human love' (*PS* 59) had died and been left in Europe. She was feeling that she had exhausted her past life, spent for love and worldly desires, and attained a desireless state of a high order: 'Something infinitely intangible but infinitely blessed took its place: a peace that passes understanding. . . . No, she no longer wanted love, excitement, and something to fill her life' (*PS* 59). However, it is gradually divulged that her remark is untrue: Kate does not shut herself up in the isolation of stillness like the island men in the previous chapter of this study. Being in Mexico, she is shocked at being betrayed by her own words: as if she is burdened with what Lawrence has taught us through the earlier stories, she realizes that she is unable to live without her insatiable desire for other people, especially for men.

Kate is asked by Ramón and Cipriano to be a member of the Quetzalcoatl religious sect which seeks the revival of ancient religion as a cult. Kate has grown tired of the European *beau monde* and resented the interaction with those who flatter with superficial excitement and consider that it is the meaning of life, so it was a second life and a new place supplied for her who had come to the foreign place to seek the true meaning of life. Ironically, however, Kate becomes buoyant with her old self-respect due to being an educated adviser to Ramón, who is a powerful man who wins Mexican citizens' hearts by his advocacy of political and religious ideals, and feels that he gives her credit for her attractiveness. Her satisfaction, therefore, is all the more irrevocably connected with her old egoism. The earlier protagonists' self-consciousness was nothing to Kate's: the self-approval and desire for recognition are the things which give the greatest pleasure to her. She keeps wishing for her old self to be satisfied, and thus contradicts her narrative which has a high regard for the eternity of stillness.

Furthermore, we witness an immense aggression explode inside Kate: getting familiar with a whole new life in Mexico, she objectively observes the class to which she belongs and develops a hatred of frivolous intellectuals of the leisured class. However, it means a negation of her own identity, and her anger gets brutal almost as if she is killing herself. She experiences a dilemma of being unwilling to admit the fact that she cannot escape from seeking recognition from other people, although she openly speaks of her misanthropy. Being unable to respond to Ramón's asking why she cannot be alone and avoid demanding earthly relationships, Kate trembles in resentment:

> She was silent, very angry. She knew she could not live quite alone. The vacuity crushed her. She needed a man there, to stop the gap, and to keep her balanced. But even when she had him, in her heart of hearts she despised him, as she despised the dog and the cat. Between herself and humanity there was the bond of subtle, helpless antagonism. (*PS* 251)

How can we explain her inconsistent manner in which she attacks herself by such self-denial? Taking her selfishness into account, it could not be explained by the theory of self-enclosure or desireless oppression of oneself which has been used to diagnose the characters in the last chapter. However, Kate's aggression can be explained again by the instinct of human beings which Freud proposes. Explaining in detail the theory which I have already referred to in discussing 'The Prussian Officer', it is well known that Freud stated that the basic aggressive instincts of human beings are tamed by the rationality of civilization, intelligence, and the acquisition of culture, with the deterrent force of the 'life instinct', or Eros, which seeks the homeostasis of organisms. However, aggression appears as a constant force from inside organisms, and is an expression of Thanatos, also named the 'death instinct'.

> . . . [M]an's natural aggressive instinct, the hostility of each against all and of all against each, opposes this programme of civilization. This aggressive instinct is the derivative and the main representative of the death instinct which we have found alongside of Eros and which shares world-dominion with it. And now, I think, the meaning of the evolution of civilization is no longer obscure to us. It must present the struggle between Eros and Death, between the instinct of life and the instinct of destruction, as it works itself out in the human species. (*SE 21*, 122)

Reflecting on Freud's remarks, it is evident that Kate's anger, which leads in the direction of death, expresses the drive of Thanatos. The instinct which emerges through repeating the experience of criticizing the civilized identity in the land of Mexico, is an expression of instinctive aggression which involves the constant renewal of one's self against the homeostasis. However, Kate cannot fit herself to the Mexican female attitude which is imposed on her, and in which she is restrained as if living in the shadow of the male. Therefore, she moves back and forth, bearing the question of whether to adjust to Mexico which critically offends her identity or to go back to England where she can live as herself. Kate postpones making the decision and exposes herself to the contradiction — it is the same as the movement caused by the death instinct which I analyzed in the orderly's conflict in 'The Prussian Officer'. Her suffering would be eased if she chose either of the two options; however, if the pleasurable stillness of the resolution would mean giving herself to the ultimate stillness of death as in the case of the orderly, she had better keep fluctuating. Although it is not clearly written that Kate is feeling an inertia in the repetitive movement like the orderly, the self-destructive friction is a self-sufficient false pleasure. Because of the anxiety of losing her self in this extreme situation in Mexico, I argue, the continual fluctuation creates a pleasure for her in the foreign environment by the stillness in the motion. Kate's repetition results from a desire to repeat her minute self-shattering and it evades death in the physical sense.

In the midst of this vicissitude, Kate is encouraged to marry the Indian general Cipriano as a requirement for entering the Quetzalcoatl organization. Cipriano, who is a pure Indian, has been a mysterious man who cannot be understood or sympathized with until the middle of the novel. He is implanted with the image of a non-individual being which sometimes even suggests the aura of a dark and savage ancient god. She suffers: 'Ah, how could she marry Cipriano, and give her body to this death? . . . Die before dying, and pass away whilst still beneath the sun? Ah no! Better to escape back to the white men's lands' (*PS* 246). Even imagining marrying Cipriano makes Kate lose the balance of her identity, and as she fails to persuade herself, the disturbance of her emotion leads her towards self-destruction again. Despite her distraught wish to run back to the land of Europe with which she is familiar, however, Kate speaks to Ramón and postpones her decision to do so. Although it is hinted that Cipriano has a romantic feeling for Kate, to express his enamoured feeling means betraying the Quetzalcoatl creed; moreover, to admit it would also kindle his pride and resentment due to not wanting her to look down on him. On the other hand, the same was true of Kate's unwillingness when she wanted to confirm that the marriage was only a religious contract and not a civil arrangement. Kate's unresponsive and disdainful reaction towards Cipriano's personality spreads a thought like the one which Swarthout describes: 'Even Cipriano Viedma . . . who is the novel's only developed indigenous character — cannot escape Lawrence's racial stereotyping [of seeing him as totally abstract and inhuman]' (133).[7] Although Cipriano pretends to be inhumanly detached, it can be suggested that he eagerly retains a personal selfhood as it has been revealed earlier in this study that the exotic men in Lawrence's fiction preserve their ego under their nonchalance. Cipriano fights for his emotional conflict with Kate, and I argue that it can never be said that Lawrence has stopped having a concern for the characters' subtleties.

In the scene in which he gazes at Kate, crying at her memory of her deceased English husband, it cannot pass unremarked that his eyes become wide open with moving awe:

> Cipriano sat motionless as a statue. But from his breast came *that dark, surging passion of tenderness* the Indians are capable of. Perhaps it would pass, leaving him indifferent and fatalistic again. But at any rate for the moment he sat in a dark, fiery cloud of *passionate male tenderness*. He looked at her soft, wet white hands over her face, and at the one big emerald on her finger, in a sort of wonder. The wonder, the mystery, the magic that used to flood over him as a boy and a youth, when he kneeled before the babyish figure of the Santa María de la Soledad, flooded him

CHAPTER THREE

again. He was in the presence of the goddess, white-handed, mysterious, gleaming with a moon-like power and the intense potency of grief. (*PS* 71; emphasis added)

Cipriano is definitely mesmerized by the sensuality of Kate's otherness — her tears make him realize that the Western womanhood, which resembles Maria, is a living wonder for him now as in the old days. Looking at her tears, Cipriano's inhuman authority is stirred and he is pulled back to his own personal memory: it evokes his young and fresh romantic feeling. The fact that Cipriano is unconsciously experiencing an inner change by realizing Kate's inner movement through her extraordinary tears, reminds us of the effect of tears that affectively bridge the gap between people, which I have discussed earlier. At this moment, however, the aspect of racial otherness intervenes. In addition to his being moved by the exposure of Kate's feebleness, Cipriano feels an authentic wonder, facing the beauty of her otherness. Since, as I have argued, the reciprocal experience of impressing and being impressed by the other being would enable the active revival of stagnant relationships, Cipriano's inhuman self-enclosure with his servile consciousness is only ineffectual before his wonder and attraction towards Kate's heterogeneous beauty. The experience of integrating one's body and mind has been facilitating a flight *from personal to impersonal* for the English protagonists. Contrastingly, for Cipriano, who is a character who represents the racial other, I would argue that it has the effect of washing him over *from the impersonal to the personal*. Kate's tears make him physically remember his personal feeling which is interestingly expressed as a passion of 'tenderness'. The notion of tenderness which I highlighted will be carried over to the analysis of the novel *Lady Chatterley's Lover* in the next chapter.

Apparently, in the text as a whole, Cipriano tries to deny Kate's identity due to his resolute subjugation of his personal feeling and binds himself in an impersonal married relationship with her. Kate senses with chagrin that Cipriano, who shows himself off with an air of macho male pride would never meet her half way and she does not expect to achieve mutual understanding with him through verbal communication. He silently teaches the virtue of not exchanging frictional looks or words, which are thought to be representations of Western methods of communication, or the achievement of self-complacent sexual orgasm related to exploitative will. Yet, I would argue that it is an unspoken paradox that he is attracted to Kate's Western womanhood and carries a self-contradiction as a matter of fact. Furthermore, the paradox connotes a foreshadowing of the ultimate ending of the novel.

Both Kate and Cipriano possess the other on an impersonal level in this way and they bind each other with the indifferent relationship of not interfering on a personal level. It seems that the blood-conscious marriage and the blood-conscious sex which Lawrence has been proposing as the ideal is achieved here. It transcends the unacceptability of the difference in race, and the female acknowledges the wonder of the phallic male force and both sexes are bound by the acceptance — therefore, the unity of blood consciousness precisely overcomes the difference in blood. Many scholars, such as the above-mentioned Widmer, have noted that the power balance of the dominant manhood and passive womanhood is inherent in the blood-conscious sexual relationship. However, it is obvious from Kate's intensified dissatisfaction and sense of self-oppression that she is unable to find real contentment in the relationship: she cannot help but feel an excitement in living in the vortex of exchanging desire with others. This is the distinguishing feature of Kate, which sets out the image of a woman who cannot be passive and controlled by the narrative force. She resists the uniformity of *Ressentiment* oppression, which demands her subordination and makes her admit her oneness of blood with the indigenous people, and her fierce conflicting emotions defeat the stillness of the blood-conscious marriage. Her old will to let men approve her independence and individuality and applaud her queenly sexuality has grown stronger and she repeats the alternative of becoming either a Mexican woman or an English woman more violently than ever.

Kate's friction gains force as the novel approaches its conclusion. She reaches the verge of a fateful dilemma as to whether she should stay in Mexico or return to England, similarly to the final action of the orderly. As T. E. Apter suggests, whereas Kate's plan to leave the country is 'an assertion of the distorted aggressiveness of her nature, which can only emerge as a deadly rejection', it is 'partly an expression of her need to be wanted and to be protected from her own self, which is at a loss' (175). However, Ramón leaves her to make the decision by herself, by saying 'Listen to your own best desire' (*PS* 444), and neglects her urgent wish for someone to ask her to stay in Mexico. Although she is nearly heartbroken, her tearful plea is defiantly targeted at Cipriano, in the cynical way which she painfully knew that he used to scorn at. Although 'she was a bit afraid of him too, with his inhuman black eyes', she pleaded, 'You don't want me to go, do you?' (*PS* 444). This seems to be parallel to the earnest demand for an answer of Romero towards Dollie in 'The Princess'. However, in contrast with that situation, Cipriano intuits what Kate really demands:

> A slow, almost foolish smile came over his face, and his body was slightly convulsed. Then came his soft-tongued Indian

speech, as if all his mouth were soft, saying in Spanish, but with the 'r' sound almost lost:

'*Yo! Yo!*' — his eyebrows lifted with queer mock surprise, and a little convulsion went through his body again. '*Te quiero mucho! Mucho te quiero! Mucho! Mucho!* I like you very much! Very much!'

It sounded so soft, so soft-tonged, of the soft, wet, hot blood, that she shivered a little.

'You won't let me go!' she said to him. (*PS* 444)

This is the last phrase of the novel and I would strongly argue that Kate and Cipriano have dynamically bridged the gap between their old stances and bound each other in the specific moment. The change he detects in Kate, the sight of her tears and her sincere plea, evoke his tenderness again, and spur him to make the action: it is shown by the various physical descriptions of Cipriano that he has summoned up all his courage to cast off his old ego. Due to the way the nerves and muscles of Cipriano's face quiver and soften to break his obstinate selfhood, Kate's supposition that he had been a detached other to her dramatically changes. From the emergence of his physical change, and furthermore, from the fact that he expressed his feelings in words, which is the Western way he used to loath, Kate understands that he meets her half way for the first time. The reason why the story is concluded by Cipriano's concession, despite the fact that he has been rejecting her Western verbal quality, has been under dispute among critics. As far as I have discovered, there is no study which discusses the couple's relationship in terms of the affective physicality of tears and also from the perspective of Cipriano's respect for Kate's otherness, and thus this is a unique feature of my study.

CHAPTER THREE

Extending our perspective to the external others and in the context of the interracial communication, through this chapter, I have suggested that Lawrence has unmasked *the sameness* of the others with the protagonists in terms of being harmed by the hierarchical consciousness or emotion. Hence, as for the unacceptable others, the fertileness of coexistence was needed in order for them to overwhelm each other by their gleam of life. I have suggested the new policy in Lawrence's texts, in addition to the momentary affect between the others: it emphasizes the reciprocal and persistent manifestation of vital energy in everyday life by highlighting the differences between individuals. It is a proactive way of dynamically destabilizing the relationship so as to counteract the stagnant or dehumanized friction, and which thus leads each to realize their vitality for living and keep organically reforming the space of their coexistence.

As we have seen, both the respect for the difference and the affective communion are achieved in *The Plumed Serpent*. It can be said that to meet half way is to pay respect to the gap between others, and is not to forcefully deny and eradicate the other's identity. I would argue that Cipriano has intuited that to enable Kate to guarantee her ontological security at this moment is to indicate that he likes the way she naturally is and to accept her innate Western identity, and it made their affect flow and connected them together. Whether the bond of the couple's hearts lasts forever or not is not mentioned. However, the collapsed relationship of the two sexes which could not absorb each others' feeling in 'The Princess' has precisely changed into success here. It must be said that Lawrence's implication of this profound quality in Cipriano's character is still unacknowledged among critics. What is worth noticing is that Lawrence has depicted Cipriano, the racial other, as endeavoring to bridge the gap of unacceptableness between humans by intuiting Kate's feeling in the end. To conclude the story by granting deep communication between the different races creates an opened prospect of the reconstruction of the relationship of the interracial lovers.

CHAPTER FOUR

Discovering the 'Internal' Other and a New Vista on Human Relationships

1. The Return to the Interior

The theme of the reconstruction of human relationships in Lawrence's fiction can be described as having started inside England, issued forth to the external world, and then returned to the inside again. Taking this progression into account, in this last chapter I will rethink the nature of the existence of the others as such. To put it briefly, why do the modernized people see the others as incompatible with them, and shrink from them with negative emotions? The others have always had a quality of *externality*, and their separation from the socially or ethnically privileged group has mainly been solved by dynamic communication which precedes the intervention of knowledge. In short, the comprehensive solution lay in the act of energizing oneself to awaken one's innermost aggression. The means of getting over the externality was in fact *inside* ourselves — this is the point which I will focus on in this chapter.

From the beginning of this study, I have steadily pointed out that the emotions are in bondage to the characters' mental attitudes which are based on socially-structured, hierarchical consciousness. Besides, my argument has suggested that these emotions can evaporate through the affective communion of dynamic consciousness. In his essay, *Study of Thomas Hardy*, Lawrence refers to the difference between emotion and dynamic feeling, stating (as Olga Desiderio paraphrases his argument) that real feeling is 'the manifestation of *the dark continent* that human beings have *within themselves* without being conscious of it' (257; emphasis added). Desiderio tactfully explains Lawrence's concept as follows:

> [I]t is from this hidden and repressed part of our soul that life springs, although man tends to hide this unknown side of his being. This attempt to suppress one's source of vitality is due to man's desire to tame himself, under the pressure of civilization, which imposes the denial of authentic feelings. All this leads man to insanity, since repression makes him degenerate like an enslaved animal. (257)

Desiderio concludes by summarizing Lawrence's ideas, though I would add to her summary by presenting a supposition. 'The dark continent', which is the inner, cryptic part of human beings, coincides with the source of vital feeling, and is separate from the mind.[1] However, the denomination 'dark' may remind us of something — it bears a close resemblance to the names which Lawrence gave to the alien races: the living, unaccountable beings whom he called the 'dark blood', or the 'dark races' in his writings. It is particularly interesting that the specific words which were used to remove the intangible others far from the European group consciousness, are also used to refer to what exists inside subjects. Could it be that what is referred to by the notion of 'darkness', which we have associated with the 'imagined' others, originally exists inside us and is even the source of ourselves? It is perhaps therefore the protagonists' quivering souls that sympathetically and gradually react to the old, dark religions which the others possess, and something responds which has been repressed by the yoke of civilization before they were aware of it.

    However, many critics define that dark power as a male, phallic, mystic force in Lawrence's fictionalized world, and John Clayton is one of these. Lawrence poses to himself the question of why human beings cannot revive the old, dark religions, and Clayton answers it by saying that it is 'Because the dark powers, male powers, are frightening. To let male force enter is part of the process of rebirth, and it is fearful' (203). Clayton explains that the reason for the fear is that this involves opening up one's self before the invasion of the male power and surrendering the world which education has allowed one to see. Here, I find two cardinal perspectives to discuss: the first point is whether the dark power or dark religion are limited to the external male power. There is a sense in which Lawrence frequently prophesies the importance of inviting in the specifically male power in love and sexual relationships. Nevertheless, his various works also insist that whether the subject is female or male, it is important to realize one's *inner* aggressive nature, hidden under the acquired self, and not only to accept the external force. Secondly, I would like to focus on the emotion of *fear*, which Clayton emphasizes. The characters have always been afraid of the others, living on another plane, as their initial attitude: they feared the differentness and were in dread of physically touching them. The fear itself is the emotion which causes human beings to contract and keeps them at a distance from the existence of others. The dread of the unknown and the unrecognizable equals the dread of being unable to sway the object by the power of intelligence; and it has been associated with the others in numerous negative concepts, both linguistically and semantically. Modernized people have equipped the unknown beings with their technology and their logical, economic, and scientific ways of thinking. Moreover, they repressed the unmanageable intuitive or carnal reaction, which is unsuitable for them as filthy and corrupted, and built the fabrication of a civilized fortress on them. Thus, what should be noted is that the destruction of the fearful emotion would facilitate an escape from modern life and would be the first step towards facing the others.

Focusing on the tactile sense in Lawrence that 'links the body to the antiquity of the other time scheme', Takamura writes that 'the text of *Lady Chatterley's Lover* does not locate this antiquity in the externality, but inside the characters' physicality' (25; my translation), though I would argue that the discovery of the externality in the interior starts at an earlier stage of Lawrence's fiction. The germ of this idea is already evident in the story 'The Blind Man'. In the story, a blind character, Maurice Pervin, and his wife Isabel are both suffering from nervous temperaments because of excessive anxiety about each other. The couple's relationship was becoming strained in the stage of anticipating the birth of their baby. Maurice himself is not distraught about his sightlessness and 'Life was still very full and strangely serene for the blind man, peaceful with the almost incomprehensible peace of immediate contact in darkness' (*EME* 46). However, when his wife goes out searching for Maurice in a dark stable, suffused with the grossness of 'hot animal life' (*EME* 52), what she encounters is 'a world of violence, turmoil and terror' (Clausson 116) and she feels horrified at standing opposite her invisible husband in the dark with her raw and defenseless physical sense without eyesight. This reveals the habitual sense of modernized people, for Lawrence compares darkness with the optical intelligence. He writes in his essay that people have familiarized themselves to seeing and being aware of themselves by their conscious egos and have become unused to the darkness 'since Greece first broke the spell of "darkness"' (*STH* 165).

> Man has learnt to *see* himself. So now, he *is* what he sees. . . . Previously, even in Egypt, men had not learned to *see straight*. . . . Like men in the dark room, they only *felt* their own existence surging in the darkness of other existences. (*STH* 165)

Facing her husband, Isabel feels that 'For a moment he was *a tower of darkness* to her, as if he rose out of the earth' (*EME* 53; emphasis added). It is precisely an expression which calls the element of the other races into our mind. The alarming emotion of fear urges Isabel to regard the unknown man as something totally external to herself, even though his substance is something she used to know well. For the modernized people, the externality, lying dormant in ordinary life, is easily emphasized by the sudden unbalanced hierarchy of physical sensation. One of the cardinal aspects of the issue of physicality in Lawrence is the importance of letting the five senses become flexible and untrammeled by the rigidity of mind; and this aspect becomes significant when it is concomitant with the act of destroying one's fear. Therefore, people are obliged to simulate the life of a human being who involves the world of 'dark minds' (*STH* 164), which is independent from visionary sight, as if mimicking the existence of the external others.

Conversely, Maurice fumbles in his own house which has turned into a world without light in his everyday life. Depending entirely on the tactile sense, he feels the *joie de vivre* of blood consciousness.

> [Maurice] Pervin moved about almost unconsciously in his familiar surroundings, dark though everything was. . . . It was a pleasure to him to rock thus through a world of things, carried

on the flood in a sort of blood-prescience. He did not think much or trouble much. So long as he kept this sheer immediacy of blood-contact with the substantial world he was happy, he wanted no intervention of visual consciousness. In this state there was a certain rich positivity, bordering sometimes on rapture. Life seemed to move in him like a tide lapping, lapping, and advancing, enveloping all things darkly. It was a pleasure to stretch forth the hand and meet the unseen object, clasp it, and possess it in pure contact. He did not try to remember, to visualise. He did not want to. The new way of consciousness substituted itself in him. (*EME* 54)

It is unnecessary to point out that the subversion of the values of the optical and tactile world is suggested here, and Maurice literally has access to the world of darkness. He feels his strength surging up in his flesh through his blood consciousness, and thus he feels a dynamic bond between himself and the substances in the room. As in the case of those characters who mitigate their existential anxiety by a sense of unity with their natural surroundings, the optical sense of difference between things is not valid for Maurice. Therefore, it can be said that the interior and the exterior are linked and intermingled as an inside-out world. It is expressed in the way in which the lightless world he sees changes his own body into an incarnation of darkness; similarly, the fear which is brought by visual sensation produces a hypothetical or fictitious externality.

However, in the same way as I described in the second chapter of this study, with his absorption into a rich self-sufficiency, Maurice is excluded from contact with other people in real life and thus his 'human eros is ever unsatisfied' (Ragachewskaya 'The Logic of Love', 112).

Since his self-contained power cannot be directed toward other people, 'at times the flow would seem to be checked and thrown back. Then it would beat inside him like a tangled sea, and he was tortured in the shattered chaos of his own blood' (*EME* 54), and we see him writhing within his self-closure like the earlier exclusive characters. There is a glass barrier between Maurice, and his non-handicapped wife and their mutual friend, Bertie, who Maurice suspects of having a relationship with Isabel. Listening to their conversation with his sharp auditory sense, 'a childish sense of desolation had come over him, as he heard their brisk voices. He seemed shut out — like a child that is left out' (*EME* 55). In revenge for his own usual situation, Maurice tries to discover the distasteful heterogeneity in them:

> He disliked the slight purr of complacency in [Bertie's] Scottish speech. He disliked intensely the glib way in which Isabel spoke of their happiness and nearness. It made him recoil. He was fretful and beside himself like a child, he had almost a childish nostalgia to be included in the life circle. And at the same time he was a man, dark and powerful and infuriated by his own weakness. By some *fatal flaw*, he could not be by himself, he had to depend on the support of another. And this very dependence enraged him. He hated Bertie Reid, and *at the same time he knew the hatred was nonsense, he knew it was the outcome of his own weakness.* (*EME* 55; emphasis added)

Maurice's strong desire to interact with the two highlights the contradiction between his physical independence and mental dependence. The emphasis on his childish isolation psychoanalytically expresses the infantile phase in which the individual is shut out from the world of verbal representation inhabited by the adults. It suggests a microcosm of human beings' growth process in which displeasing stimuli have severed one's initial unity with the outer world — or the mother — in which one was satisfied by blood-consciousness. Generally, the infant acquires mental consciousness as an inevitable result, and the discord with physicality develops inside oneself. Although Maurice has once gained a sense of self-sufficiency by his blindness, his mental weakness was a blot on his maturity. I would argue that the phrase 'fatal flaw' in the quotation above not only refers to his physical disability, but also to his shifting of his weakness into a hatred of able-bodied others.

In the last part of the story, Maurice lets his enemy Bertie finally touch his body and he obtains a pleasure through the physical contact with the other, as distinct from contact with lifeless furniture, and it is a clue to his regeneration. In contrast with Maurice, Bertie is a person who is entrapped by the morality of the optical world, and his fear is depicted as a display of the pathological state of modernized people. As Shirley Rose indicates, his pity towards Maurice, and the fact that Maurice feels no empathy towards him on the other hand, is noteworthy. Bertie feels Maurice's hurt as if it is his own personal affair and he even states that all people have a deformity somewhere. Though nothing more than a 'sanctimonious . . . bystander', Bertie is 'exquisitely tortured by the trauma of actual contact with Maurice's wound' (Rose 78). Maurice unreservedly touches Bertie's head and face, dependent only on tactile sense, and Bertie 'shrank away instinctively' (*EME* 61) from the immoral barbarity of the outrageous gesture. Imprisoned in the common practice of the civilized world that one should not recklessly touch the body of another person, Bertie feels terror at the sudden savageness as if he will be ravished by the other man, though

Maurice 'is completely unaware of Bertie's misery' (Rose 78). Making a bold approach of physical contact to his vexing rival in love, I would insist that Maurice has succeeded in tying himself to Bertie, beyond his superficial emotion of either liking or hate. In a way that makes him antithetical to Maurice, who has conquered his weakness and received pleasure, Bertie is 'mute and terror-struck, overcome by his own weakness' (*EME* 62). Unable to free his selfhood, he feels himself to be a victim and has gone numb with his feeling of the destruction of his civilized self like 'a mollusc whose shell is broken' (*EME* 63). Nils Clausson interestingly points out that 'the mollusc image here echoes the earlier *positive* sea image comparing Maurice's new consciousness to an enveloping tide' (120). Whereas Maurice's satisfaction is produced by his contact with his detestable mate, Bertie, 'the comparison of Bertie to a mollusc incongruously places him in the *same* dark world as Maurice, even though thematically the two men are opposites' (Clausson 120). I would argue that the intention of the text which suggests that the two men's 'differences dissolve into similarity' (Clausson 121) in the end, implies the conclusion of the male relationship in 'The Prussian Officer' and is sublimated into a more or less desirable result in this story.

Although 'The Blind Man' was written in the middle period of Lawrence's career, it includes a suggestion that is relevant to the author's entire creative activity in terms of acknowledging the latent quality of darkness inside one's self. Passing through the stage of frictional contact with the racial others, it can be said that Lawrence's works toward his later period concentrate on the issue of internality again. The short story 'Sun' emphasizes the reformation of one's interior and is rare among Lawrence's fiction in showing a path to the successful achievement of the relationship of a nuclear family, centralizing the mother. As one can guess from its title and the timing of its composition, the tale was written under the influence of the Indians' heliolatry. Lawrence describes the sun as a symbol of dark religion in *The Plumed Serpent* and many of his essays. However, this tale is interesting in that it does not particularly deify the sun or describe exposure to sunlight as soaking up one's desire to live, as embodied in the island men in the earlier chapter. The sun, I would argue, can be compared to a surgeon, who refines the heroine's body, which is stiffened by her mental impoverishment, into a condition in which she is ready to reformulate the relationship with her little son and her husband. Since there is a description of the heroine as feeling a wish to 'have intercourse with the sun' (*WWRA* 21) and her contracted womb gradually opens due to the infiltration of the sun's rays, the sun represents the external, phallic power in one sense. However, far from Barbara Ann Schapiro's argument that the story 'reflect[s] a masochistic fantasy — Juliet finds herself only by worshipful surrender to the more powerful male force' (60), what is really reflected is not only the heroine's symptom but, more generally, modernized people's fear of the massive vitality of the sun:

> They were so un-elemental, so un-sunned. They were so like graveyard worms. . . . There was a little soft white core of fear, like a snail in a shell, where the soul of the man cowered in fear of death, and still more in fear of the natural blaze of life. (*WWRA* 24)

The fear of the sun exactly mirrors the fear of their own instinctive and natural way of living. The heroine Juliet tells her toddler son to play naked in the sunshine like her, though she finds in his eyes a colour of misgiving, in spite of his immaturity, 'which she believed was at the centre of all male eyes, now. She called it fear of the sun. And her womb stayed shut against all men, sun-fearers' (*WWRA* 25).

The other major issue of this story is that it shows how the relinquishing of the duty of benevolence becomes a gateway to the liberation of one's physical consciousness. The essence of this tale is analogous to that of 'The Blind Man' in this respect. The sun has metaphorically changed the heroine into a blind woman so that it has made her blind to and unconcerned about the mental world which was too much visible to her: 'So, dazed, she went home, only half-seeing, sun-blinded and sun-dazed. And her blindness was like a richness to her, and her dim, warm, heavy half-consciousness was like wealth' (*WWRA* 22). After this experience, Juliet notices that she has lost her will to respond to her son's attention-seeking behaviour or to be overly concerned about his trifling plea. She has become free from the duty of responsibility, and as Judith Ruderman also notes, the release from self-afflicting compassion is a fruition of the ideal mother-child relationship which can scarcely be found in Lawrence's works (158-59). Yet, it should be noted that Juliet's love for her son has not ceased, but appears in a different way. Realizing that her young boy is about to freeze and shut his tiny spirit tightly before the sun, Juliet gathers that he is starting to be molded into a miniature of her husband and many other men. Judging that there is still time for the little child, she pushes him forth to play fearlessly and to splendidly salute the sun, so 'That little civilized tension would disappear off his brow' (*WWRA* 25). The more the boy gets to accept the sun, the more he becomes able to play alone in a self-reliant manner. Juliet teaches her son the necessary things to live, and she dashes to help him when he is in physical danger, moving intuitively like a serpent or a wild cat. The mother and child have unknowingly become like a family of feral animals, living under the sun. Returning to *The White Peacock*, I would argue that Juliet's animal-like child-rearing is a practical demonstration of the game-keeper's idealized education. The keeper Annable who has nine children instructs them to be natural, to "'Do as th' animals do'" (*WP* 132), and he wishes them to "'fend for themselves like wild beasts do'" (*WP* 132) instead of dirtying themselves as the modernized people do. Nevertheless, no concrete, feasible action was indicated by Annable's words. His wife was merely rude and violent and the naughty children shouted in tears and the family atmosphere was effectively in chaos, and beyond management. However, the animal-like way of raising children, which seemed to be an empty theory, is profitable for the healthy relationship of mother and her child in 'Sun'. Diminishing the excessive burden of caring for the other and obtaining an animal-like indifference, which could be seen as being potentially beneficial for our contemporary, mutually sympathetic, surveillance society, the characters can take time for the rehabilitation of their own physicality and can concentrate on the nature inside themselves. The mother and the child have become psychologically independent and opened their bodies to the sun. They were able to regain their natural wild power which had been numbed by evil customs. If Juliet's son keeps living in this same circumstance, it can be supposed that he will not yearn for mental love from his mother and will direct his dynamic consciousness towards other people. Juliet feels certain that the power is not given externally but awakes inside herself.

> Something deep inside her unfolded and relaxed, and she was given to the cosmic influence. By some mysterious will inside her, deeper than her known consciousness and her known will,

she was put into connection with the sun, and the stream of the sun flowed through her, round her womb. She herself, her conscious self, was secondary, a secondary person, almost an onlooker. The true Juliet lived in the dark flow of the sun within her deep body. . . .

She had always been mistress of herself, aware of what she was doing, and held tense in her own command. Now she felt inside her quite another sort of power, something greater than herself, darker and more savage, the element flowing upon her. (*WWRA* 26)

The sense of one's self being linked with the universe is no longer a novel incident now; though what this quotation conveys anew is the necessity of heating up the inner aggressiveness which has been restricted by fear or social responsibility as a mother. In Lawrence's post-colonial works, the aggression and vitality are extracted by the stimulating communication with other beings. Yet, it is necessary to notice its internality at first hand, before receiving the outside intruder. It can be considered that Lawrence's works in his later period teach the importance of having an attitude which is open to preparing the ground for contacting others.

2. Encountering the Pan, or the Internal Other [2]

Through his journeys to countries which maintain viewpoints external to Western modernization, Lawrence magnified his criticism of people who immerse themselves in the materialistic and mind-oriented civilization and encouraged them to throw their complacent consciousness into turbulence. However, he neither severed himself from his contemporary companions in his homeland nor left the immobile English people to their fate, as can be seen from the fact that his trajectory led him back to England and that he kept searching for a way to enlighten people who had lost their awe at nature due to their rational minds.[3] Therefore, in short, the theme of building organic human relationships in Lawrence's works started from England, moved to its exterior, and returned back to its interior.

The short story, 'The Last Laugh' is especially unique among his late works in that the characters encounter an absolute other in spite of continuing their daily life in London. The otherness the story depicts is allegorically emphasized: it is not even a human, but a supernatural being, and the characters are disorientated by being unable to visually inspect its figure. However, the interesting thing is that the tale develops with no direct physical contact between the characters and the other, such as tactile sensation, which was previously a counterpart to optical knowledge in Lawrence's novels. I will come back to this point and examine it later. Although the characters do not step into the outer world, their in-group norms are thrown into a wild commotion and by taking a different approach from the other works, 'The Last Laugh' is successful in intensifying the same theme. Moreover, the story encourages us to wonder and reconsider what exactly is the 'imagined otherness' which we fear so much.

The story begins with the scene in which a man and a woman, Marchbanks and Miss James, stand on a wintry street one night in Hampstead. The forest-like Hampstead heath in front of them and a towering, deserted church effectively evoke a hushed dark world where there is no sign of human activity. Suddenly, Marchbanks hears a strange neighing sound like an animal laughing, ringing shrilly from the holly bushes, and he gets exceedingly excited as if possessed by the laugh and begins to mimic it. Miss James is a woman with an auditory disability and can hear nothing with her Marconi listening machine which she carries around with her. Therefore, one can guess that the enigmatic laugh is not the kind of sound which can be delivered through a machine. A young police officer suspiciously approaches the couple, though he cannot hear the laugh either, and turns pale and becomes terrified by their extraordinary reactions to it. In the meantime, Marchbanks becomes intrigued by a seductive Jewish woman who unexpectedly appears from her house nearby and who distracts his attention from the voice, and he follows her to spend the night in her house. On the other hand, Miss James finally hears the laugh and even witnesses a floating man's face in the darkness, due to not fearing it intellectually but sensing it with awe. Before she realizes it, she regains her hearing ability and a strong vital force has formed within her feeble body: it is clear that she has been invested with those powers by the preternatural master of the laugh. As she accepts the unknown other with a fearless manner and becomes attracted to it, she is liberated from the physical disability which was oppressing her. Her aggressiveness flowers both physically and mentally, and her character and attitude change radically. She sneers in her heart at the mercy of the policeman stretching his arm to her in order to support her walking and she ridicules his insensibility to the mystery. She has a burning sense of her omnipotence in imagining that she can easily run faster than the officer and even that she is capable of killing him.

> She was surprised herself at the strong, bright, throbbing sensation beneath her breasts, a sensation of triumph and of rosy anger. Her hands felt keen on her wrists. She who had always declared she had not a muscle in her body! Even now, it was not muscle, it was a sort of flame. (*WWRA* 129)

CHAPTER FOUR

As she meets the eyes of the uncanny being, Miss James's extremities brim over with fiery power. In contrast, the policeman finds the next morning that his feet have strangely changed into the claws of an animal, and being unable to walk, he has nothing to do but weep. It is plain to see that it is a penalty for his weakness, inflicted by the master of the laugh. Marchbanks is also struck by a mysterious heart attack and suddenly dies. Whereas Miss James is blessed, the men who are distracted by fear or who indulge in depraved and indiscreet sexual behaviour receive the opposite effects of merciless punishment involving the impairment of their physicality or even the loss of their life. The characters' fate is determined by their act of regarding the laugh as merely extraordinary and a gross deviation from rational understanding, or alternatively of affirmatively accepting it with an open mind.

It is quite obvious that this story aims to condemn the modernized value of rejecting things that are unrecognizable to scientific knowledge, and people whose physical senses have grown dull by being too rationally orientated. Lawrence gave the role of prompting such fear to a being who is characterized as the god Pan. Pan is a half-man, half-beast god in Greek mythology whose torso is that of a human male with horns and a beard, and who has goat's legs, and was born in Arcadia as a son of Hermes. As a god who governs the rich vital force of nature, Pan originally appeared in the idyllic tone of Romantic art and was depicted as playing a syrinx, a panpipe made from reeds, at his ease. However, as suggested by the well-known phrase 'The Great Pan is dead', Pan in later ages stands for an anti-Christian quality. As the name 'Pan' is derived from the Greek word for 'every' or 'universal', Pan — who represents 'pantheism' in the natural world — contradicts monotheistic religion. Moreover, Pan's fondness of drink and dance and his energy of prosperity and reproduction that sometimes exposes its instinctive aggressiveness, were reinterpreted as indecent and vicious things by the moral values which Christianity professes to hold. Lawrence laments the fact that since people started to move into cities and to love people more than trees in the forests, 'They liked the glory they got of overpowering one another in war. And, above all, they loved the vainglory of their own words, the pomp of argument and the vanity of ideas', and that caused Pan to get old and to be reduced into a devil by Christianity, and 'his passion was degraded with the lust of senility' (*P* 23).

The god Pan, who symbolizes the premodern notions and values that were lost by the dissemination of Christianity, had a vogue in the art world in the West. The Pan motif, which has two opposing faces of good and evil, god and demon, enlivened the world of novels from the late Victorian to the Edwardian period with a free and destructive impact. Richard Stromer explains this phenomenon by stating that Pan's image of aggression and the release of sexual desire turned into an influential motif which released the bottled-up feeling of Europe in the wartime, though it was expressed in some negative ways in the novels. Pan originally embraces a furious element in his vitalistic nature, though it has deteriorated into a negative and fearful quality in the intimidated eyes of the mass of repressed people. Therefore, although Pan envelops ambivalent qualities, his devilish, occult quality is partly foregrounded, as if dispelling the aspect of a benevolent god from the viewpoint of people with the values of later periods.

The attitude of judging the other's external quality as evil, contrastingly illuminates the realities of the subject. Zygmunt Bouman states that the objects of our fear should lead us to contemplate the spirit of the age we live in, rather than the feared objects themselves.[4] When the evil-looking ones revolt against people and endanger them, it is also a moment when the concepts of right and wrong, and the inside and the outside of the dominant values, which are unconsciously and collectively determined, are subverted by the displaying of the antithesis of civilization. Citing Saki's Pan story as an example, Tabish Khair notes as follows:

> [Much that has been said] about the Gothic and Otherness in a colonial or post-colonial context can also be said to some extent in a 'fully' British context. . . . In stories like Saki's . . . 'The Music on the Hill', the normative is fully European in location, and so is the 'Otherness' confronting it: actually, . . . it [the normative] is even seen as partly heroic. . . . [I]t is restrictive and blind to Other aspects of reality even *within* a British / European context. (38)

The otherness in Gothic tales is often seen as depending on the externality in the postcolonial context, though in fact the issue is thoroughly developed inside England, and it questions the normativity of which the Europeans wave the banner. The way in which the fearfulness of Pan is amplified indicates that something which originally existed inside civilization has been separated and chased away to the periphery, and become recognized as an object of fear in consequence. The fear which is attached to the quality of otherness results from modern people's mental tendency and is distinct from Pan's original nature. Therefore, I would argue that Pan is an 'imaginary other' which emerges from the interior of the modernized people.

However, it can be pointed out that many of the stories which merely draw attention to the frightfulness of Pan, end up strongly marking a boundary between inside and outside. Examining E. M. Forster's 'The Story of A Panic' (1902), for example, the words which evoke the devilish side of Pan are spoken by people who fear his preternatural sign and the contrast between Pan and divine protection.

> 'The Evil One has been very near us in bodily form. Time may yet discover some injury that he has wrought among us. But, at present, for myself at all events, I wish to offer up thanks for a merciful deliverance.'
> With that he knelt down, and, as the others knelt, I knelt too, though I do not believe in the Devil being allowed to assail us in visible form, ... ('The Story of A Panic', 18)

Moreover, the fact that the boy named Eustace has acquired a vigorous temperament through contact with Pan is not described as a good omen. The boy is judged by the adults to be in an ill condition and haunted by a terrible sign, and he disappears in the darkness of the night in the end. Hence, the antithesis which Pan proposes does not appear as having a magnetic quality and it ends within the realm of an external, vicious element.

Returning to 'The Last Laugh', we can see how Pan is vividly depicted and filled with the power to destroy the duality of inside / outside or self / other through Miss James's change. For her who does not fear Pan, he is not a demon which provokes panic nor an enraged god of revenge. The sequence of phenomena which is presented through the encounter of Pan and Miss James is a sequence of two liberations both on the macrocosmic level of the civilization and on the microcosmic level of the individual. Although Pan originally existed in the interior, he has been expelled to the outside of modernity in the developing civilization. However, as the oppressed 'internal other', as it were, is restored to the present world, Miss James's keen physicality awakens and the internal other inside her, which has been held dormant in her individual self, also breaks out. As I have highlighted in the quotation in the early part of this section, the 'rosy anger' has awakened inside her through the contact with the mysterious laugh: this, I would argue, represents the flourishing of the Pan quality inside her. Earlier in this study, I suggested that Lawrence's works do not depict the tactile sense as a first prerequisite as many critics believe. Significantly, this tale does not include the essence of touch as a counteracting element to optical-oriented thinking. The characters could scarcely catch Pan's appearance and are also deprived of their will and ability to judge it from the visual information. So why is there no description of Pan and Miss James touching each other in order to have a dynamic contact, which is the common practice in Lawrence's other tales? Takamura proclaims that the act of touch 'represents the active contact of the human body with its environment and connects heterogeneous qualities and has an open quality for relating the inside and outside of life' (36; my translation). However, the notion of 'internality' which I argue is set forth in 'The Last Laugh' shows that the discernment of the active quality inside one's self does not even require touch. Because the 'imagined otherness' exists inside one's self, there is no more need to have a tactile contact with it in order to reconcile oneself with the external.

The internality of Pan recalls Patricia Merivale's comments which refer to the Pan in poems of Robert Browning (1812-1889): '[His Pan *is not*] a goat-god outside ourselves, but as the goat-god *within ourselves*, not exclusively sexual, but largely so, because sexuality is

... the most vivid aspect of our *animal natures*' (90; emphasis added). Besides, Lawrence himself projects this internality in his letter to Forster by bitterly criticizing Forster's description of Pan.

> Don't you see Pan is the undifferentiated root and stem drawing out of unfathomable darkness, ... No plant can live towards the root. That is the most split, perverse thing of all.
>
> All that dark, concentrated, complete, all-containing surge of which I am the fountain; and of which the well-head is my loins, is urging forward, like a plant to [its] flower or a fountain to its parabola. . . .
>
> But your Pan is a stooping back to the well head, a perverse pushing back the waters to their source, and saying, the source is everything. . . . One must live from the source, through all the racings and heats of Pan, ... (*2L* 275-76)

It can be said that the Pan which Lawrence assumes has an internal quality like the root of a plant or the source of a fountain which sends power and has a primordial quality that is irreversible. However, he claims that Forster's Pan represents the past, towards which he encourages people to run back. The difference of recognition between the two novelists, which Lawrence's comments highlight, critically shows the essential disparity between the boy Eustace who has undergone a negative mutation and Miss James who has found her innate Pan-like quality inside herself. Her vital force gains massive energy like a fountain which increases its water pressure by turning on the tap.

Furthermore, it can be said that Lawrence's insight into the physical senses of human beings is reflected in the way in which Miss

James possesses an aptitude for demonstrating her inner Pan-quality. The three human characters are tested as to whether they preserve the ancient, so-called unscientific sense of acknowledging this omnipresent and supernatural laugh, not by intelligence but with a physical sense. In spite of her deafness, the excellence of Miss James's intuitive powers, in contrast with those of the policeman and Marchbanks, is traceable to Lawrence's cherished theory of the five senses.

> We have some choice to refuse tastes or smells or touch. In hearing we have *the minimum of choice*. Sound acts direct upon the great affective centres. We . . . have really no choice of what we hear. Our will is eliminated. Sound acts direct, almost automatically, upon *the affective centres*. . . . We are always and only recipient. (*PUFU* 103; emphasis added)

In Lawrence's view, the sense of hearing is the most open to the outer world among human bodily senses and the ear is an organ unsusceptible to suppression. Since the enigmatic laugh is not audible to the policeman's ears, even the sense of hearing has become petrified in the physicality of modernized people; nevertheless, Miss James's reaction to it can be interpreted as implying that she is far better prepared to release her 'internal other' than the other civilized people, due to her not possessing the arrogance of believing in the perfection of human beings.

Lawrence advocates the idea that the lower part of the human body has to do with sensuality, and is a center of a strong reaction and repulsion, in lieu of the sympathetic upper nerve tissue. He writes: 'The legs and feet are instruments of unfathomable gratifications and repudiation. The thighs, the knees, the feet are intensely alive with love-desire, darkly and superbly drinking in the love-contact, blindly. Or they are the great centres of resistance, kicking, repudiating' (*PUFU* 99). However, he deplores the idea that it is the activation of these lower nerves of the human body which is lacking in the over-theoretical modernized people. The reason why Lawrence recommends opening up one's sense of hearing is that he thinks that it cooperates with the nerve tissue which controls sensuality.

> The singing of birds . . . acts direct upon the upper, or spiritual centres in us. So does almost all our music, which is all Christian in tendency. But modern music is analytical, critical, and it has discovered the power of ugliness. Like our martial music, it is of the upper plane, like our martial songs, our fifes and our brass-bands. These act direct upon the thoracic ganglion. Time was, however, when music acted upon the sensual centres direct. We hear it still in savage music, and in the roll of drums, and in the roaring of lions, and in the howling of cats. *And in some voices still we hear the deeper resonance of the sensual mode of consciousness.* (*PUFU* 103-4; emphasis added)

The description of the archaic past when sounds acted directly on the body with no mediation of mind, can be linked to Miss James's irrational mutation. Reflecting Merivale's words, it can be related to the liberation of Pan-like elements of sensuality and the animal nature inside human beings. Lawrence's idea, expressed through the Pan image, is therefore not the resurgence of the past but the necessity of being aware of the internality of the living body. Moreover, he approvingly states in the quotation that even nowadays we could hear the sensual sound in 'some voices': the allusion to the voice would be the prototype of the laugh like the sound of a goat in the tale which surprises us with the extraordinariness of its bestiality, rending the stillness of the ordinary night. Lawrence suggests in his essay that the wild creatures survive in the 'dark continent' inside ourselves.

> [S]ince the forest is inside all of us, and in every forest there's a whole assortment of big game and dangerous creatures, ... We've managed to keep clear of the darkest Africa inside us, for a long time. We've been so busy finding the North Pole and converting the Patagonians, loving our neighbor and devising new means of *exterminating him, listening in and shutting out.*
>
> But now, my dear, dear reader, Nemesis is blowing his nose. And muffled roarings are heard out of darkest Africa, with stifled shrieks. (*STH* 202; emphasis added)

Furthermore, Lawrence writes,

> In the very darkest continent of the body, there is God. . . .
>
> Now we have to educate ourselves, not by laying down laws and inscribing tablets of stone, but by . . . listening-in to the voices of the honorable beasts that call in the dark paths of the veins of our body, from the God in the heart. Listening inwards, inwards, not for words nor for inspiration, but to the lowing of the innermost beasts, the feelings, that roam in the forest of the blood, from the feet of God within the red, dark heart. (*STH* 205)

To whom does Lawrence refer with the personal pronoun 'him', who is inside us and has been persecuted by the territorial expansion, the progression of technology and the spread of the Gospel? The one to whom we listen while shutting out his voice? Although the word Pan is not used in this essay, comparing it with 'The Last Laugh', I would argue that what Lawrence implicitly refers to is a straining to hear the voice of the animal inside one's self, that is, to release one's Pan-like quality. The animality in 'The Last Laugh' unearths the internal otherness in the two spheres of the social and the individual: the next section will focus on the animal quality which is both represented in the Pan motif and disclosed through the characters' encounter with the laugh.

3. The Pure Animal Man

The method of using animal metaphors is widely employed in Lawrence's later works for the purpose of illustrating the alien others who have an image contrasting with that of Europeans. There, such metaphors are used in order to emphasize the ethnicity as seen by Western eyes, in alliance with images of the earth spirit which each animal symbolically owns. The animal images are a suitable form of rhetoric to express the figures and behaviour of external others who bear differences of race, class, and custom that seem queer to English people. As William M. Harrison points out, Lawrence was suspicious of the habit of personifying animals as Romantic writers did, for the reason that it removed the vitality from the animals by its anthropocentric manner (353-54). On the contrary, Lawrence allows his Western narrator authoritatively to liken the Australians and Indians to animals such as kangaroos, reptiles, and birds. Drawing a demarcation line between animals and people is a political act of defining the propriety of mankind and fixing the others as heterodox, though the reason why Lawrence ventures to do this, I argue, is his intention to expose the nonsense which accompanies the subjective looks and representational acts of the English narrator.

However, as already indicated in the last section, in 'The Last Laugh' there is an effect of animalizing human beings in the absolute power which Pan wields; it is the English people who face the other that are expressed through an animalistic image in 'The Last Laugh'. It can be said that Lawrence has the definite purpose of making a clear distinction between this tale and his other fiction which intensifies the awareness of difference between the self and others by giving a bestial quality to these characters. The animalization deservedly influences the two men but not Miss James. Miss James, already turned into a Pan-like woman, observes the enfeebled and terrified policeman as follows:

> She was looking at him [the policeman] almost angrily. But then the clean, fresh animal look of his skin, the tame-animal look in his frightened eyes amused her, she laughed her low, triumphant laugh. He was obviously afraid, like a frightened dog that sees something uncanny. . . . He stood cowed, with his tail between his legs, listening to the strange noises [the voices resonating like seagulls which praise the master of the laugh] in the church. (*WWRA* 130)

Finally, the laugh turns into a gust of fierce wind and breaks the church windows and then the altar cloth blows up like a crazy bird. These descriptions are evidently meant to show that Pan defeats the authority of Christianity in a series of effects.

What is most eminent is the change that has taken place by the next morning. When Miss James looks out of the window of her room, 'Suddenly, the world had become quite different: as if some skin or integument had broken, as if the old, mouldering London sky had cracked and rolled back, like an old skin, shrivelled, leaving an absolutely new blue heaven' (*WWRA* 132). The reference to the vanishing of this skin or integument can also be comprehended as implying the animalization of the whole city of London, and it seems that Pan is changing not only human characters but also the materials of the modernized society which deny his existence. Then, the feet of the policeman, who has been taking shelter in Miss James' house, have swelled and been transfigured into the claws of an animal. In contrast with Miss James who has been freed from her physical disability, he has been deprived of the human privilege of walking with two legs and changed into an awkward being. Simultaneously, Marchbanks, who happened to be there, suddenly loses his life and his death cry is described as animal-like: 'Marchbanks, gave a strange, yelping cry, like a shot animal. His white face was drawn, distorted in a curious grin, that was chiefly agony, but partly wild recognition' (*WWRA* 137). The two men have superficially changed into beasts as a punishment, in contrast with Miss James who has released the inner wildness curbed inside her. However, it is noticeable that Miss James, who alone does not experience the impact of animalization, is introduced as possessing bestial elements from the beginning of the story: 'She had an odd nymph-like inquisitiveness, sometimes like a bird, sometimes a squirrel, sometimes a rabbit: never quite like a woman' (*WWRA* 123). The comparison of her to a nymph seems to make the readers anticipate the affinity between Pan and her; yet the fact that she is compared to various animals, with the additional reference to her unlikeness to a woman, shows that the borderline between animal and mankind is made vague inside Miss James from the start.

As I have explained, Pan has two faces of god and demon, and the figure of Pan is unforgettable in terms of its double meanings: its features which combine animal and human contain many metaphors. The impossibility of deciding the hierarchy of men and animals is a crucial problem which Christian civilization has demonstrated. As the fable of The Garden of Eden is said to be the watershed of the separation of animal and human species, men have borne an inferiority by their original fault and thus, by acquiring the propriety of human beings, they created the dominant value-system which makes animals into scapegoats of civilization in the anthropocentric ideology.[5] Criticizing the paradox of placing the burden of misery on animals, Jacques Derrida cites the fable of a huntsman, Bellerophon, which figuratively demonstrates the relationship of men and animals. Bellerophon chases Pegasus, the archetypal horse, and molests it by putting into its mouth a golden bit given by Athena, though it turns out that Pegasus was a half brother of his since Poseidon was the father of both.

> [Pegasus] is therefore the half-brother of Bellerophon, who, descending from the same god as Pegasus, ends up following and taming a sort of brother, an other self: I am half (following) my brother, it is as if he says finally, I am (following) my other and I have the better of him, I hold him by the bit. What does one do in holding one's other by the bit? When one holds one's brother or half-brother by the bit? (*The Animal That Therefore I Am*, 42)

I would argue that the relationship of Pegasus and Bellerophon can be replaced with that of Pan and human beings. Pan originally existed in the West, and moreover, the vitality which Pan possessed used to be an innate quality of human beings. Therefore, why do people in the modern world fear its resurrection? — It can be said that our attitude of forcing Pan to succumb, eliminating the exterior world, and unilaterally thrusting otherness upon it has come to intimidate us in return, being felt as fear on the mental and intellectual level. Similarly to Derrida's fable, although human beings themselves are also animals, and have the same wild nature as animals, we have followed them and put them in an inferior position: the gesture of seizing and making the brother succumb as an other is disclosed. Therefore, I would argue that Miss James's deficiency of hearing, the element which makes her reconciled to being an inferior human, has just turned into an animal like power and overflowed from inside her.

Derrida anxiously examines the fact that human beings in the long-lived Western philosophy recognized that animals are not endowed with the faculty of making a response. Animals have been thought not to understand but to imitate or react unthinkingly, and thus they deserve to be seen as inferior in terms of their incapability of exchanging any responsible answer. However, what is interesting is that we can find a scene in which the communication of the mutual response has occurred between Miss James and Pan. She admits that she had acknowledged the bodiless master of the laugh and claims: 'What a wonderful being! I suppose I must call him *a being*. He's not a person, exactly' (*WWRA* 132-33; emphasis added). The act of showing her stance of acknowledging Pan as a being, more than a phenomenon, triggers a big change. Induced by the mysterious contact, Miss James decides to stop her old benevolent way of living, like Juliet in 'Sun', and tries to radically reform her past relationships. She is suddenly enlightened by noticing the absurdity of the compassionate love with which she keeps supporting Marchbanks in a mental way, and she laughs at it and says to herself that it is the encounter with the laughing man that made her become aware of the nonsense of the pseudo-affection. Then, a mysterious voice responds to her self-questioning only once. "'Is love *really* so absurd and *infra dig.*?" She said aloud to herself. "Why of course!" came a deep, laughing voice. She started round. But nobody was to be seen' (*WWRA* 133). A reciprocal conversation between Pan and the modernized characters had never occurred in the contemporary Pan stories, such as in Forster, or Algernon Blackwood's 'A Touch of Pan' (1917) and Saki's 'The Music on the Hill' (1911), for instance. This is an intimate response towards Miss James, who has previously responded to the call from the laughing man. It can be said that the act of responding is equivalent to incorporating the other into one's self. The fact that Pan has become incorporated into Miss James's dialogue proves that he is present as the internal being of the woman. Therefore, reading the story in a Derridean manner, the notion of the Pan motif which tends to be read with the dichotomization of the self and the other, or inside and outside, can be overturned by the discovery and reintegration of the other inside one's self.

The encouragement to dismantle the quality of otherness in 'The Last Laugh' depends on redefining the existence of the laughing man. In actuality, there is no affirmative description in the story that the man is identified with mythological Pan. Although Lawrence mentions in a private letter that he was keeping Pan in mind while writing the tale (*5L* 50), he had erased from the text the literal name of Pan, which he used in the first draft, only retaining one word, 'pan-pipe'. For what reason did Lawrence avoid the directness of the name Pan? — I would argue that it is a manifestation of his attitude of trying to imply something more than the image which the name of Pan provides us with. It is the deconstruction of the otherness which is expressed through the interpenetration of the master of the laugh and Miss James, who has risen above the stereotypical modernized attitude of having a fear of the unknown.

I have argued so far that 'The Last Laugh' is shaped by a suggestion that the external other, set up by human beings, was in fact an internal other. Naturally, however, this does not imply that Lawrence's idea reduces human beings and animals into the same entity. It does not involve the idea that a variety (heterogeneous species) is a fantasy and that external others are altogether internal constituents of the self. As I have shown in the last chapter, in the natural pluralistic space which Lawrence experienced in Mexico, people could not psychologically communicate with the parrots, and the birds showed off their living energy by imitating the voices of dogs and human beings. In that specific space, each of the external others was striving to pay respect to the abyss of difference between them, and activating an intimate relationship by taunting each other and expressing their vitality. However, what I have repeatedly focused on in this chapter is the importance of having an insight into one's interior nature before having contact with those external others. The civilized people live self-restrainedly by reason and make themselves accustomed to this life, which does not allow their aggressiveness to come out into the open, and are also unaware of their inmost vitality. They live as if the wild nature is unnecessary to the sophisticated species and as if it is a sin to have this nature. Therefore, it is challenging for people who have expelled their own natural aggression to understand the qualities' actual innateness. As long as we relinquish the vitality, it is impossible for us to actively communicate with the true external others. Naturally, the animals do not have language and representational abilities like human beings. Precisely for this reason, the innate nature is a commonality that makes us able to communicate with the others in the realm of the Real, or on a non-human level.

It is inaccurate to say that Lawrence totally negates human development and strongly recommends a retrogression, without benefitting from evolution. This is confirmed by Lou's words, again in *St. Mawr*. She considers that the deadly dull human male and female, including herself, are not drawing the great burning life straight from its source: 'It's the animal in them has gone perverse, or cringing, or humble, or domesticated, like dogs. I don't know one single man who is a proud living animal . . . clever men are mostly such unpleasant *animals*' (*StM* 61). She insists that 'the animal has gone queer and wrong' in men and they are all tame dogs and 'We seem to be living off old fuel, like the camel when he lives off his hump' (*StM* 61). However, Lou proclaims,

> '[D]on't misunderstand me, mother. I don't want to be an animal like a horse or a cat or a lioness, though they all fascinate me, the way they get their life *straight*, not from a lot of old tanks, as we do. I don't admire the cave man, and that sort of thing. But think mother, if we could get our lives straight from the source, as the animals do, *and still be ourselves*.' (*StM* 61; emphasis added)

It is not that she should act like animals or a brutish and degenerate primitive man, but rather that she should let life rush into her like them, and still maintain her personal self at the same time.

What can be said through the analysis of Lawrence's works is that while people are trying to escape from fixity and stagnancy, he recognizes the way they still struggle on a personal level and their inclination to return to their old position and consciousness. Looking back at the earlier chapters of this study, we cannot prevent the contingent effect of affect and epiphany disappearing in a short while and we also cannot abandon our class, even if a bond is created which bridges class consciousness. Although one finds the key to a solution in the dynamic motion, one cannot move permanently as far as to consume one's energy, and also needs the comfort of stillness. Although Lawrence's texts encourage us to acknowledge the invisible darkness and to bathe in the sun to regain the animal-like life style, they do not oblige one to discard every convenience of human lives and to sleep and eat together with animals. Lawrence is not propagating the extremist ideal of becoming backward beings, merely inhuman and impersonal, but he looks steadily at the fact that we are modernized human beings to the end. Lou seems to be somehow envisaging Pan-like human beings: 'A pure animal man would be as lovely as a deer or a leopard, burning like a flame fed straight from underneath. . . . *He'd be all the animals in turn, instead of one, fixed, automatic thing*' (*StM* 62; emphasis added). I would argue that this is not a condition which grows in an unbalanced way in human beings but a lifestyle which dynamically encompasses mankind and various animals, and that this is the real reason for the use of animal metaphors in Lawrence's works. It is well known that Julian Moynahan has written that Lawrence 'tries to show that the most valuable human enterprise is the dual fulfillment of the social and the inhuman selves within a single integrated experience of life, and at the end envisions the transformation of society into a new form within which just such saving fulfillments could work themselves out' (42). What Lawrence means by becoming an animal man, I would conclude, is a coexisting or synchronized lifestyle of personal and impersonal, and human and inhuman. It is a worldview which distinguishes the individuals, and does not trespass on or devour the difference between the self and other and involves having a lively relationship with flexible motion.

It can be said that Lawrence has used the motif of Pan as a way of manifesting the internal otherness as a dynamic representation to the readers and it is already personified by the gamekeeper, Annable, in *The White Peacock*. As I have already suggested, although the gamekeeper is an English man like the main characters Cyril and George, he is a being who dedicates himself to a life that is closer to nature than the human moral life. He sternly stands in the way of the men who treat nature with their egoistic purpose and puts pressure on them as an intimidating other, criticizing their acts by beating them to the ground with his astounding physical power. Cyril and George, who feel the difference of strength as a lesson, give in to the captivating physical power of the gamekeeper. Yoshihiro Nakanishi proclaims that Annable has all the necessary qualities to constitute a Pan motif in his character and the semiotical traits of his existence. Due to the double aspect of his role as a guardian of the forest and his ruthless, demonic manner toward people, and also to his death in carrying out his duty of vengeance against the modernized world, Nakanishi argues that although the emblem is undeveloped yet, Annable is shaped as 'a pale foetus of an image of Pan' (97; my translation) which emerges more fully in Lawrence's later works.[6] Although he is a key character who insinuates the internal otherness and attempts to put the theory of living as a pure animal man into practice, the gamekeeper was yet unable to achieve actuality as a rounded-out character and thus he disappears from the novel before long. He tried to be animal-like, though he seems to have been too careless for his hermit life as a person. However, one would never fail to admire the consistency and faith in Lawrence's creativity whereby the uncanny character has accomplished a profound development in his human aspect, so much that he comes to play opposite the heroine in *Lady Chatterley's Lover*, Lawrence's last passionate novel which instructed his readers about the deep cross-class communion between the man and woman.

Is it possible for us who live in the actuality of time and society to be aware of the wild nature in ourselves? Is it possible to draw the life straight up from the source, and then mingle with others while still being ourselves? In the final section of this study, I will examine this ideal and the harsh friction with reality through Lady Chatterley, running in 'the *inwardness* of the remnant of forest, the unspeaking reticence of the old trees' (*LCL* 65) — which makes one recall Lawrence's suggestion that modernized people who love the mass more than trees should reenter into the forest to meet Pan again.

4. 'Be tender to it, and that will be its future'

One may say that we can see a compilation of the arguments of this study in *Lady Chatterley's Lover*, Lawrence's last masterpiece that deals with male and female relationships. Numerous failures and successes depicted in Lawrence's earlier works, issuing from troubled relationships involving mental and physical incompatibilities, paved the way for this novel of romance. Moreover, I would suggest that the novel takes a step further from the usual solution of a momentary fullness with the release of dynamic consciousness — it provides a guide to a sustainable, future relationship which has hitherto not been found.

The upper class Chatterleys, Sir Clifford and his wife Constance, who possess a fair amount of property and collieries in the Midlands, were involved in the sad plight of being unable to expect a child or

CHAPTER FOUR

even have physical intercourse due to the husband's disability caused by the war. Having no way of venting his mental energy, Clifford calls his philosophizing friends to the mansion named Wragby Hall and becomes absorbed in debating with them. Through the depiction of him, we see how Clifford is submerged in his own class as if living in a vacuum of nothing but intelligence and reacts against actually communicating with the lower class people. Reflecting self-consciously on his loss of sexual potency, he feels shame about physical or sexual things. Although Connie was a thoughtful woman who could participate in her husband's and the controversialists' talk (though they were arguing while ignoring her presence in the same room), she was originally a powerful woman, and being immersed in the empty ideas with Clifford, day after day, was too stifling for her. Clifford expressed himself in writing stories in order to maintain his dignity and acquired a considerable reputation in his own way. However, his life was no more than vagueness and the life of producing money from nothingness had hardly any meaning for Connie. Rapidly, she came to be gnawed by intolerable despair, and having become physically ill from anyone's viewpoint, she is finally brought to the doctor. The doctor diagnoses, 'Your vitality is much too low: . . . You're spending your life *without renewing it*. You've got to be amused, properly healthily amused' (*LCL* 78; emphasis added), and his words clearly prove how Lawrence takes the vitality of human beings seriously in his late works.

    Knowing at last that her depression is due to their incapability of having a child, Clifford is also chagrined at being unable to bring an heir to the Wragby estate into the world. Therefore, he proposes to Connie one day that he would give tacit approval to her having a child with another man and then he would rear the child as a legitimate son. He makes a speech full of flowery words saying that the act of sex is only temporary and that kind of momentary relationship by no means has any influence on the bond of their enduring wedlock and their own integrated lives.

> 'It is what endures through one's life, that matters: my own life matters to me, in its long continuance and development. But what do the occasional connections matter? . . . We have the habit of each other. And habit, to my thinking, is more vital than any occasional excitement. The long, slow, enduring thing — that's what we live by — not any occasional spasm of any sort.' (*LCL* 44)

Many points at issue are hidden in these flourishing words which apparently express a soft compassion for Connie. At first, these include Clifford's disdain for sensuality and unwillingness to recognize that the sexual sensation would bring a big change and strong satisfaction to a human being's physical consciousness, and furthermore to his or her relationship with others. Moreover, thinking that 'one can just subordinate the sex thing to the necessities of a long life' (*LCL* 45), Clifford minimizes every sexual interaction as 'temporary excitements' (*LCL* 45). What is more, I would argue that the exhortation to stagnancy is salient in his words: his comment expresses his attitude of reducing marriage to a habitual thing, though it should be a vital connection between the sexes, and his way of speaking equates their marriage with a mere vacant mental bond. Clifford says: 'After all, *do* these temporary excitements matter? Isn't the whole problem of life the slow building up of an integral personality through the years? living an integrated life? There's no point in a disintegrated life' (*LCL* 45). This is also an inconsiderate claim which belittles and suspects the act of pursuing an existence that finds vital presence in the moment which transforms one's life, which Lawrence's earlier fiction had proposed. Being indifferent to the possibility that the trivial 'occasional connections' should profoundly change people's consciousness, he values the act of preserving established personal matters as a form of righteousness. Theoretically, Connie could understand the steadily-lived, harmonious life-unison which her husband proposes. However, Clifford was merely entangling her in his *immobile* life and forcing her to follow the same destiny as him. Now, his life itself was in a state of paralysis, not only physically, and Connie's instinctive voice was frantically calling for help from the pit of vague nothingness which she had already been dragged into with Clifford.

    One day when she is pushing Clifford's wheelchair — the fateful day of her first contact with the gamekeeper, Oliver Mellors — Connie is suddenly occupied with a mood of running to open the gate of the hazel grove. Her limbs, which have been used only for Clifford's nursing care and were wholly numbed by the monotonous life with him, were craving to move freely. However, Clifford blames her for not having made the gamekeeper do the subordinate work and shows an unpleasant attitude to her in displaying an unrestrained and degrading manner in front of the man. The disappointment with Clifford who tries to shut her up with the class-consciousness and every torment of their depressing daily life, showers down on Connie all of a sudden and she physically feels a fatal discontent: 'A strange, weary yearning, a dissatisfaction had started in her. Clifford did not notice: those were not things he was aware of. But the stranger knew. To Connie, everything in her world and life seemed worn out, and her dissatisfaction was older than the hills' (*LCL* 48). It can be said that it is a Bovary-like, fierce existential despair for Connie at being forced to live a stagnant life inside the enclosure of their class with him. From the description of the gamekeeper who was silently monitoring everything around the couple, whereas Clifford does not notice the change in her feelings, it can be said that the scene suggests the development of the story of Connie and the man being intuitively and actively connected with each other.

Taking the earlier works into account, it can be considered that Lawrence does not depict Clifford as a person who is at fault in relation to Connie's life only because of his physical deficiency. In 'The Blind Man' and 'The Last Laugh', the physically disabled characters were precisely more acute to their dynamic consciousness and were beings who are nearer to their release from selfhood than the rest of the people. In a short story 'The Thimble' (1917), the war-disabled man whose face has been pathetically disfigured even initiates his shocked wife into reviving their marriage relationship which was once dead, as if he has obtained a far-sighted, philosophical view. However, it will be obvious from my analysis throughout this study that the problem is that Clifford's mind and spirit are full of the stultifying elements of lethargy, the human pathology which Lawrence is concerned about, due to his obsession with binding Connie to his life. There is no hope of Clifford gaining a physical revival, and the paralysis of the lower half of his body satirically symbolizes the loss of the inner power and sexual vitality which Pan teaches as precious, as implied by Inniss, who comments that 'Riding upon "the achievements of the mind of man", Clifford, in his motorized wheel-chair, can be seen as a mechanical centaur' (191).

It is unnecessary to refer to the aftermath of the war which causes tremendous damage to human beings both physically and psychologically: 'the bruise of the war . . . [it] would take many years for the living blood of the generations to dissolve the vast black clot of bruised blood, deep inside their souls and bodies' (*LCL* 50). Furthermore, the novel evokes the uneasiness of all the modernized people, who launch into the worship of money through activities ranging from manual mining to the mechanical processing of its products while aiming at further industrialization. Like Clifford, the Tevershall men who are embroiled in the gear wheel of industrialized society are metaphorically described as 'weird fauna of the coal-seams' or 'Men not men, but animas of coal and iron and clay' (*LCL* 159), wrongly dehumanized into sacrificial animals which are far removed from wild nature. Moreover, as if demonstrating exactly the opposite of Lawrence's ideas, Clifford treats the individual lightly and believes that the repletion of industry is more important than individual life. He begins to consider that it is not the miners themselves who make them alive, but himself in the ruling aristocracy, and he silently calls Connie to account for the fact that she is going to abandon the responsibility of their class by descending from her upper-class position and demanding a free life (*LCL* 181, 183).

It is obvious that the secret meetings with the gamekeeper Mellors give a release of dynamic consciousness for Connie; however, his existence cannot be reduced into a symbolical dynamo which revives her energy to live. In terms of the fact that his legs are full of power and that it injects a physical repletion into the afflicted Connie, the existence of Mellors can be seen to play the role of a Pan motif. However, it is actually Mellors who is sensitively anxious about the aforementioned current state of British society and its members which the novel carries in its background. In truth, he fears people's rumours and the eyes of the society more than Connie or anybody else and is trapped in class consciousness. The character of the forest dweller had to be an embodiment of Pan and an active representation of instincts which the modernized people have forgotten. Yet, as if betraying the image of the gamekeeper, he shows the delicacy of his emotion, and the shadows of his solitude in his past life are gradually exposed.

Mellors was an educated and wise man who could speak the standard, good English in spite of his birth in a collier family and thus Connie comes to be surprised by her impression of him as if he has a quality of handsomeness like a gentleman. She is told by Clifford that although Mellors had risen to the position of a lieutenant in the army during the war, he observed the reality of the people in India and he chose to hide himself in the working class again as a blacksmith after returning to his home country. Having an ulterior antagonism towards the insentient iron Midlands which have fallen into the hands of 'the Mammon of mechanised greed' (119) and a disillusionment with the future of English society, he gets employed by Clifford and secludes himself in a hut in the woods after separating from his wife. He expresses an indifferent coolheadedness towards Connie at first that even frightens her a little, and he detests her unbending will that leads her to make a spare key for the hut and violate his private territory: it was an authoritative womanhood which he loathed. Mellors had been abiding in a dried stillness, having no tenderness or passion for women for a long time and his self-enclosure was half threatening.

> Especially he did not want to come into contact with a woman again. He feared it: and he had a big wound from old contacts. He felt, . . . if he could not be left alone, he would die. His recoil away from the outer world was complete. His last refuge was this wood. To hide himself there! (*LCL* 88)

CHAPTER FOUR

What is revealed here is that while Mellors puts the anti-modernized way of life into practice — that is, is uninterested in chasing after profits and a higher position — he has lost the strength of life and has not been freed from his mental consciousness in the least. Camouflaging himself as if he is rootless and capable of moving between classes, he was no more than feigning his working-class disposition and his inhuman self, as noted by Connie's sister Hilda, who sharply detects that 'He was no simple working man, not he: he was acting! acting!' (*LCL* 243). Whereas Clifford's persistency in the mentality of the upper class is emphasized, Mellors was also failing to get into the opened state of an animal man.

However, the relationship of the lady and the gamekeeper changes due to an incident. Being afraid of the invading, maniacal dependence of Clifford who tries to make her swear not to leave him, Connie came to see Mellors' poultry house. Then 'she found two brown hens sitting alert and fierce in the coops, sitting on pheasants' eggs, and fluffed out so proud and deep in all the heat of the pondering female blood' (*LCL* 113) and she was stricken with amazement and awe by seeing the hen expressing her untaught motherhood and natural dignity to protect the eggs. The mystery of life, fundamental to animals, maternity, and the physical womanhood which is not mental, was all withered inside Connie through her life with Clifford. Her heart moved as if nearly broken by 'their warm, hot, brooding female bodies' (*LCL* 114). When Mellors hands over the faintly peeping chick and she touches the quivering new life in her palms,

> Suddenly, he saw a tear fall on to her wrist.
> And he stood up, and stood away, moving to the other coop. For suddenly he was aware of the old flame shooting and leaping

up in his loins, that he had hoped was quiescent forever. He fought against it, turning his back to her. But it leapt, and leapt downwards, circling in his knees. . . . And there was something so mute and forlorn in her, compassion flamed in his bowels for her. (*LCL* 115)

As I have repeatedly noted through this study, it can be declared that tears are an important physical tool in Lawrence's works which enables the affective inner communication between people. Having been inwardly swayed by Connie for the first time here, Mellors' physical desire which seemed to be unmoved forever has reignited and he feels that he has begun his life again by being drawn back to the 'old connecting passion' (*LCL* 118) with a woman. Simply stating that Connie and Mellors are brought together 'through the agency of the hens and the baby chicks' (78), John B. Humma does not see through that the immediate cause is the vital interaction between Connie and the fowls and that the sight of her tears has triggered the big change inside the man. And then they make love, though the fact that he detected Connie, breaking her heart with the inspiration from the animal life, has made him feel the living womanhood inside her, and not as Lady Chatterley. Mellors' heart and his lower body get filled with hot fluid passion by knowing that Connie is still a woman who is not the common 'celluloid women of today' (*LCL* 119) in spite of her oppressive situation. He feels a need 'to preserve the tenderness of life, the tenderness of women, and the natural riches of desire' (*LCL* 120) and he is convinced that she is the exact woman to enable him to do this. As for Connie, who has been struggling to find what was lacking in her life with Clifford and had found the light of a saviour in Mellors, his fortuitous encounter with her causes an immense commotion in Mellors' life. The novel expresses the change and liberation in a man's life, more than depicting the sexual freedom of a woman, as Charles Michael Burack states that since Mellors 'is badly in need of revitalization', 'The development of his relationship with Connie transforms him as much as it does her' ('Revitalizing the Reader', 107). Repeating clandestine meetings with Mellors, Connie realizes that he is the first man who has been affectionate to her womb, that is, to her body as a single female and not as a person with the embellishment of her social position (*LCL* 121). She finds a rare physical tenderness in him which contemporary men have lost and gets comfort from his warm touch and tenderness for her inner, impersonal sensuality. On the other hand, Mellors feels a deep pleasure in and gratitude for his encounter with a woman who solaced him and renewed his passion, in spite of the long days of preserving his past sorrow and solitude and pretending to be inhuman. Their contact has redeemed each of them from their sense of lack, and consequently they can actively set their lives in motion.

The hut in the woods which is the cradle of their love is a secluded place which is withdrawn from the outer industrial world and the social reality. However, I would suggest that this space does not have the same literary effect as the isolated islands had. The woods are a place of resuscitation for Connie who was fenced in at Wragby Hall, and she has not realized the internal significance of the dark inner space which is spoiled by the fixed intellectual life. She physically feels the vibrating pulse and breath of the forest as if they are inside her (*LCL* 121-22). On her way home from an intimate night with the gamekeeper, she feels as if 'the trees in the park seemed bulging and surging at anchor on a tide, and the heave of the slope to the house was alive' (*LCL* 178). The moment when she senses the connection of the forest with the rhythms of the body is the moment when the tide of nature and the human body coincide, which is exactly what I have discussed in the second chapter. It is the passage which most dynamically shows the differentness of Connie and Mellors from the mechanized human bodies in the outside world of Wragby Hall.

Furthermore, a scene in which Connie and Mellors dance naked and make love in the forest in the rain is famous, or even notorious, in the novel. The rain is seen in earlier studies as a means of purification or a ceremony for purging their earlier lives and facilitating their rebirth. For the readers who see it negatively, the scene ends by producing an impression of inflammatory obscenity, and has prompted the criticism that this abrupt unreasonable act would never be a plausible solution to the predicaments of social human beings in reality. However, I suspect that such criticisms have emerged as a result of not reading the novel thoroughly. Looking at the passage directly before this scene, we see Mellors lengthily relating his reprobation of contemporary men who exhaust their bodies for work and moneymaking: 'Connie was uneasy. He had talked so long now — and he was really talking to himself, not to her. Despair seemed to come down on him completely, ... She knew her leaving him, which he had only just realised inside himself, had plunged him back into this mood' (*LCL* 221). Therefore, it is revealed that Connie's running out into the woods gives succour to Mellors who is tormented by his mental agony again. Connie showed her reckless and freed behaviour in order to make him forget the torture of shutting himself up in the shell of his thought, and I would argue that she disturbs his inertia by surprising him with her bold action. Then she dances in the heavy rain which blurs the outline of her body, which expresses in a visionary manner a human being losing the contours of her individual identity,

CHAPTER FOUR

and precisely shows her inhuman unity with nature.

> It was a strange pallid figure lifting and falling, bending so the rain beat and glistened on the full haunches, swaying up again and coming belly-forward through the rain, then stooping again so that only the full loins and buttocks were offered in a kind of homage towards him, repeating a wild obeisance.
> He laughed wryly, and threw off his clothes. It was too much. He jumped out, naked and white, with a little shiver, into the hard, slanting rain. (*LCL* 221)

Her action makes him remember that he should not be isolated but should communicate with her in a natural animal way. This act, therefore, should not be understood directly as an indecent image but should be appreciated as a metaphorical encouragement to dynamically change the other person's inert condition. In another scene, Connie is made to feel a real sensuality by Mellors through sex and she feels that she has reached the utmost limit so that her fear and shame have burnt down to ashes. As I have argued earlier in this chapter, fear is an emotion which the modernized people immediately feel toward the unknown or something that is oppressed and thus they are deservedly criticized in Lawrence's works. Besides, it is fresh in our memory that fear and shame are emotions which Clifford shows toward other people in an excessively self-conscious way. Through the intercourse with Mellors, Connie undergoes the experience of aggressively transcending those emotions with physical consciousness; hence, they reciprocally teach each other the importance of freeing themselves.

During her trip to Venice, Connie realizes that she has conceived Mellors' child and feels an immense pleasure at feeling him inwardly in her body as a germ of life. Although they are apart, she feels him as an inner vitality inside her womb. However, she is informed about the cruel reality by a letter from Clifford: it is about Bertha, the gamekeeper's separated wife, suddenly entering into his hut and subsequently spreading a rumor that he takes women to his place. Because these claims became known to the local community, Clifford had no choice but to discharge the man. Mellors has gone back to his cynical temperament and shut his heart again due to his weariness with the world. Reuniting with him in London, Connie manages to open his eyes and make him revivify. Mellors exposes his unbearable disbelief: 'I don't believe in the world, nor in money, nor in advancement, nor in the future of our civilization. — *If there's got to be a future for humanity,* there'll have to be a very big change from what now is' (*LCL* 277; emphasis added). However, Connie confidently informs him, '"Shall I tell you what you have that other men don't have, and *that will make the future?* Shall I tell you? . . . It's the courage of your own tenderness, that's what it is: like when you put your hand on my tail and say I've got a pretty tail"' (*LCL* 277; emphasis added). She reassures him that it is a tenderness which he conveys from his body to hers, and an awareness of her flesh and genitalia, and that it kindles 'the bowels of compassion' (*LCL* 279) between them. The specific phrase, 'the bowels of compassion', was precisely what Mellors felt towards Connie at the poultry house for the first time. This notion of physical compassion replaces the mental compassion which has become a target of ferocious criticism in Lawrence's late works in terms of its exploiting or binding the other person. The mental compassion is a self-sufficient complacency and a plea for one's freedom against the other 'that ends in the most beastly bullying' (*LCL* 279). However, 'the bowels of compassion' is not a self-insistence that involves neglecting the other but a direct gentleness towards the other's body and a touch involving dynamic consciousness with warmth and solace for the inner sexuality. Connie reassuringly appeals to Mellors to bless their child: 'Kiss it! Kiss my womb and say you're glad it's there.'

> But that was more difficult for him,
> 'I've a dread of puttin' children i' th' world,' he said. 'I've such a dread o' th' future for 'em.'
> 'But you've put it into me. Be tender to it, and that will be its future already. Kiss it! Kiss it!'
> He quivered, because it was true. 'Be tender to it, and that will be its future.' — At that moment he felt a sheer love for the woman. (*LCL* 278)

It is exactly this word that lightens Mellors' anxiety about the future and encourages him. To be tender to what has born between them — it does not just indicate the child itself — it includes the immaterial passion or the dynamic bond. I would argue that this intention critically overturns the obtrusive idea, which Clifford had emphasized and was persistent about, that the intercourse of male and female is no more than 'occasional connections' and its momentary passion would swiftly be lost. 'The world goes on. Wragby stands and will go on standing. The world is more or less a fixed thing, and externally, we have to adapt ourselves to it' — the comments of Connie's father, Sir Malcolm, are based upon the same thoughts as Clifford's: 'Emotions change. You may like one man this year and another next. But Wragby still stands. Stick by Wragby as far as Wragby sticks by you' (*LCL* 273). However, the way male and female live on, which Connie teaches Mellors, breaks the view of life which considers that immovable status is stronger than the relationships of human beings.

Furthermore, I would argue that the notion of tenderness is a revolutionary solution which overcomes the flaw in the temporal connection between humans which Lawrence's works had hitherto explored. The experiences of affect or epiphany, and the life-competition of expressing vitality reciprocally were filled with a power which changes one's consciousness and actively changes one's relationships with others. On the other hand, however, their temporality involved the issue that it cannot be maintained in the sense of reality and time, and the means to overcome this flaw had not yet been presented concretely in Lawrence's works. The tenderness is also a solution to the question of what connects the father and mother, who were a man and a woman with discrepancies, which was a crucial and traumatic question in *Sons and Lovers* and also cast a shade over Lawrence's boyhood, as already noted in the first chapter of this study. It is known that the original title of *Lady Chatterley's Lover* was *Tenderness*, though it is my distinctive argument in this study that Lawrence put an end to his life-long inquiry into this issue with the notion of tenderness in this novel. The dynamic ties that were born between the lovers are a momentary thing. However, no matter how much time has passed and how their respective mental consciousnesses start to diverge again, to face and always be physically aware of the bond and to be tender to it will extend its momentariness into a sustainable temporality. It can be said that *Lady Chatterley's Lover* is therefore a feat in its meaningfulness since it strongly indicates the futurity of the solution to the problem which underlies Lawrence's works.

The novel is concluded by a letter from Mellors, who moved away in silence to prepare for divorce and beginning the new life with

Connie and their expected child. He writes in the letter to Connie, 'I don't like to think too much about you, in my head, that only makes a mess of us both. But of course what I live for now is for you and me to live together. . . . You can't insure against the future, ... So I believe in the little flame between us' (*LCL* 300). This undoubtedly shows that Mellors is expressing by the way he behaves, as Connie has taught him, the aim of protecting the bond between them.

> . . . [T]he little forked flame between me and you: there you are! That's what I abide by, and will abide by, Cliffords and Berthas, colliery companies and governments and the money-mass of people all notwithstanding. . . . We'll really trust in the little flame, and in the unnamed god that shields it from being blown out. There's so much of you here with me, really — that it's a pity you aren't all here. (*LCL* 301)

Mellors is trying to keep the physical feeling between them and this act would protect their momentary passion for the future. I would argue that the value of tenderness increases when it is acknowledged as a phenomenon that exists beyond the momentariness of dynamic consciousness. The intense sensation by which human beings become aware of life moves their relationship when it is conveyed by dynamic consciousness from one individual to the other, and aggressively breaks down the smothering sense of reality. Tenderness gives the power of duration to this concept, which has been thoroughly investigated through Lawrence's works, and takes away people's fears and anxieties and initiates them into the power of believing in the future.

CONCLUSION

The clue in Lawrence's works to restoring the vitality of modernized people and to recreating their relationships is to keep having an active energy and will to be involved with others instead of settling down in static mental consciousness and relationships. While expressing the difficulty of drawing out such energy in modern times and society, Lawrence's various works propose methods of escaping from the stagnation. In this study I have called the energy 'aggression': it is a representation of the primitiveness which has been oppressed by modernized society, and besides, the inner motion which is instinctively produced inside one's self. I have used the term 'aggression' as the central notion of the study in order to discuss how Lawrence teaches his readers to renew their recognition of this energy, and moreover, his attitude of manifesting it as having the potential to actively and interactively reform both one's self and the other.

We have seen two major ways in which the aggressive energy is effectively used in Lawrence's works. Firstly, the youths who are entrapped in the community inside England and swayed by the values of the city and of the countryside, are in need of energy to escape from their old selves and open up the intuitive communication which is prior to intelligence and mental consciousness. Secondly, the colonized countries which involve deep-rooted discrepancies in terms of race and class, to a much greater extent than in domestic British society, are in need of another kind of solution. In order to overcome the hierarchy (or enable the other to get over it), I argued, one impresses the other by actively revealing his or her living energy, which enables them to create a dynamic coexisting space of multiple lives.

As a preparatory stage of these relationships, it can be said that Lawrence's works, as a whole, teach the importance of being aware of the physical internality of aggressive energy which breaks the adhesive relationships and the old social ego, and also of the existential affirmation of the individual. It is my distinctive argument that this attitude is consistently expressed from the earliest stage of his works, dating back to the short pieces, written before *The White Peacock*, which have been relatively little discussed in Lawrence studies. Generally, in Lawrence studies, the energy of opposition to modernity which is involved in the author's thoughts is based on his adulation of the primitive which he encountered during his travels to foreign countries. However, his recognition of the fact that the primitiveness has existed inside human beings from the beginning is evident from his earliest works as much as from his latest writings — a discovery which I aimed to demonstrate through this study.

My distinctive opinions and arguments from the chapters of my study can be summarized as follows. In the first chapter, I have mentioned affect and epiphany as examples of the dynamic interaction between people which the unrepresentable experience involves. These key experiences, depending on physical sensation, have attracted noticeably increasing attention in recent years in the academic world due to the introduction of theories of physicality and affect. However, it is a cardinal argument of this study that Lawrence, who attempts to restore people's way of living by dynamic consciousness, in place of mental consciousness, aims at bridging the gap between human beings whose relationships are hindered by the differences in their social status and living environment. Besides, noting the problem that the difference between affect and epiphany has not been clearly defined in earlier studies, I have specified their ranges. Affect has a fluidity that dissolves the distance between individuals with an intersubjective quality, and epiphany produces a sense of direct connection between the individual and the truth. The two phenomena are considerably different in that in the former, the individual is lost and has a characteristic of being blindly restored to the whole, while in the latter, the existential consciousness of the individual is intensified and the affirmation is accompanied by a sense of enlightenment. In 'The White Stocking' and 'Goose Fair', it is shown that affect is well matched with physicality and primitive elements. However, in examples such as that of Ursula in *The Rainbow*, who is a representative of the new woman, epiphany does not make her return to primitiveness, but is depicted as an affirmative sensory knowledge, which precedes intelligence, and which does not negate modernized individuals.

However, my discovery is that Lawrence experimented with combining the two experiences in addition to his acknowledgement of their differences in quality. Being intent on depicting the experience of escaping from the old self, Lawrence creates a state of metaphorical (and occasionally physical) death and rebirth as a rite of passage. As we have observed the process, when encountering the other in the unknown space, the individual's experience of epiphany which accompanies his or her rebirth is conveyed to the other through affect. Therefore, we have witnessed the destruction of the established recognition of the self and the other and the rebuilding of a whole new relationship which it was impossible even to imagine by preserving social consciousness. Ultimately, Lawrence's affect is not a blind condition of losing one's individuality but has an immense influential power which even changes the other person's recognition by the new knowledge gained through epiphany and the ecstasy with which the affirmation of the new self is disseminated. Although it is a deep-rooted opinion in previous studies of Lawrence's ideas that the abandonment of the self is required in his stories, I have shown that it is an innovative aspect of physical experience in Lawrence that the existential experience of the individual is more important and the extinction of the self is rather undesirable. Although the relationship had started with the impossibility of unity, the mutual difference or distance between the characters could be resolved in the momentary experience of the communication and exchange of epiphany and affect. Therefore, a kind of hope is depicted in the ecstatic communication which departs from the spell of the old egoism.

Furthermore, I have shown that the extinction of the self in Lawrence's island stories risks the worst situation of death with no rebirth of body and mind. Lawrence's tendency to seek peace in stillness during wartime is expressed in the works of his middle period; though, on the other hand, the island stories particularly sounded an alarm that immobility would lead one to the state of having no desire and of a retrogression which obliterates the self. The human relationship with dynamic consciousness which Lawrence advocates encourages us to return to the ground of direct physical experience, apart from human beings' intellectual development and powers of representation. Nevertheless, when the relationship is linked to excessive stillness, one returns to the satisfaction of the unity of mother and fetus which is the primordial condition of the Real. It makes one lose the distinction between the self and other and deters one from the possibility of individual reformation and development. Therefore, the island fiction vividly evokes the way in which soaking too much in the satisfactory inertia of unification with the outer world deprives the individual of independence and precipitates one into a false, inactive inertia in which one loses the desire to interact with others — the death in life which is an inhumanity of the wrong sort. In other words, dynamic consciousness must be expressed in the active space, and I have concluded that, for Lawrence, it is necessary for the individual to exist independently and keep actively challenging the other. Supporting this claim, in 'The Prussian Officer', the story which deals with physicality in the army and the homosocial relationship, I have argued that the passive submission of the central character weakens his vital energy and moreover, that the loss of his opponent becomes a trigger for the complete loss of the existential sense of the subject.

The next topic I have focused on is the active exchange of vitality which is the essence of life in the battle with the external others who still possess values outside Western modernity, and which accompanies the advance of Lawrence's fiction into the geographical outer world. In Lawrence's late works, there evidently exist fables in which the non-western characters seek to annihilate the Westerners' identity and their power of will and encourage them to turn into passive beings in a self-abandoning manner. Moreover, there has been a vague, uniform way of describing the external others as being customarily enveloped in an inhuman aura. However, I have pointed out that it is these racial others who maintain the historical and hierarchical tensions with the race of the masters; therefore, the racial others are not overly idealized nor disdained as barbarians in distinction from the Westerners as many critics argue. Rather, I have claimed that they are positioned as equal to the central characters in possessing historical emotions and will. As proof of this, Lawrence writes conclusions which include depictions of the formerly-colonized people's unacceptableness to Western characters, owing to their emotions and wills, and stories in which the relationships end in their destroying each other. Although each of the stories ends in discord, Lawrence's inquiry and his aim become evident when we observe his late works inclusively.

As Lawrence himself discovered during his stay in Mexico, what enables the organic coexistence of different species, such as Westerners, the colonial others, and animals, is the relationship of mutually exchanging energy by showing their vitality as individuals, in addition to acknowledging their essential differentness. Therefore, the Lawrentian road to living in symbiosis is not to deny or turn one's back on the other, but rather to highlight their difference. As Lawrence often finds in the lives of animals, although they are the weak in relation to human beings from a racial perspective, they occasionally astonish us by expressing their inspiring vitality. At that specific moment, we are surprisingly attracted to the other in the context of being, as if transcending the social consciousness, and the relationship among individuals reveals a sign of vital change and the static power balance is destabilized. As this suggests, even after setting eyes on the world outside England, Lawrence considers that losing one's self has its drawbacks, and demonstrated, rather, how the act of forcefully attracting the other with the natural alterity initiates a process of the destruction and renovation of the relationship between racial others.

Lawrence in his declining years, in which his perspective returned from the outer world to the internal, has shown that the dark place which had lurked inside the imagined other actually existed in the metaphorical internality of the modernized West and originally in the bodies of human beings. In his late works, it has been considered that Lawrence's inclination toward primitiveness, wilderness, and animality becomes even more conspicuous. However, as was already demonstrated by the affective dancing of the English man and woman in the earliest period of his fiction, the unknown darkness which we fear and hesitate to approach does not suggest an escape to the uncivilized past, but reveals that the darkness was virtually inside ourselves. The attitude of disturbing the interior of the established framework and believing in the possibility of resuscitating the internality becomes obvious when we look inclusively at Lawrence's works. Moreover, Lawrence finally presents a solution to the issue of the unsustainable effect of the dynamic-conscious relationship, which is the weakness of the momentary connection. The male and female who have auspiciously formed a connection by profound consciousness tend to be unable to maintain its repletion. However, in a way that is not limited to the vanishing momentary connection, what has produced the possibility of the couple's relationship being sustained in the future was the 'bowels of compassion'. No matter how the relationship was hindered by the mental consciousness or various obstacles in the society, Lawrence has evoked through Connie the necessity of not quenching the little flame of physical consciousness which has arisen between different sexes. To open up one's physical consciousness is to get out of the stable consciousness of the self and make an aggressive approach to the other, or conversely to accept the approach. And to cherish the new bond, born by the reformed awareness of self and other, with the physical sense and keep facing it would change the momentary connection into a sustainable connection. Although Lawrence is a prolific and experimental author, it should be known as his excellence that his works make a great impression by being thoroughly read. As has become clear through this study, Lawrence determinedly grappled with the issue of the life of human beings and their interaction and coexistence with others with a consistent literary attitude. The path of his thoughts is solidly expressed in each of his works, which tried to be faithful to the sense which arises from actual human relationships and their friction; the notion of tenderness which he had reached, solemnly exists in the end.

I have been presupposing that Lawrence devoted himself to drawing out the positive value of aggression on the level of the individual, as having the potential for eliminating the fetters of mind and emotion that make one overly aware of otherness. However, it goes without saying that Lawrence did not wish to create an offensive society. It is clear that his reaction to the vicious practices of modernized society and the energy which facilitates human beings' vivacious life is a motive power of his works, and I consider that to give motion to stability and to recreate the relationship with a new recognition and acceptance of the other, which was never accomplished in the former condition, was what he attempted through his works. The study has proved that the dynamic energy which fills the text chiefly operates as a reaction against the existing cognitive framework, which is constituted and historicized, and thus produces a contrastingly radical approach toward peace and humanity.

Japan, the country which I live in, is not the same as the Western society which is the origin of Lawrence's viewpoint, though our present age has gone to extremes of dependence on machines, and the poverty of mind and physicality has become much worse than that which prompted Lawrence's concerns. It has moved too rapidly to the grave situation of dependence on other people by means of mechanical devices. The society has become more and more characterized by mutual aid and sympathy and the individuals have lessened their sense of self-affirmation and always crave an object to sympathize with, and earn their peace of mind by enclosing themselves in their secure lives and relationships. People, who have become still more unable to abandon machines, refuse to actively engage with others and live by controlling their aggression or vitality and even being unaware that they own it by nature.

    The direct physical experience which the communication with others provides in Lawrence's texts, I argue, is simultaneously an achievement of the independence of the individual, and an active, organic integration with nature and others. We are impressed through his writings by the vividness of the way in which the self and others remarkably change, while facing the others as individual beings and having a profound life interaction involving the exchange of energy. When we realize that the aggression which his works project is a dark place or an internal other of ourselves, we feel convinced of our own living power, although we are entangled with our present conventions on a daily basis. If we open up ourselves, we can create a profound bond with the others through the unknown interaction and affective communication: as long as we can maintain the heat of the incendiary spark, I believe — as Lawrence does — that we can practically live a dynamic life as both social beings and impersonal animal beings. There is a true value in Lawrence's depiction of aggression and the representation of its dynamics which we intuitively feel from his works, and a need for it to be read in our age, a hundred years after his works were written.

Endnotes

INTRODUCTION

[1] Charles Michael Burack suggests that Lawrence's 'reference to "the fourth dimension" demonstrates his acquaintance with Einstein's theory of relativity' and that Einstein's 'understanding of time as "the fourth dimension of space" supports the religious idea of the "Eternal Now"' (*D. H. Lawrence's Language*, 160).

CHAPTER ONE

[1] However, it has been revealed that Arthur had a fair amount of income when he married and Lydia was in fact from the working class so there was no economic gap in the couple. Hence there is a growing opinion that it was actually Lawrence himself who fabricated the illusion of difference between his parents. Noting in advance that 'The myth of the Beardsall family, however, became enshrined in both family and literary history; it became an established fact in the early 1930s that the writer D. H. Lawrence had had a working-class father and a middle-class mother', though 'In actuality, both families were working-class', John Worthen argues that 'the most powerful class distinctions always operate in borderline areas; and what divided the Beardsalls from the the [*sic*] Lawrences was ideology, myth and expectation: that made for a deep and lasting division' (26).

[2] The intersubjective quality which Albright points out as the unique aspect of twentieth-century novels is notably similar to the concept of 'affect' which I deal with in the next section, though it is interesting that he wrote this before the development of that specific theory. Moreover, the words of W. B. Yeats (1865-1939), which Albright quotes, also coincide with the fluidity in the description in 'The White Stocking' and imply a presentiment of 'affect': '[In those novels, we find] mental and physical objects alike material, a deluge of experience breaking over us and within us, melting limits whether of line or tint; man no hard bright mirror dawdling by the dry sticks of a hedge, but a swimmer, or rather the waves themselves' (20).

[3] By 1892, being named 'Bovarysme' by Jules de Gaultier and widely shared as a symptom among readers, this phenomenon had reached the impasse of an uncategorizable categorization.

[4] Manning quotes Baker's suggestion that 'the unconscious, the foreign, the supernatural — are declared "other" to realist narrative' (par. 4).

[5] Young also refers to Courbet, the painter of *The Stone Breakers* (1849), alongside Flaubert, though I omitted this from the quotation in order to focus on the discussion of Flaubert.

[6] Iwai refers to letters sent from Lawrence to Cynthia Asquith in 1916 or to his literary agent J. B. Pinker.

[7] Much of the study of epiphany developed hereafter is a revised version of my essay (Oyama, 'Epiphany, Transformation, and Communication').

[8] See also Beja, for the details of the definition of the modernist epiphany.

[9] Compared to 'Chronos', the chronological notion of measurable time, 'Kairos', which reflects a qualitative and subjective moment, expresses the moment of epiphany. See Kermode, for the explanation of the two terms (46-51). 'Kairos' is thus similar to affect which is seen in the intensity of a 'perpetual present'.

[10] Abbie Garrington writes that skin sensation is used 'as a means of epistemological investigation' and that many of Lawrence's works 'can be seen to link touch to salving, and thence salvation' (156). She also explains that they offer 'a truly corporeal corpus, deeply invested in the experiences of the somatic system, and the philosophical and spiritual insight which consideration of the human body may bring' (Garrington 155).

[11] Haruo Tetsumura attributes revelation to physical contact as an experience of inseparableness and assumes that the immediate cause of Fergusson's epiphany which empties his realistic consciousness is the touch of the girl's skin. He comments that: 'Although there was nothing which predicted such a deep connection between the couple, the distance between them before the "physical contact" does not even matter. Here we see the allegory: when we look into the depths of humanity through "epiphany", we realise that every realistic thing we have ever supposed turns vacant and we find an utterly different value instead' (Tetsumura 202; my translation). Other scholars also conclude that the tale is a

double sleeping-beauty story in which a man and a woman resuscitate each other on a level beyond the manipulation of emotion or will. See, Sarah Betsky-Zweig and Keith Cushman.

[12] Asai discusses the difficulty and the effort of preserving epiphanic experience (Asai, *Jizokusuru Epiphany*).

CHAPTER TWO

[1] Schneider cites the letter of 1913 written when Lawrence was writing *The Sisters* which is the earlier version of *Women in Love*. Reflecting on the chronology of his writing, it is reasonable to suppose that the aestheticism of stillness is highlighted in his works from *The Rainbow* to *Women in Love* (Schneider, 'Alternatives to Logocentrism' 40).

[2] Granofsky sees that the positive challenge of preserving a balance is 'an understandable defensive move for Lawrence under the stress of the war' (186).

[3] Jill Franks remarks that the principle of the party has 'metamorphosed from a socialist state without money, to a place to love and create, to a male getaway' (107).

[4] It should be added that this demarcation made by Tagata is based on the description in *Women in Love*. Since she does not attach special importance to each of the three elements, I intentionally changed their order in this study.

[5] Maria Ferreira states that Lawrence's desire for the womb / tomb is particularly seen in his late works, and positively argues that Lawrence got this idea from the lifestyle of the Etruscan people who cherished the notion of 'the death-journey' and 'the sojourn in the after-life' that he learned of through his experience in the region once known as Etruria (165). However, it is unnecessary to say that it does not suggest a good way of living in the island novels.

[6] 'Mimetic desire' is a psychoanalytic notion of René Girard which explains the relationship between the social structure and the self.

[7] Kalaidjian points out that coal mining is reproached as representing an industrial negative inertia in *The Rainbow* and *Women in Love*, and he indicates that it is opposite to the generative aesthetics of positive inertia due to its loss of organic production for the next generation.

[8] In a novel which is like a vortex of abstract perception, *The Waves* (1930), Woolf frequently presents a concept of the disappearance of the self, while the material world and people remain. The epiphany which lacks self-approval stresses the impossibility of survival through existential despair.

[9] Stoltzfus psychoanalytically discusses the direction of aggression and desire by adapting the famous game of *Fort! Da!* of Freud's grandson Ernst; 'The game manifests itself symbolically as the murder of the thing (*Fort!*) and this death guarantees the persistence of desire'. Therefore, the duration of desire is assured by directing it to the object. However, due to the extinction of the precious object, the 'desire has been redirected as a death-wish and, instead of the thing being murdered, it is now the self' (Stoltzfus 34).

CHAPTER THREE

[1] The discussion of Mexican stories in the first and second sections of this chapter partly overlaps with my published essay (Oyama, 'The Description of the Indians' Longing for Identity').

[2] In Lawrence's works, most of the characters who are led to abandon their old will are women, and they passively accept the change and submit to this more easily than male protagonists. Furthermore, an offensive attitude can be suspected in the process whereby the heterogeneous values are implanted in the female characters, and the misogynistic impression of the fiction has naturally triggered feminists' fierce resentment. See Williams, for the history of the relationship between Lawrence and his women readers.

[3] See Roux, for the comparison of the females' fascination and repulsion in 'The Woman Who Rode Away', 'None of That!', and 'The Princess'.

[4] Octavio Paz, an illustrious Mexican poet and essayist, analyses the disposition of fundamental duality which Mexican nationality involves. He writes: 'The Mexican tells us that human beings are a mixture, that good and evil are subtly blended in their souls' (Paz 34), and he interestingly introduces this as an idiosyncratic ethnic force in which the contradictory desires are both proved to be real and the duality has an impact on the people's existential pleasure. In Mexico, politics, the meanings of words, or fiestas, and many other things are a

tangle of contradictions, as the nation's cry of independence 'possesses the same ambiguous resonance: an angry joy, a destructive affirmation' (Paz 75).

[5] See also *5L*, 176-78.

[6] The argument for the fluctuation of Kate's egoism in this section partly coincides with that in my essay (Oyama, 'Desire for Love and Recognition'). In this essay, I developed the argument that Kate's persistence in her Western character can be attributed to her love for Ramón, whom she regards as a Western man, and thus similar to her, which also overlaps with her attitude towards her former husband.

[7] Swarthout's comment hints at the fact that it has hardly been considered that Juana is a character who is incarnated with rich living energy, as I have noted in the last section. The Mexican people depicted in *The Plumed Serpent* have been evaluated as not fully human over a period of decades and, for example, Hirokazu Yoshimura rashly judges that 'originally, there was no ego to abandon for Cipriano' (66-7; my translation) and therefore there is no need for the general to take pains to communicate with Kate.

CHAPTER FOUR

[1] Lawrence writes, 'I'm supposed to be a sensible human being. Yet I carry a whole waste-paper basket of ideas at the top of my head, and in some other part of my anatomy, the dark continent of my self, I have a stormy chaos of "feelings"' (*STH* 202).

[2] The discussion of 'The Last Laugh' and Lawrence's idea of Pan in the second and third sections of this chapter considerably overlaps with my published essay (Oyama, 'Naiteki Tasya tositeno Bokusin').

[3] Ferreira writes that Lawrence's desire to return to the revival inside England is 'vividly dramatized in "A Dream of Life", where the narrator returns to the warm embrace of the maternal cave in Newthorpe, a fictional Eastwood' (166). The unfinished story 'A Dream of Life' (1927) is known as an uncanny compilation of Lawrence's thoughts which deals with the idealized society and the resuscitation of a human being from the level of sensory nerves.

[4] Bauman's argument is summarized by Khair: 'as Zygmunt Bauman suggests, the object of our fear tells us more about the epoch we live in than the substance of

the fear itself' (3).

[5] In ancient Greece, in the service of reinforcing the city, evil things were evicted to the outside of the system of the city as scapegoats. This is a coded sacrifice with the aim of giving immunity to the city and firmly rebuilding it; hence, the concept of the protective inside and disordered outside was created. However, Patrick Llored argues that this aim has been concealed in Western civilization, and animality has been extinguished as an evil otherness which harms and contaminates the interior.

[6] Like the occult quality of the Pan symbol in the last section, the inhuman fearfulness is obviously connected with Annable who barely appears in the novel. He does not speak in the scene of his first appearance and the scene ends by instantly highlighting the way 'the saturnine keeper smiled grimly' (*WP* 58) beside the selfish people who call the rabbits which increased excessively in the farm 'quails and manna'. From the way in which his creepy smile is highlighted right after the reference to the Bible, it can be said that the occult quality of the symbolic keeper is emphasized like that of Pan.

Works Cited

Works by D. H. Lawrence

'The Blind Man.' *England, My England and Other Stories*. Ed. Bruce Steele. Cambridge: Cambridge UP, 1990, 46-63.

'Hadrian [You Touched Me].' *England, My England and Other Stories*. Ed. Bruce Steele. Cambridge: Cambridge UP, 1990, 92-107.

'The Horse-Dealer's Daughter.' *England, My England and Other Stories*. Ed. Bruce Steele. Cambridge: Cambridge UP, 1990, 137-52.

'The Thimble.' *England, My England and Other Stories*. Ed. Bruce Steele. Cambridge: Cambridge UP, 1990, 190-200.

Lady Chatterley's Lover: A Propos of 'Lady Chatterley's Lover'. Ed. Michael Squires. Cambridge: Cambridge UP, 1993.

The Letters of D. H. Lawrence. Vol. 1. Ed. James T. Boulton. Cambridge: Cambridge UP, 1979.

The Letters of D. H. Lawrence. Vol. 2. Ed. George. J. Zytaruk and James. T. Boulton. Cambridge: Cambridge UP, 1981.

The Letters of D. H. Lawrence. Vol. 5. Ed. James. T. Boulton and Lindeth Vasey. Cambridge: Cambridge UP, 1989.

Mornings in Mexico and Etruscan Places. London: Heinemann, 1970.

'Pan in America.' *Phoenix: The Posthumous Papers of D. H. Lawrence*. William Heinemann, 1961.

The Plumed Serpent. Ed. L. D. Clark. Cambridge: Cambridge UP, 1987.

'Goose Fair.' *The Prussian Officer and Other Stories*. Ed. John Worthen. Cambridge: Cambridge UP, 1983, 133-42.

'The Prussian Officer.' *The Prussian Officer and Other Stories*. Ed. John Worthen. Cambridge: Cambridge UP, 1983, 1-21.

'Second-Best.' *The Prussian Officer and Other Stories*. Ed. John Worthen. Cambridge: Cambridge UP. 1983, 113-120.

'The White Stocking.' *The Prussian Officer and Other Stories*. Ed. John

Worthen. Cambridge: Cambridge UP. 1983, 143-64.

Psychoanalysis and the Unconscious and Fantasia of the Unconscious. Ed. Bruce Steele. Cambridge: Cambridge UP, 2004.

The Rainbow. Ed. Mark Kinkead-Weekes. Cambridge: Cambridge UP, 1989.

Reflections on the Death of a Porcupine and Other Essays. Ed. Michael Herbert. Cambridge: Cambridge UP, 1988.

'The Princess.' *St. Mawr and Other Stories.* Ed. Brian Finney. Cambridge: Cambridge UP, 1983.

St. Mawr. St. Mawr and Other Stories. Ed. Brian Finney. Cambridge: Cambridge UP, 1983.

Sons and Lovers. Ed. Helen Baron and Carl Baron. Cambridge: Cambridge UP, 1992.

Study of Thomas Hardy and Other Essays. Ed. Bruce Steele. Cambridge: Cambridge UP, 1985.

The Trespasser. Ed. Elizabeth Mansfield. Cambridge: Cambridge UP, 1981.

The White Peacock. Ed. Andrew Robertson. Cambridge: Cambridge UP, 1983.

Women in Love. Ed. Lindeth Vasey and John Worthen. Cambridge: Cambridge UP, 1987.

'The Last Laugh.' *The Woman Who Rode Away and Other Stories.* Ed. Dieter Mehl and Christa Jansohn. Cambridge: Cambridge UP, 1995.

'The Man Who Loved Islands.' *The Woman Who Rode Away and Other Stories.* Ed. Dieter Mehl and Christa Jansohn. Cambridge: Cambridge UP, 1995.

'Sun.' *The Woman Who Rode Away and Other Stories.* Ed. Dieter Mehl and Christa Jansohn. Cambridge: Cambridge UP, 1995, 19-38.

'The Woman Who Rode Away.' *The Woman Who Rode Away and The Other Stories.* Ed. Dieter Mehl and Christa Jansohn. Cambridge: Cambridge UP, 1995.

The Virgin and the Gipsy. Vintage Books, New York: Random House, Inc., 1984.

Other Books and Essays Consulted

Albright, Daniel. *Personality and Impersonality: Lawrence, Woolf, and Mann*. Chicago and London: The U of Chicago P, 1978.

Apter, T. E. 'Let's Hear What the Male Chauvinist is Saying: *The Plumed Serpent*.' *Lawrence and Women*. Ed. Anne Smith. London: Vision Press, 1978.

Aristotle. *Metaphysics*. Trans. Hugh Lawson-Tancred. London: Penguin Books, 2004.

Asai, Masashi. 'How to Have Meaningful Relationships with the Other: Lawrence, Sade, Bataille.' *D. H. Lawrence: New Critical Perspectives and Cultural Translation*. Ed. Simonetta de Filippis. Newcastle upon Tyne: Cambridge Scholars Publishing, 2016a.

-----. *Jizokusuru Epiphany: Bungaku ni Hyosho sareta Eroticism to Reisei* (*Sustained Epiphany: Literary Representations of the Erotic and the Spiritual*). Tokyo: Shohakusha, 2016b.

Auerbach, Erich. 'On the Serious Imitation of the Everyday.' in Flaubert, *Madame Bovary*. Ed. Margaret Cohen. New York: Norton, 2005.

Bataille, Georges. *Inner Experience*. Albany: State U of New York, 1988.

Bauman, Zygmunt. *Life in Fragments: Essays in Postmodern Morality*. Oxford and Cambridge, MA: Blackwell, 1995.

Beja, Morris. *Epiphany in the Modern Novel*. Seattle: U of Washington P, 1971.

Bell, Michael. 'Lawrence, the "pure present" and *les années de pèlerinage*.' *Études Lawrenciennes* 48, 2017.

Bergson, Henri. *Time and Free Will: An Essay on the Immediate Data of Consciousness*. Trans. F. L. Pogson. New York: Dover Publications, Inc., 2001.

Bersani, Leo. *A Future for Astyanax: Character and Desire in Literature*. London: Marion Boyars, 1978.

Betsky-Zweig, Sarah. 'Floutingly in the Fine Black Mud: D. H. Lawrence's "The Horse-Dealer's Daughter."' *Dutch Quarterly Review* 3 (1973): 159-65.

Bown, Alfie. 'Losing the Self: Transgression in Lawrence and Bataille.' *Études Lawrenciennes* 43 (2012): 259-80.

Brennan, Teresa. *The Transmission of Affect*. New York: Cornell UP, 2004.

Brooks, Peter. *Realist Vision*. New Haven: Yale UP, 2005.

Brown, Keith. 'Wales no Red Indian — Lawrence to *St. Mawr* (Red Indians in Wales: Lawrence and *St. Mawr*).' *D. H. Lawrence Hihyochizu — Feminism kara Bakhtin made (The Critical Map of D. H. Lawrence: From Feminism to Bakhtin)*. Trans. Yoshimura Hirokazu and Sugiyama Yasushi. Tokyo: Shohakusya, 2001. (Originally, *Rethinking Lawrence*. Maidenhead: Open UP, 1990.)

Burack, Charles Michael. *D. H. Lawrence's Language of Sacred Experience: The Transfiguration of the Reader*. New York: Palgrave Macmillan, 2005.

-----. 'Revitalizing the Reader: Literary Technique and the Language of Sacred Experience in D.H. Lawrence's Lady Chatterley's Lover.' *Style* 32. 1 (1998): 102-126.

Callow, Philip. *Son and Lover: The Young D. H. Lawrence*. New York: Stein and Day, 1975.

Camelia, Anghel. 'Exilic Dimensions of Modernism: D. H. Lawrence's "Island"-Characters.' The Proceedings of the *Ovid, Myth and (Literary) Exile* Conference. Constanta, September 10-12 (2009): 75-82.

Carpenter, Rebecca. '"Bottom-Dog Insolence" and "The Harem Mentality": Race and Gender in *The Plumed Serpent*.' *The D. H. Lawrence Review* 25. 1/3 (1993, 1994): 119-29.

Clausson, Nils. 'Practicing Deconstruction, Again: Blindness, Insight and the Lovely Treachery of Words in D. H. Lawrence's "The Blind Man."' *College Literature* 34.1 (2007): 106-28.

Clayton, John J. 'D. H. Lawrence: Psychic Wholeness through Rebirth.' *The Massachusetts Review* 25. 2 (1984): 200-21.

Clough, Patricia T. 'The Affective Turn: Political Economy, Biomedia, and Bodies.' *The Affect Theory Reader*. Ed. Melissa Gregg and Gregory J. Seigworth. Durham and London: Duke UP, 2010.

Coates, Kimberly. 'Eros in the Sick Room: Phosphorescent Form and Aesthetic Ecstasy in D. H. Lawrence's *Sons and Lovers*.' *Journal of Narrative Theory* 38. 2 (2008): 135-176.

Cushman, Keith. 'The Achievement of *England, My England and Other Stories*.' *D. H. Lawrence: The Man Who Lived*. Ed. H. T. Moore and R. B. Partlow, Carbondale: Southern Illinois UP, 1980.

Derrida, Jacques. *The Animal That Therefore I Am*. Trans. David Wills. Ed. Marie-Louise Mallet. New York: Fordham UP, 2008.

Desiderio, Olga. 'The Flowing of Emotion. Sentiment and Ressentiment in *The Trespasser*.' *Études Lawrenciennes* 42 (2011): 255-80.

Endo, Fuhito. 'Affect, Realism, and Utopia: Fredric Jameson's Dialogues with De Man, Karatani, and Williams.' *Bulletin of the Faculty of Humanities Seikei University* 51 (2016): 115-25.

-----. *Jyodo to Modernity: Eibeibungaku/ Seishinbunseki/ Hihyoriron (Affect and Modernity: Literature/ Psychoanalysis/ Theory)*. Tokyo: Sairyusha, 2017.

Ferreira, Maria Aline. '"Glad Wombs" and "Friendly Tombs": Reembodiments in D. H. Lawrence's Late Works.' *Writing the Body in D. H. Lawrence: Essays on Language, Representation, and Sexuality*. Ed. Paul Poplawski. Westport CT: Greenwood P, 2001.

Flaubert, Gustave. *Madame Bovary: A Study of Provincial Life*. Ed. Dora Knowlton Ranous. New York: Brentano's Publishers, 1919.

Fleming, Fiona. 'Encountering Foreignness: a Transformation of Self.' *Études Lawrenciennes* 47, 2016.

Forster, E. M. 'The Story of A Panic', *Collected Short Stories*. Harmondsworth: Penguin, 1954.

Franks, Jill. *Islands and the Modernists*. Jefferson, North Carolina and London: McFarland & Company, Inc., 2006.

Freud, Sigmund. *The Complete Psychological Works of Sigmund Freud Vol. 18: Beyond the Pleasure Principle, Group Psychology and Other Works*. London: Vintage Classics, 2001.

-----. *The Complete Psychological Works of Sigmund Freud Vol. 21: The*

Future of an Illusion, Civilization and Its Discontents and Other Works. London: The Hogarth Press, 1961.

-----. *The Complete Psychological Works of Sigmund Freud Vol. 22: New Introductory Lectures on Psycho-Analysis and Other Works*. London: Vintage Classics, 2001.

Garrard, Greg. 'Nietzsche *contra* Lawrence: How to be True to the Earth.' *Colloquy text theory critique* 12 (2006): 9-27.

Garrington, Abbie. *Haptic Modernism: Touch and the Tactile in Modernist Writing*. Edinburgh: Edinburgh UP, 2013.

Gordon, David J. 'Sex and Language in D. H. Lawrence.' *Twentieth Century Literature* 27. 4 (1981): 362-75.

Granofsky, Ronald. 'Attachment and Autonomy in *The White Peacock*: D. H. Lawrence Read through Margaret S. Mahler.' *DH Lawrence Study* 14. 2 (2006): 185-204.

Gregorio, Giuseppina Di. 'Carbon Identity: A Lawrencian Reading of Thomas Hardy's Novels.' *FATHOM* 4, 2016.

Grmelová, Anna. '"The Prussian Officer" in the Context of D. H. Lawrence's Short Fiction.' *Brno Studies in English* 24 (1998): 141-46.

Gurko, Leo. 'D. H. Lawrence's Neglected Novel.' *College English* 24. 1 (1962): 29-35.

Haegert, John. 'D. H. Lawrence and the Aesthetics of Transgression.' *Modern Philology* 88. 1 (1990): 2-25.

Harris, Janis Hubbard. *The Short Fiction of D. H. Lawrence*. New Brunswick, NJ: Rutgers UP, 1984.

Harrison, Andrew. *D. H. Lawrence: Selected Short Stories*. Tirril: Humanities-Ebooks, 2008.

-----. *The Life of D. H. Lawrence: A Critical Biography*. NJ: John Wiley & Sons, 2016.

-----. 'The Regional Modernism of D. H. Lawrence and James Joyce.' *Regional Modernisms*. Ed. Neal Alexander and James Moran. Edinburgh: Edinburgh UP, 2013.

Harrison, William M. 'Thinking Like a Chicken — But not a Porcupine:

Lawrence, Feminism, and Animal Rights.' *LIT* 10 (2000): 349-70.

Hayles, Nancy Katherine. 'The Ambivalent Approach: D. H. Lawrence and the New Physics.' *Mosaic: An Interdisciplinary Critical Journal* 15. 3 (1982): 89-108.

Humma, John B. 'The Interpenetrating Metaphor: Nature and Myth in *Lady Chatterley's Lover.*' *PMLA* 98. 1(1983): 77-86.

Inniss, Kenneth. *D. H. Lawrence's Bestiary: A Study of His Use of Animal Trope and Symbol.* The Hague: Mouton & Co. N. V., Publishers, 1971.

Irwin, Alexander C. 'Ecstasy, Sacrifice, Communication: Bataille on Religion and Inner Experience.' *Soundings: An Interdisciplinary Journal* 76. 1 (1993): 105-28.

Iwai, Gaku. 'Yubinuki wo Homurisaru koto ha dekiruka?: Senji Romance to D. H. Lawrence ni okeru Aikoku to Hanaikoku no Syoso (Can We Banish the Thimble to Oblivion?: Romance in War Time and the Aspects of Patriotism and Anti-patriotism in D. H. Lawrence).' *21 Seiki no D. H. Lawrence (D. H. Lawrence in the 21st Century).* Ed. The D. H. Lawrence Society of Japan. Tokyo: Kokushokankokai, 2015.

Jameson, Fredric. *The Antinomies of Realism.* London and New York: Verso, 2013.

Jeffers, Thomas L. 'Lawrence's Major Phase.' *The Yale Review* 90. 3 (2008): 148-58.

Janik, Del Ivan. 'D. H. Lawrence and Environmental Consciousness.' *Environmental Review* 7.4, Special Issue: A Cumulative Index to the First Seven Years of Environmental Review (1983): 359-72.

Kalaidjian, Andrew. 'Positive Inertia: D. H. Lawrence and the Aesthetics of Generation.' *Journal of Modern Literature* 38.1 (2014): 38-55.

Kearny, Martin F. *Major Short Stories of D. H. Lawrence: A Handbook.* New York and London: Garland Publishing Inc., 1998.

Kermode, Frank. *The Sense of an Ending: Studies in the Theory of Fiction: With a New Epilogue.* Oxford: Oxford UP, 2000.

Khair, Tabish. *The Gothic, Postcolonialism and Otherness: Ghosts from Elsewhere.* London and New York: Palgrave Macmillan, 2009.

Kinkead-Weeks, Mark. 'D. H. Lawrence and the Dance.' *Dance Research: The Journal of the Society for Dance Research* 10.1 (1992): 59-77.

Lacan, Jacques. *Ecrits: A Selection*. Trans. Alan Sheridan. London: Routledge Classics, 2001.

Llored, Patrick. *Jacques Derrida — The Politics and Ethics of Animality*. Trans. Yuji Nishiyama and Kei Kiritani. Tokyo: Keisoshobo, 2017.

Lowenthal, David. 'Islands, Lovers, and Others.' *Geographical Review* 97. 2 (2007): 202-29.

Lyotard, Jean-François. *Inhuman: Reflections on Time*. Cambridge: Polity, 1993.

Manning, Nicholas. 'Can Realism Speak of Affect?: Forces of Emotional Alterity in Realist Modes.' *L'Atelier* 8. 1, 2016.

Massumi, Brian. *Parables for the Virtual: Movement, Affect, Sensation*. Durham and London: Duke UP, 2002.

McCabe, Thomas H. 'Rhythm as Form in Lawrence: "The Horse Dealer's Daughter."' *PMLA*. 87.1 (1972): 64-68.

Merivale, Patricia. *Pan the Goat-God: His Myth in Modern Times*. Harvard Studies in Comparative Literature 30, Cambridge: Harvard UP, 1969.

Michelucci, Stefania. 'D. H. Lawrence's (Un)happy Islands', *Études Lawrenciennes* 46, 2015.

Milton, Colin. *Lawrence and Nietzsche: A Study in Influence*. Aberdeen: Aberdeen UP, 1987.

Moynahan, Julian. *Deed of Life: The Novels and Tales of D. H. Lawrence*, Princeton: Princeton UP, 1966.

Nakanishi, Yoshihiro. 'D. H. Lawrence to "Atarashii" Bokuyoshin Pan (D. H. Lawrence and the "New" God Pan).' *Bulletin of Tenri University* 40 (1988): 95-116.

Nichols, Ashton. 'Browning's Modernism: The Infinite Moment as Epiphany.' *Browning Institute Studies* 11 (1983): 81-99.

Nietzsche, Friedrich. *On the Genealogy of Morality*. Ed. Keith Ansell-Pearson, Trans. Carol Diethe. Cambridge: Cambridge UP, 2007.

Okano, Keiichi. '*Urin no Hebi* no Haikei: Mexico no Rekishi to Syakai (The

Background of *The Plumed Serpent* — The History and Society of Mexico).' *Lawrence Kenkyu: Urin no Hebi (Lawrence Studies: The Plumed Serpent)*. Tokyo: Asahi Syuppansha, 1994.

Okuma, Akinobu. *D. H. Lawrence no Bunkajinruigakuteki Kosatsu — Seiai no Shinpishugi, Post-colonialism, Tandokusya wo megutte (The Cultural Anthropological Study of D. H. Lawrence — The Mysticism of Sexual Love, Post-colonialism, and Singleness)*. Tokyo: Kazamashobo, 2009.

Orwell, George. *The Road to Wigan Pier*. Harmondsworth: Penguin Books Ltd, 1962.

Osborn, Marijane. '"Strangely Jumbled": Attitudes Toward the Native Other in Melville's and D. H. Lawrence's Captivity Narratives.' *Leviathan: A Journal of Melville Studies* 11.2 (2009): 57-70.

Oyama, Miyo. 'Epiphany, Transformation, and Communication in D. H. Lawrence's Short Stories; with Particular Reference to "The Horse-Dealer's Daughter."' *Bulletin of the Research Center for the Technique of Representation* 12 (2017a): 17-29.

-----. 'Naiteki Tasya tositeno Bokusin: D. H. Lawrence no "Saigo no Warai" (Pan as an Internal Other in D. H. Lawrence's "The Last Laugh").' *Hiroshima Studies in English Language and Literature* 63 (2019): 49-62.

-----. 'The Description of the Indians' Longing for Identity in D. H. Lawrence's *The Plumed Serpent* and His Other Mexican Writings.' *Studies in English Literature*. Regional Branches Combined Issue 9 (2017b): 255-63.

-----. 'Desire for Love and Recognition in D. H. Lawrence's *The Plumed Serpent*: A Resistance to Abandoning Western Ego.' *Studies in English Literature*. Regional Branches Combined Issue 10 (2018): 267-74.

Paz, Octavio. *The Labyrinth of Solitude and Other Writings*. New York: Grove Press, Inc. 1985.

Ragachewskaya, Marina S. '"The Man Who Loved Islands" and "The Woman Who Rode Away": Turning a Moment into Eternity.' *Études Lawrenciennes* 48, 2017.

-----. 'The Logic of Love: Deconstructing Eros in Four of D. H. Lawrence's Short Stories.' *Études Lawrenciennes* 43, 2012.

Roberts, Neil. *D. H. Lawrence, Travel and Cultural Difference*. Basingstoke: Palgrave Macmillan, 2004.

Rose, Shirley. 'Physical Trauma in D, H. Lawrence's Short Fiction.' *Contemporary Literature* 16. 1 (1975): 73-83.

Roux, Magali. 'Emotions and Otherness in D. H. Lawrence's Mexican Fiction.' *Études Lawrenciennes* 43, 2012.

Ruderman, Judith. *D. H. Lawrence and the Devouring Mother: The Search for a Patriarchal Ideal of Leadership*. Durham, NC: Duke UP, 1984.

Santos, José Dos. 'Self and the Other: Mimetic Desire and Violence in Stephen Crane's "Maggie: A Girl of the Streets" and D. H. Lawrence's "The Prussian Officer."' *SIGNÓTICA* 17. 1 (2005): 91-102.

Schapiro, Barbara Ann. *D. H. Lawrence and the Paradoxes of Psychic Life*. Albany: State U of New York P, 1999.

Schneider, Daniel J. 'Alternatives to Logocentrism in D. H. Lawrence.' *South Atlantic Review* 51.2 (1986): 35-47.

Shklovsky, Viktor. 'Art as Technique.' *Russian Formalist Criticism. Four Essays*, Ed. L. T. Lemon and M. Reis. Lincoln: U of Nebraska P, 1965.

Snyder, Carey. '"When the Indian was in Vogue": D. H. Lawrence, Aldous Huxley, and Ethnological Tourism in the Southwest.' Modern Fiction Studies 53.4 (2007): 662-696.

Squires, Michael. 'Modernism and the Contours of Violence in D. H. Lawrence's Fiction.' *Studies in the Novel* 39. 1 (2007): 84-104.

Stoltzfus, Ben. '"The Man Who Loved Islands": A Lacanian Reading.' *D. H. Lawrence Review* 29. 3 (2000): 27-38.

Stromer, Richard. 'An Odd Sort of God for the British: Exploring the Appearance of Pan in Late Victorian and Edwardian Literature.' 23 Nov. 2018. <www.soulmyths.com/oddgod.pdf>.

Swarthout, Kelley R. *'Assimilating the Primitive' — Parallel Dialogues on Racial Miscegenation in Revolutionary Mexico*. New York: Peter Lang Publishing, Inc., 2004.

Takamura, Mineo. *Fureru koto no Modernity (Tactility and Modernity): D. H. Lawrence, Alfred Stieglitz, Walter Benjamin, and Maurice Merleau-Ponty*, Tokyo: Ibunsha, 2017.

Tagata, Midori. 'Lawrence Bungaku ni okeru Kinndaijiga no Yukue — "inhuman" to "impersonal" toiu Kotoba wo Otte (The traces of modern ego in Lawrence's fiction — following the terms of "inhuman" and "impersonal").' *D. H. Lawrence to Genndai (D. H. Lawrence and Our Age)*. Ed. The D. H. Lawrence Society of Japan. Tokyo: Kokushokankokai, 1995.

Tetsumura, Haruo. *Souzouryoku to Image: D. H. Lawrence no Chūtanpen no Kenkyū(Imagination and Image: A Study of D. H. Lawrence's Novellas and Short Stories)*. Tokyo: Kaibunsha, 1984.

Toth, Naomi. 'Disturbing Epiphany: Rereading Virginia Woolf's "Moments of Being."' *Études Britanniques Contemporaines* 46, 2014.

Ueda, Kazuo. 'Kaisetsu (Afterword).' *Shinban Lawrence Tanpensyū (New version of A Volume of Thirteen Short Stories)*. Trans. Kazuo Ueda. Tokyo: Shinchosha, 2000.

Whiteley, Patrick J. *Knowledge and Experimental Realism in Conrad, Lawrence, and Woolf.* Louisiana State UP, 1987.

Widmer, Kingsley. *Defiant Desire: Some Dialectical Legacies of D. H. Lawrence*. Carbondale and Edwardsville: Southern Illinois UP, 1992.

Williams, Linda Ruth. 'The Trial of D. H. Lawrence.' *Critical Survey 4* (1992): 154-61.

Worthen, John. *D. H. Lawrence: The Early Years 1885-1912*. Cambridge UP, 1992.

Yoshimura, Hirokazu. 'Fascism, Leadership, *Urin no Hebi* (Fascism, Leadership, *The Plumed Serpent*).' *Lawrence Kenkyu: Urin no Hebi (Lawrence Studies: The Plumed Serpent)*. Tokyo: Asahi Syuppansha, 1994.

Young, Michael. 'The Affects of Realism: Or the Estragement of the Background.' *Evoking through Design: Contemporary Moods in Architecture* 244 (2016): 58-65.

Index

A
affect 8, 29, 30, **32**, **35-39**, 43, **44**, 51-53, **55-57**, 64, 65, 75-76, 92, 130-31, 155-56, 201, **210-12**
aggression 4, **7**, 8, 10, 11, **28**, 29, 36, 57, 69, 76, 78, 102-04, 107, 110, **128-130**, **133-35**, 139-40, **142**, 148-49, 154, 159, 161, 171, 173, 175, 189, 204, 208, **209**, 210, 216-17
Albright, Daniel 26, 38, 219
animality 11, **24**, 27-28, 85, **170**, 179, 182-87, **189-91**, 204, 215
animal man 12, 191-92, 200
anthropocentrism 11, 137, 186
Apter, T. E. 154
Aristotle 26
Asai, Masashi 58, 64-65, 221
Auerbach, Erich 34

B
Baker, Geoffrey 36, 220
Balzac, Honoré de 33
Bataille, Georges 58, 62, 64-66
Bauman, Zygmunt 175, 223
Beja, Morris 220
Bell, Michael 78
Bergson, Henri 5-6, 72
Bersani, Leo 104
Betsky-Zweig, Sarah 221
Blackwood, Algernon 188
'The Blind Man' 11, 27, 37, 162-67, 169
blood-consciousness 3, 15, 17, 95-96, 112, 114, 153
Bown, Alfie 144
Brennan, Teresa 39
Brooks, Peter 32
Browning, Robert 50, 178
Brown, Keith 122
Burack, Charles Michael 202, 219

C
Callow, Philip 40
Camelia, Anghel 50, 84
carbon identity 46-47, 119
Carpenter, Rebecca 131, 133
Christianity 129, 139, 175, 184, 186
Clausson, Nils 162, 167
Clayton, John J. 4, 11, 161
Clough, Patricia T 30
Coats, Kimberly 9
Cushman, Keith 221

D
the Death Instinct 103-04, 109, 149-50
Derrida, Jacques 12, 186-88
Desiderio, Olga 159-60
'A Dream of Life' 223
dynamic 3, 4, **6**, 16, 28-29, 36, **39**, 52, 57, 76, 80, 86-87, 91, 104, 159, **191**, 204, 210, 216-17
dynamic consciousness 2, **3**, **4**, 15, **16**, 18, 27, **28**, 32, 44, 55, 100, 110, 197, 208, 210, 212-13, 215
dynamic relationship 2, 11, **17**, **18**, 20, 92, 110-11, 124, **156**, **164**, 206, **207**, 210
dynamism 7, 30, 36, 72, 104, 110

E
Endo, Fuhito 30, 36, 45, 68, 89
Engelberg, Edward 142
England 11, 14-15, 24, 28, 40, 72, 77, 118, 172, 176
the Enlightenment 2
epiphany **49-53**, 57, 68, 106, 118, 120, 210-11

F
Fantasia of the Unconsciousness (Psychoanalysis and the Unconscious and Fantasia of the Unconscious) 15-17, 89-90, 146, 180-81

237

feminism 117, 119
Ferreira, Maria Aline 221, 223
the First World War 9, 71-72, 197
Flaubert, Gustave 33, 37
Fleming, Fiona 112, 119-20
Ford, Madox Ford 40
Forster, E. M. 177, 179, 188
Franks, Jill 92, 221
Freud, Sigmund 9, 98, 103-04, 148-49, 222
G
Garrard, Greg 11, 51
Garrington, Abbie 220
'Goose Fair' 8, 39-44
Gordon, David J. 100
Granofsky, Ronald 80, 221
the great affective centre 16, 45, 180
Gregorio, Giuseppina Di 48
Grmelová, Anna 106-07
Gurko, Leo 87
H
'Hadrian [You Touched Me]' 8, 52-53
Haegert, John 109
Hardy, Thomas 48-49
Harris, Janis Hubbard 40, 56-57
Harrison, Andrew 41, 50, 129, 141
Harrison, William M. 183
Hayles, Nancy Katherine 80
'The Horse-Dealer's Daughter' 8, 57-68
humanism 2-3, 96, 216
Humma, John B. 201
I
impersonal 2, **24-28**, 48, 53, 65, 75, **86**, 88, 112, 116-17, 125, 128, 135, 152-53, 191, 202, 217
Indians 27, 116, 118, 130, 139, 141, 150-51, 154
inertia 8, **72-74**, **76**, **79**, 82-83, 92, 100, **102-05**, 140, 144, **203**, **204**, 213
inhuman 2, 10, 24, 27, 45, **85-88**, 96, **104**, 112, 114-15, 120, 122, 124-26, 128, 138, **151**, **152**, 154, 190-91, 202, 204, 213

inner experience 62, 66
Inniss, Kenneth 144, 197
internal other 178, 180, 188, 189, 192
intuition 6-7, 39, 50, 134, 180, 209
Irwin, Alexander C. 62, 66
Iwai, Gaku 47, 220
J
Jameson, Fredric 30-31, 33-34, 37, 74
Janik, Del Ivan 2
Jeffers, Thomas L. 73
Joyce, James 49-50
K
Kalaidjian, Andrew 72-74, 79, 221
Kearny, Martin F. 60
Kermode, Frank 220
Khair, Tabiṣh 176, 223
Kinkead-Weeks, Mark 23
L
Lacan, Jacques 9, 95-97
Lady Chatterley's Lover 11, 162, 193-208
'The Last Laugh' 11, 172-89
Letters of D. H. Lawrence Vol.1 20
Letters of D. H. Lawrence Vol.2 46, 179
Letters of D. H. Lawrence Vol.5 188, 223
Llored, Patrick 224
Lowenthal, David 97
Lyotard, Jean-François 96
M
Madame Bovary 34-35, 39
Manning, Nicholas 36, 220
'The Man Who Loved Islands' 9, 92-98
Massumi, Brian 30, 35, 38-39
McCabe, Thomas H. 73, 80
mental consciousness 1-4, 6, 15-16, 18, 207, 209, 215
Merivale, Patricia 178, 181
Mexico 27, 132, 145, 147-49, 189
Michelucci, Stefania 84
Milton, Colin 139-40
Mornings in Mexico and Etruscan Places 141-43

Index

Moynahan, Julian 191

N
Nakanishi, Yoshihiro 192
Nichols, Ashton 50-51
Nietzsche, Friedrich 11, 128-29, 135, 139-40, 142

O
oceanic feeling 98
Okano, Keiichi 133
Okuma, Akinobu 137
Orwell, George 19, 67
Osborn, Marijane 115
Oyama, Miyo 220, 222-23

P
Pan 174-88, 192-93, 198
Paz, Octavio 222
Phoenix: The Posthumous Papers of D. H. Lawrence 175
physical consciousness 3, 12, 15, 25, 71, 91, 134, 169, 204, 215
physicality 1, 7, **8**, 11, **18-23**, 25, 28-29, 32-33, 35, **37**, 43-44, **55**, 63, 68, 71, 84-85, 90-91, 102, 114, 118, **155**, 162-63, 166, 170, 174, **180**, 197, 200, 202, 205, 210-12, 217
The Plumed Serpent 10, 27, 113-15, 130-35, 138-40, 145-57
post-colonialism 10, 117, 119, 130, 171
primitiveness 24, 27-28, 112-14, 209-11, 214
'The Princess' 10, 125-29, 154, 156
'The Prussian Officer' 9, 101-04, 106-10, 149-50, 167
psychoanalysis 9, 23, 95, 165

R
Ragachewskaya, Marina S. 118, 164
The Rainbow 9, 51, 71, 74-75, 77-78
realism 29-31, 33, 35-36, 40, 43
Reflections on the Death of a Porcupine and Other Essays 136, 138
Ressentiment 128-29, 134-35, 142, 154
The Road to Wigan Pier 19

Roberts, Neil 127
Romain, Rolland 98
Rose, Shirley 142, 166-67
Roux, Magali 222
Ruderman, Judith 169

S
Saki 176, 188
Santos, José Dos 101-02
Schapiro, Barbara Ann 168
Schneider, Daniel J. 75, 221
'Second-Best' 8, 53-57
Shklovsky, Viktor 91
Snyder, Carey 125
social Darwinism 135-37
solar plexus 16, 18, 89
Sons and Lovers 8, 13, 17, 21-22, 26, 38
Squires, Michael 127
stillness 8-9, **72-77**, 79, **80**, **81**, 83, 87, 90-91, 100, **104**, 105, **109**, 110, 145-48, 150, 154, 199, 212
St. Mawr 10, 121-28, 130, 134-35, 144, 146, 190-91
Stoltzfus, Ben 95, 97-98, 222
'The Story of A Panic' 177
Stromer, Richard 175
Study of Thomas Hardy and Other Essays 2-4, 13, 31, 49, 58, 79, 131, 159, 162-63, 182, 223
'Sun' 11, 167-71
Swathout, Kelley R. 115, 151, 223

T
Tagata, Midori 86-87, 221
Takamura, Mineo 26, 162, 178
Tetsumura, Haruo 220
Theory of Three Orders 95-100
'The Thimble' 197
Toth, Naomi 106
The Trespasser 9, 82-92, 94, 98-99, 105, 108
Twilight in Italy 119

U
Ueda, Kazuo 60, 63

unrepresentable experience 8, 32, 34, 68, 76, 96

V

The Virgin and the Gipsy 112-13
vital energy 11, 28, 100, 110, **128-29**, **137**, **138**, **142**, 144, 147, 156, 160, 171, 173, 175, **189**, 197, 201, 207, 209, 213, 214

W

Whiteley, Patrick J. 46-47
The White Peacock 8, 13-14, 24, 170, 224
'The White Stocking' 8, 23-29, 38
Widmer, Kingsley 145, 153
Williams, Linda Ruth 222
'The Woman Who Rode Away' 10, 115-20, 127
Women in Love 62, 77
Woolf, Virginia 106, 222
Wordsworth, William 49, 86
Worthen, John 219

Y

Yeats, W. B. 219
Yoshimura, Hirokazu 223
Young, Michael 36-37, 220